SPECIAL ... ADERS

THE ULVERSCROFT FOUNDATION
(registered UK charity number 264873)
was established in 1972 to provide funds for
research, diagnosis and treatment of eye diseases.
Examples of major projects funded by
the Ulverscroft Foundation are:-

- The Children's Eye Unit at Moorfields Eye Hospital, London
- The Ulverscroft Children's Eye Unit at Great Ormond Street Hospital for Sick Children
- Funding research into eye diseases and treatment at the Department of Ophthalmology, University of Leicester
- The Ulverscroft Vision Research Group, Institute of Child Health
- Twin operating theatres at the Western Ophthalmic Hospital, London
- The Chair of Ophthalmology at the Royal Australian College of Ophthalmologists

You can help further the work of the Foundation
by making a donation or leaving a legacy.
Every contribution is gratefully received. If you
would like to help support the Foundation or
require further information, please contact:

THE ULVERSCROFT FOUNDATION
The Green, Bradgate Road, Anstey
Leicester LE7 7FU, England
Tel: (0116) 236 4325

website: www.foundation.ulverscroft.com

THE LOVE THAT I HAVE

Margot Baumann has left school to work in the mailroom of a large prison. But this is Germany in 1944, and the prison is Sachsenhausen concentration camp near Berlin. Margot is shielded from the camp's brutality, as she has no contact with the prisoners. But she does handle their mail; and when given a cigarette lighter and told to burn the prisoners' letters, she is horrified by the callous act she must carry out. Intending to send some letters in secret, she is drawn to their heart-rending words of hope, of despair, and of love. This is how Margot comes to know Dieter Kleinschmidt: through the beauty and the passion of his letters to a girlfriend, also named Margot — which become the catalyst for a huge act of courage.

JAMES MOLONEY

THE LOVE
THAT I
HAVE

Complete and Unabridged

AURORA
Leicester

First published in Australia in 2018 by
HarperCollins*Publishers* Australia

First Aurora Edition
published 2020
by arrangement with
HarperCollins*Publishers* Australia

*A catalogue record for this book is available
from the British Library.*

ISBN 978–1–78782–258–0

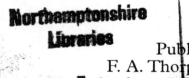

Published by
F. A. Thorpe (Publishing)
Anstey, Leicestershire
Set by Words & Graphics Ltd.
Anstey, Leicestershire
Printed and bound in Great Britain by
T. J. International Ltd., Padstow, Cornwall

This book is printed on acid-free paper

For Margot Frank who died, aged eighteen, in Bergen-Belsen along with her sister, Anne.

And for Margot Rieth who, at a similar age, has the world at her feet.

MARGOT

JULY, 1944

1

For as long as I can remember, I've loved three things: the long summer holidays, my brother Walther and Adolf Hitler.

Out loud, I always put the Führer first, of course, and it's such a natural thing to thrust out my arm when teachers give the salute at the start of each lesson. Heil Hitler, I say, looking up at his picture above the blackboard, the same one that hangs in our hall at home. But sometimes I sense he knows my guilty secret — that warm, sunny weeks at the beach mean more to me than his portrait on the wall.

When I confessed this to my friend, Lili Martin, she grabbed my arm and said, 'You too, Margot? I'm the same! This war is going on so long. They said it would be over in months, but it's been years and years. We hardly ever have strawberries or anything nice to eat. There's barely enough bread some days and nothing at all to wear in the shops. Worst of all, we never have fun anymore.' Fun for Lili means boys. It does for me as well, if I'm honest and I'm as unhappy as Lili that there aren't any to dance with or kiss if we're daring, but holidays by the sea still top my list of treasured things.

There'll be no summer holiday this year, though. The Führer has other plans for me. Today I take my sister's place in the mailroom at the konzentrationslager because she has been ordered upstairs to type letters and file reports for the officers. I even have her uniform which I pressed last night before going to bed and again this morning until Renate scoffed, 'Oh, for heaven's sake, Margot. You're not going on parade in front of the commandant.'

It's natural to be nervous, though, isn't it? I was a schoolgirl only last week and today I'll be working for the Reich. I'm glad about that, actually. At sixteen, I've had enough of school. Lili left months ago to train as a nurse and I thought about doing the same until Renate got in my ear. 'Please, darling, they won't let me be a secretary until I find someone to do my job in the mailroom.' And then the plea that I couldn't ignore. 'The Führer needs workers, even if the work isn't what you imagined yourself doing.'

I didn't eat any breakfast in case it all came up again and the same dread is back in my stomach now as Renate and I ride through the streets of Oranienburg, swerving to miss the puddles left by last night's rain. Already the sun is breaking through and since it's July the heat draws wisps of steam from the dampened road.

I used to ride these streets all the time when Walther and my other brother, Franz, took me to the Lehnitzsee to sail or swim. I wonder if Walther thinks of those times while he waits for the war to end in his prisoner-of-war camp. He's the oldest and I can't remember a time when he didn't tower over me, the youngest, casting a protective shadow that I basked in happily whenever I walked beside him. Will I ever walk beside him again?

These memories of my favourite brother push me towards a sadness that only makes life seem harder than it is. I sit up straighter on the saddle and tell myself: even if there'll be no lazy days at the beach for me this year, at least I can enjoy the summer green of the trees lining our way. They don't care about shortages or how long it will be before they see their brothers again. Sunshine and rain are all they ask for, the roses too, their pinks and yellows in full bloom, and in the next street there'll be the red of cherries and the heavily laden arms of Herr Koder's apple tree, which Lili and I robbed so many times on our way home from school.

The houses we pass are steep-roofed with twin windows staring down into the street from the upstairs bedrooms — much like ours in Wilhelmstrasse. These days, most have a dejected look because there's no one to repair the shutters and window frames damaged during the winter or slap on the fresh coat of paint so many of them need. All the men are at the war, and the boys, too, down to the age where they need as much looking after as these houses.

We ride north through the outskirts of town and for a little way there are only trees and brambles on either side of the road. Then, new houses, built for the officers from the konzentrationslager and beyond them I can see its dull grey walls growing closer. My stomach tightens. I've never been this close before; close enough to see the way the concrete blocks have been thrown on top of one another in a brutal rush, as though the workmen didn't care how the mortar

5

oozed out between each one.

'What are those white cones above the wall?' I ask.

'They're conductors. All the barbed wire here is electrified. Don't ever go near it.'

'On the other side is where the prisoners live, isn't it?' I ask.

Renate glances across at me, as though she has finally noticed how scared I am. 'Don't worry. I've worked here for two years and never had to go into that part.'

We turn a corner and suddenly I'm riding between wooden huts towards a tall, white building. Except for the guard towers, it's the only thing higher than the walls. In fact, it's built into the wall, I see as we glide closer, with a gateway cut through the middle. On the other side of the heavy, iron gate I glimpse an enormous parade ground and then rows and rows of barracks.

'You'll be working in the gatehouse,' my sister tells me as we lean our bikes against the last of the wooden huts. Then, before I'm quite ready, she leads me into a room filled with men older than our father. I didn't expect them to be my own age, but these men look half dead! For a moment I hope Renate will whisper, 'I've changed my mind, you can't have my old job after all.' I'd be pedalling back to Oranienburg before she'd finished speaking.

'Guten morgen,' she trills, and at the sound of her voice it's as though sunshine has burst into the room. The weary heads of the old soldiers lift and turn her way, and I see that one of them is actually a woman.

'They all love me here,' my sister announces. 'A few dream I'm their girlfriend and the rest treat me like a favourite daughter, isn't that right?' Her teasing draws sheepish smiles. 'Listen everyone, this is Margot. Today I'll show her what to do and then she can be your dream girl the way I was.'

Hot blood flushes my cheeks and I grin like an idiot, as I always do when Renate embarrasses me.

'Come on, I'll introduce you to the boss,' she says to me.

We walk the length of the room until we are standing in front of a desk that would take four men to lift. The man behind it is younger than the rest and he wears his jacket formally buttoned.

'Unteroffizier Junge, may I present Margot Baumann, my replacement as mail clerk.' Renate's tone is respectful as she addresses him.

When he stands, his body is crooked and he winces as he tries to straighten up. 'Welcome, Margot,' he says, and there's even a friendly smile. 'The work we do here is important. All mail in and out of Sachsenhausen comes through this office. We regularly handle letters from Reichsführer Himmler, himself, for example.' He pauses and I notice a sly glint in his eye. 'Perhaps you will be a better worker than your sister.'

Once we've moved out of earshot, Renate whispers, 'He used to drive a tank. Injured his spine — shrapnel or something.'

We're in the centre of the mailroom now, where two of the workers are sorting envelopes then tossing them into sacks. Sitting beneath the windows, two more are reading letters. While I watch, one crosses out half a line using a thick black pen. The most active worker in the room is a square-headed man standing at a counter covered in parcels. He pokes hopefully at a package he's just opened, then reaches in to draw out something that's caught his eye.

'Are you listening?' Renate asks in annoyance.

'Oh, sorry,' I splutter, returning my attention to her, but I can't help stealing a glance at the counter. The prize turns out to be a sausage. The man sniffs at it. Then, clearly liking what he smells, he takes out a pocket knife to cut a slice from one end. When he rewraps the parcel, the sausage is left on the counter.

Renate takes me outside and points to the huts I'm to visit with my sacks. My job is to collect new mail as well, it seems. There are ink pads to be replenished and I learn where fresh envelopes are stored. 'Oh, and I'd better show you this,' she says, heading for the corner of the room furthest from the door. A barrel standing as high as my waist sits beneath a slot cut into the wall.

'When this fills up with letters, it's your job to scoop them out. Don't worry about getting them all — besides, if you reach in too far, these old crocks will get a good look at your legs.'

'Why shouldn't I take all of them out of the barrel?' I ask. 'The ones at the bottom will have been there the longest, won't they?'

'That doesn't matter,' Renate answers lightly. 'These letters are from prisoners. When the censors have time they check a few and send them on.'

'Just a few? But you told me to scoop out as many as I can reach.'

'Yes, to burn them.'

'Burn them?'

Renate sighs in frustration, as though she can't believe how stupid I am. 'Prisoners' letters don't count. They are mostly written by filthy Jews, or by communists or deviates and other enemies of the Reich. Their letters are a nuisance, really, because everything has to be censored and so many of our censors have been sent off to join fighting units.'

She points to the man I'd been watching at the counter. 'They concentrate on mail coming into the camp, especially parcels. Only if there's enough time after that do they look at letters from this barrel.'

'Then why do the prisoners bother to keep writing?'

'Because they don't know, of course.'

'Why not tell them?'

'Why do you care?' Renate asks with a puzzled frown. Then she leans in close. 'There are benefits,' she whispers. 'The prisoners have to buy the stamps and the paper and the envelopes. We split the money with the guards inside the camp, of course, but there *are* little perks we keep to ourselves.'

She nods towards the counter where the parcels are examined. The sausage! Now I understand.

2

It's Sunday, after my first week at the konzentrationslager and I'm lying beside Lili on the grassy slope we used to roll down, like dizzy, squealing logs, all the way into the waters of the Lehnitzsee. The war had barely begun back then; the younger of my brothers, Franz, was still living at home and Lili had thought she was in love with him. She's like that.

Lili's slim, almost skinny, and blonde like the girls you see around the Führer in newsreels. She has an open-mouthed way of staring out at the world, as though everything she sees would be amazing and full of fun if she could just find the key to open it up. I can't imagine life without her, even if we fight occasionally, which she says is a sign of strong character. I'm miserable when we're not speaking and always want to go to her house and apologise, whether I was responsible for us falling out or not. She's just that little bit more daring than me, and God knows I need a bit of excitement in my life.

Right now, she's smoking a cigarette rather grandly, as though an audience is watching her shoot grey streams towards the sky. When she offers it to me, I take it, even though Mutti will smell it on my breath and we'll have another row about how respectable German girls should behave. Respectable is just another word for dull, if you ask me.

'If the Russians knew how boring this place is, they'd go back to Moscow,' I say to Lili.

'Maybe we could bomb them with it,' she replies. 'There's enough boredom in this town to kill the entire Red Army!'

'I wish we could drop my mother on them. One of the Führer's secret weapons.'

Lili stares at me wide-eyed, that I could have said such a thing. Good. She might know me better than anyone else, but I can still jolt her image of me now and again.

I look out over the lake. When the sun is shining, the Lehnitzsee is so blue I want to eat up all its colour with my eyes and keep it for the dreary winter.

'If Jens were here, he'd take us sailing,' says Lili, drawing her boyfriend into our conversation — and not for the first time today. Jens is a good sailor, I'll admit that much, but after years of family holidays on Rügen Island, I can handle a boat pretty well myself.

'I could ask Herr Koder to lend us his,' I say.

Ah, but it's Jens Lili wants, not the sailing. He's in training for the navy and hasn't been home since Easter, although Lili had decided he'd be hers the Christmas before — and when Lili wants something, a line of tanks couldn't stop her. I doubt I'll hear Jens's name at all by *next* Christmas, though. It's not that Lili will discover his faults and fall out of love with him; rather, she's like a fire I saw once, burning through a field of summer-browned grass. 'There's no danger in it,' one of the men watching assured me. 'The flames will rush to the edge of the

11

meadow then die down once there's no more fuel.' And he was right, there were limits the fire couldn't go beyond. That's the difference between Lili and me. I dream of love that keeps burning until it lights up a whole landscape.

'Do you think love can last forever?' I ask her.

This is a question I've thought about a lot lately. I had a sort-of boyfriend last year, Ferdy, who told me that he loved me while we kissed. 'I love you too,' I said and let him explore inside my sweater until we both became embarrassed about being so intimate. Only weeks later I cringed at the sight of him.

'Love lasts forever in the movies,' says Lili.

'Movies only go for an hour or two.'

She snorts loudly. 'You certainly look convinced when we come out afterwards. Go on, admit it — you see yourself up on the screen kissing those men.'

I deny it, of course, shaking my head furiously, but Lili's right and she knows it. She jumps on top of me, pinning my hands to the grass. 'Go on, say you do,' she demands.

'Kissing's not love,' I say, remembering Ferdy.

'It's close enough for now,' Lili replies, rolling off me. 'Your problem is you expect too much, Margot. Underneath, you're a bigger romantic than I am.'

'Then why do you have all the boyfriends?'

'Because falling in love is fun, and why should we have fun like that only once in our lives? Love should be light, see-through, something to drape around yourself and test how it feels, don't you agree?'

'I do,' I answer immediately, and it's true that love should be so light in your heart it can lift you into the air. See-through, though, something to drape over myself like fabric for a summer dress — that sounds flimsy. I want more than that.

'Do you still write to Jens?' I ask.

'Every week, sometimes twice.'

'Is he any better at writing back?'

Lili makes a face. 'Boys aren't natural letter writers. I don't expect him to.'

'Letters are my job now,' I say with a sigh. 'They fall like snow in my dreams.'

'What do you do? Sort them into piles all day?'

'Not me,' I tell her. 'Mostly I'm a pair of legs, so the others can stay in the mailroom. They're all old or crippled, so they do the sorting while I lug sacks from building to building and into the barracks.'

'Not the prisoners' barracks!' Lili looks horrified.

'No, only the soldiers' barracks outside the barbed wire. I don't even know how the prisoners get their mail. I know how they post letters though — through a slot in the wall. They end up in a big barrel and just sort of sit there . . . ' My voice trails off as I think about it.

I never actually see letters being posted, but each morning the level in the barrel is higher, as though the prisoners are pixies in a fairy tale who do their work at night and leave it for me to find in the morning.

Lili is watching me, waiting, like I've left the

story half told. And I have, I suppose. I don't tell her what happens to those letters. Or what is *meant* to happen; I've put off that task so far. It doesn't seem right.

'So the letters sit there . . . ' Lili prompts me.

'I was thinking of Walther,' I say, giving her an answer at last. 'What happens to the letters he writes from his prisoner-of-war camp?'

'You said he hasn't written any.'

'No, I said that we haven't received any.'

Lili shrugs. 'Because he hasn't written any, that's why. He's a boy, like Jens.'

It can't be as simple as that. Even the most reluctant writer would let his family know where he was, what they could send to him; he would at least let them know that he was alive. I think of all the soldiers captured with Walther, thousands of them, dropping letters into a barrel like the one in Sachsenhausen and wondering why no one writes back. The ache of Walther's silence is suddenly a livid pain in my chest.

★   ★   ★

If I thought I could avoid burning the prisoners' letters altogether, Unteroffizier Junge soon sets me straight. 'The barrel is almost full,' he says when I'm barely through the door on Monday morning.

'I'll take care of it once I've made the first round of deliveries,' I promise.

No more putting it off then. When I return from the barracks I go to the barrel and stuff a handful of letters into an empty bag. What do I

14

care? I ask myself, trying to sound like Renate, yet even as I remind myself the letters are from filthy Jews and others who've betrayed Germany, I know the answer. Somewhere in Russia a hand like mine might be shovelling letters into a bag for burning, with a note from Walther among them saying: *I long to hear from you. Please write back soon.* I can hear the plea in my head, as clearly as if he's standing behind me.

The sack is full, the tide in the barrel has receded to halfway. That's enough for now. 'Where should I take them to be burned?' I ask the unteroffizier. 'Over there, where the smoke is?' I point out the window. 'There must be an incinerator or something on the far side of the camp.'

Unteroffizier Junge turns quickly to look, then shudders with pain from the abrupt movement. 'Smoke?' he repeats, before easing his body back to face me again. He stares into my face for a full five seconds before saying finally, 'No, that furnace is for a different purpose. There's an old oil drum between the huts outside. Here, you'll need this.' He hands me his cigarette lighter. 'Make sure each letter is completely destroyed.'

Completely destroyed! As if the job isn't hard enough already because of Walther. The unteroffizier doesn't just want me to get rid of these letters, it's to be like they were never written at all.

Standing before the drum a few minutes later, I take a fistful of letters from the sack then click my thumb on the lighter to create a flame. Or I try to anyway. The lid keeps falling onto the

15

spark before it can catch. I take a closer look and see the cigarette lighter has twin lightning bolts spelling SS on both sides, not engraved but raised up a few millimetres — to give a better grip, I suppose. I know what those letters stand for. The Schutzstaffel is a special division separate from the army. Renate told me it's their job to run all the camps like this one. There're dozens of them, she says.

Mutti wanted Walther to join the SS, but he refused. 'I want to fight on the front line, not round up Jews and Bolsheviks after the battle is over,' he said. There'd been a terrible argument about it, but Walther stood up for himself against all the shouting — a sign my brother had grown into a man, I decided. 'When I wear my uniform I want to see respect in people's eyes, not fear,' he told me afterwards, although I didn't understand what he meant. To me, one soldier was like all the rest.

With a flame burning at last, I light the first handful of letters and drop them into the barrel. It seems so callous, though. I wrote a letter to Franz only yesterday. My letters are important to him. He tells me so in every letter he writes back. And they're important to me, as well. They've made a big difference to the way I think about this other brother of mine who always used to take Renate's side against me. At times I hated him, but our letters have changed that, just like the past year has changed Franz. He's in France doing work he's not allowed to tell us about. He tells me other things, though, things I'm surprised to read — about how scared he is

16

that he'll die slowly, in terrible pain, like he's seen others do. 'I didn't think this war would kill so many,' he wrote in his last letter. He says he can't tell these things to Mutti or Renate because they'll think he's a coward, but he trusts me to understand.

Of course, I never really hated Franz himself, only his teasing. I didn't *know* him as a person, that was the thing. He was just this big loud boy who was forever kicking a ball or charging down the hall with his friends. It's strange, but being so far apart has made it easier for me to see him and, as each letter peels away a little more of who he really is, I'm discovering a second brother to love along with Walther.

All his letters end with the same words, *Write again soon*, so yesterday, after I got home from the lake, I sat for an hour making sure my words let him know how much we miss him. Now I'm dropping letters just like it into the fire, watching as the connection each writer hoped to make to a brother, a mother, a child gets eaten up until ashes are all that remain.

I begin to read the names on the front of the envelopes before letting each one slip from my fingers, and immediately regret it because now the writers of those letters are transformed from pixies working away in the secret night into human beings. 'Don't be so lily-livered, Margot,' I whisper. The Führer deserves steel in his people, not sentiment, and these people are enemies of the Reich. If only this scene were taking place in a newsreel.

A handful of letters remain in the sack. I

rummage around to grab all of them in one fistful, and even as I do it the violence of my fingers closing over the last of the letters seems a travesty. I draw out my hand to stare at them, crumpled and at my mercy, the last ones with their words still alive. I look around; no one is watching. I stroll the few paces to where my bicycle stands against a hut and slip the surviving letters inside the rolled-up raincoat tied to the carrier rack.

★   ★   ★

On the ride home I lay down strict rules for myself. Anything that could possibly be a coded message I'll destroy. The letters I send on will be ones like my family longs to receive from Walther.

At home I carry the letters to my room still hidden in the raincoat, which keeps them safe from my mother's gaze, but not that of the Führer in the hallway. For a moment I want to run into the vegetable garden and burn them after all. But then it occurs to me that, while the Führer is a great leader who deserves obedience, he's a compassionate man, too. I know this from everything I've heard about him at school and from the newsreels I see when Lili and I go to the cinema. He would understand what I'm doing.

After dinner, Renate goes off with her friends and I have our bedroom to myself. I lock the door and take the letters from under my mattress. I read a postcard first:

Dear Merte,
Gunter and I still have our health. The
summer warmth is helping. Please send as
many pairs of socks as you can because my
only pair is mostly holes, and grit from the
quarry gets inside my shoes. Parcels seem
to come more often than letters. Gunter is
cold at night. A cardigan for him and any
food you can spare. With God's help I will
be free soon to hold you close.
With love,
Herman

What a letdown! It could be a note sent by boys
from the Hitler Youth hiking through the Black
Forest. A cardigan and a pair of socks; it doesn't
take much to make prison life more bearable,
then. I choose a second postcard and read:

My darling,
I doubt I will see you again unless you can
send more to keep me going. The rations
here aren't enough to keep a man alive
and they work us so hard. These days, I
look like Uncle Ludy — do you remem-
ber? Please don't forget me. I don't want
to take food out of our children's mouths,
but whatever you can spare, even peelings.
I love you and want only to be with you
and our little ones. Give my love to Gissy,
Marta and Eva.

I drop the card onto the bed beside me before its
desperation leaks onto my fingers. This can't be

19

right. The man is blackmailing his wife with pathetic pleas for food. Everyone's on rations these days; it's just part of the war, part of the sacrifice we all make for victory. I stare down at the card, not sure what to think. Cooking smells drift across the konzentrationslager all day long. How can anyone be starving, and who would post vegetable peelings in a parcel?

Then I think of the Führer's merciful heart and decide to send this card on anyway. The prisoner's wife can decide whether it's a trick.

Feeling good now, I take a letter from the pile this time. The handwriting is neat and stays precisely between the lines marked on the page so the writer could fit in as many words as possible.

Peter, my friend. I send this letter to you in the hope you'll know where my darlings are living. If you can see it into their hands, I will thank you from heaven.

My dearest love,
With this letter I bid you farewell. I have struggled to stay alive these three years only for you and Jordy. Last night at roll-call, all hope that I will see you again was snuffed out. I try not to think of it in the time I have left. Instead, I remember our love, from when I first saw you in your father's bookshop, until my eyes lost sight of you waving from the train in Hamburg. I thank your father every day that he saw how things would go before it was too late and that you were able to reach Sweden.

How I wish I had trusted his judgement and gone with you.

I hope you remember dinners around my parents' table as fondly as I do. Dear Vati and Mutti are surely gone already, I know. I saw them crowded onto the wagons myself before it was my turn. If there is anything good ahead of me with-out you, it is that I will be with them again. My darling, my heart longs for you; it thanks you for your love and devotion and especially for the happiness you gave me every day and each time I saw your face. It's what I will see at the last. Raise Jordell as we would have done together. It will be hard alone, but I know you have the strength. You are young and might find someone to share the task with you.

Farewell, love of my life. If you meet Leah or Sam, Tante Devorah and Onkel Benjamin or any of those who loved me years ago, kiss and hug them for me.

Jacob

I read those last lines through welling tears. *Farewell.* How could a man write that word so calmly when he was about to die? I try to guess how long the letter has been in the barrel. If it was at the bottom of my sack then it must have been near the top, posted only last night. The man might be still alive, or he might have died while I was standing over the oil drum. How many of the letters I burned this afternoon were like this?

I didn't know words on a page could be so sad — and yet they're beautiful as well. *The happiness you gave me every day and each time I saw your face.* This is a better answer to my question about love than anything Lili said yesterday beside the lake.

I want to know more about this man. Where did he live? Could I have come across him in the street? I look again at the name. Jacob. But that's a Jewish name, and so are the names he added as though with a final breath. Devorah, Leah, Benjamin. It doesn't seem possible that a filthy Jew could feel affection like this. They lack the human feelings for such tender emotions, but knowing that doesn't stop me folding the page as carefully as if it had come from Walther. If I don't send this one to its destination, I'll be the one without human feelings.

3

Those are just the first letters I save from the fire. I try not to think too much about what I'm doing. Is it really such a big thing, anyway? I'm just sending letters to anxious people who are eager to receive them, telling myself that if I do this in Sachsenhausen, then someone like me will do the same in a camp near Stalingrad. It's silly, I know, to imagine that life evens things out like that, but every time I go out to the rusty oil drum to burn another sackful of letters I hide a few in my raincoat. No one knows, no one cares.

I was about to post the first seven at Oranienburg's post office when I saw how the konzentrationslager stationery would stand out among the other letters. If anyone became suspicious, they would quickly see there was no censor's stamp, either, so I used an entire week's pay to buy fresh white envelopes and stamps to go on them. Once inside, the rescued mail would look like all the rest. Until I started reading their letters, the prisoners were no more than distant figures on the other side of the appelplatz. Now I catch myself watching through the window of the mailroom, hoping for a glimpse.

'How many prisoners are there?' I ask Bruno, the censor who stole the sausage on my first day.

'Thirty thousand in this main part of the camp,' he answers.

'No, there can't be. How could they fit so

23

many? There aren't enough barracks!'

'Haven't you seen sardines in a can?' he replies, smirking.

I stare through the window again and find proof right in front of me. The appelplatz, where the prisoners line up for rollcall, is enormous. Bigger than a football field. Not that I've seen a rollcall; that takes place before I arrive in the morning, then the inmates are marched off to work in the factories and the quarry north of the camp and they don't come back until after I've gone home. Not all of them go; a few are made to stand at attention all day in the sun, which seems cruel and if they collapse, they're dragged away by the guards with feet trailing on the gravel.

Sometimes, Lili and I would see a squad marching along a street in their striped uniforms when we were on our way home from school. No one in Oranienburg speaks about them — the thing is to pretend they're invisible, sort of non-people who don't belong among the rest of us. But reading their letters makes that harder.

Then, at the end of August, I find a letter addressed to me.

Dear Margot,
There is not enough space on this page to express the ache in my heart whenever I think of you. And you are never out of my thoughts, so the pain stays with me always. Yet it is a pain that keeps me breathing, because life in this camp is unbearable and without you alive in my imagination I

24

would give way to despair. I have seen it happen to others. The Mussulman look, they call it. The death of hope kills more men in my block than hunger or typhus. They have forgotten how to imagine, how to create something better in their heads. It's what separates them from me. I imagine you walking beside me on the daily march to the quarry, laughing in that gentle way of yours that I love. In the year we had together, we were never able to laugh loudly, were we? Not in the way I wanted to, anyway. So in my mind the two of us can be heard all over the camp. I sit in the weary evenings with my eyes closed, believing the sound of us together brings hope to others who witness the happiness we have. Maybe it helps them remember what it was to feel heart-free and close to the one they love. For me, that is you, Margot. Stay alive in my head and that way you will keep me alive. Without the thought of you I will die here in Sachsenhausen.

With all my love,
Dieter

The world has gone silent and still. I can barely breathe. None of the poems I read at school ever moved me like the letter trembling in my fingers.

After a few moments I take back control of my body because it's not just my hands shaking, but my shoulders and around my middle, even my legs. For a minute I'd believed those loving,

25

longing words were for me. But I'm not the Margot they're meant for and now I'm fighting a twinge of shame that I let myself pretend, even for an instant. It's no crime to read the envelope, though — and I have to, in any case, so I can copy the address onto a fresh one.

I look for the sender's name. Dieter Kleinschmidt. I picture him — tall, twenty-five, maybe thirty at the most. No one older could have that much emotion in his heart. More important is the address of the recipient. I turn the envelope over and read *Margot Lipsky*. Lipsky sounds like a Jewish name, but Kleinschmidt isn't. Is this a letter from a proper German to a Jew? It's illegal for Jews to marry Christians, but this letter makes me think these two are still boyfriend and girl-friend. Is that against the law? It doesn't matter. I'm sending it on because it's beautiful and filled with love. I take a plain white envelope and begin with the name, aware of how easily my hand writes *Margot*. Now for the street address.

Oh! I sit up on the bed. It's not going to a house or an apartment; it's going to *Konzentrationslager Auschwitz*. According to the address, the camp is in Poland. I wonder if there's a barrel and a young mail clerk and a rusting oil drum there, too. The best I can do is send the letter and hope this other Margot's reply gets through.

I turn the envelope over to write *Dieter Kleinschmidt* on the back along with his prisoner number: *A73901*. Then I realise what's missing. I snatch up the original envelope. No, it's not there. Not on the letter, either. If Margot Lipsky is in a konzentrationslager then she should have a

26

number too, yet there's no sign of it.

'They won't let you have your boyfriend's letter,' I say out loud. No mail in or out of a camp can be delivered without the prisoner's number. It's the first rule I learned. I feel sick deep in my stomach. The most heartfelt letter I've saved from the flames so far and I can't send it on. I'm fighting tears now for this other Margot who'll never see the loving words meant for her. She's a Jew and a prisoner, yet I envy her.

*   *   *

One of my tasks is to stack letters delivered to the mailroom into neat piles of twenty, ready for the censors. I find myself looking for any addressed to Dieter Kleinschmidt. I'm not going to read it. That's a promise I make to this pair of lovers I've stumbled across. I just want to make sure any letters from her get through because the censors don't care any more about incoming mail than they do about letters in the barrel. After a week I find one — not from Poland, but from Anna Kleinschmidt; his mother, or maybe a sister. I slip it into my pocket, hoping it contains a prisoner number for Margot Lipsky.

At home I steam open the envelope.

Dear Dieter,
We hope and pray that you are well. Gab-
riele and Silke send their special love and
the three of us miss you and Vati more
than we can say, for we are not a family
anymore without you. The girls often

27

speak of last summer and how you took them sailing along the island shore to Binz and camped overnight on the beach. The memory helps them endure all that has befallen us. I have found work at last, which means we have enough money to use all of our ration cards. I will try to send you something in a week or two.

The girls are no longer called horrible names at school, which is a relief. It used to upset Silke especially. Father Blike never shunned us. Even in the terrible days afterwards he came to sit with me and assure me things would get better once people had more pressing troubles to worry about. He was right about that. Thank God they let us stay in our apartment for I don't know what we would do otherwise.

The air raids are terrible and we spend most nights in the cellar with dozens of others, hoping our homes will survive until morning. Last week, the entire block between Goseriede and the train line was destroyed and many died, even though they had taken shelter below ground.

I seem to write only of our woes when yours are much greater. We love you, darling Dieter, and more than anything we want you home with us.

With love,
Your Mutti

No number; not even a mention of Margot Lipsky. I think about this for a minute and decide that it makes sense. His mother's mention of the priest means Dieter is a Catholic and if Margot Lipsky is a Jew then they must have kept their romance a secret.

I read the letter again. Dieter's a sailor, like me, and the island he took his sisters sailing around is sure to be Rügen Island. I've spent whole days on the beach at Binz. We might have passed each other on the sand! There's something else, too. The sisters sound young, only eleven or twelve maybe. Dieter went on holidays with them, which makes me think he's a university student, and that means he's closer to my own age than I thought.

I return the letter to the mailroom and make sure it's approved by a censor in time for delivery in the evening. In the days afterwards, I scan the incoming mail every chance I get and Unteroffizier Junge never has to remind me that the barrel in the corner is getting full.

4

By September I don't feel heat from the road anymore as I ride home from the konzentration-slager. Before October has ended, I'll make this journey in twilight and at Christmas there'll be snow. Not that I care much right now. An hour ago I filled a sack with letters from the barrel and, as I do every time now, slipped a handful into my rolled-up raincoat. Today, one of those letters is addressed to Margot Lipsky.

At home, with the letters hidden safely under my mattress, I go downstairs to the kitchen, where Mutti is bending over the sink. Stooped like this and with her back to me, she seems small, when actually a column of pencil marks inside the pantry door shows she's many centimetres taller than me. Mutti wears her braids pinned on top of her head, too, which adds to her height, but at the sink tonight her shoulders are slumped as though she's caving in on herself. That's not unusual. Mutti's never happy in the kitchen these days, now that rationing makes it hard to put a decent dinner on the table and power cuts mean there's sometimes no hot meal at all.

I take the plates out to where Vati is waiting, but there's no sign of Renate, so if my mother is in the mood that overcomes her more and more these days she will take out her anger on the daughter who *has* come home. It won't be the first time.

We eat dinner in silence broken only by the sound of cutlery scraping on plates until finally my father says, 'I had a meeting in Berlin today. The drive used to take less than an hour, but with thousands fleeing the city the roads were crammed. Around the bahnhof, fires were still burning from last night's bombing raid. So many buildings destroyed. Terrible, terrible.' And he shakes his head as though scarcely able to believe what he'd seen.

I never see Vati in anything but a suit these days, but when my brothers were younger he'd join us in shorts for a sail on the Lehnitzsee. One of my strongest memories is riding on his shoulders as he walked into the lake, deeper and deeper until his head submerged completely beneath me and I was left to bob on the surface, still clutched safely in his hands. Where has that father gone? He's losing his hair, which makes him seem older, and so do the round frames of the glasses he uses to read the war news, sighing away a little more of himself each time.

'Will our army take Paris back from the Americans?' I ask him.

'Take it back?' he replies, surprised. He looks like he's going to give me a lecture about tactics then lets the air out of his lungs as though his heart isn't in it. 'No, Margot. Paris is lost to us.'

I used to dream of visiting Paris with Lili. I imagined myself dancing with the exotic Frenchmen we've heard so much about — and they would be men, not boys. What's the use of a daydream if you can't be daring? The thrill of what I might have got up to, so far from home,

31

without Mutti or even Renate to pull me back
. . . but the city isn't ours anymore so I've lost
my chance.

'Paris isn't important anyway,' says my father,
more to Mutti than to me. 'It's the parts of
France we still control that hold the key.'

If Franz is still in France then he'll be in the
parts Vati is talking about. 'Why are they so
important?' I ask.

'To stop the Americans from crossing the
Rhine.'

I sit back so forcefully my chair almost topples
over. 'But if they reach the Rhine they'll already
be in Germany!'

My parents stare at me for long seconds,
saying nothing, then go back to shifting the
cutlery around their plates. Enemy boots on
German soil. It's never occurred to me before.
The Russians are moving westwards, I know that
much, forcing our army out of Poland, but
they'll stop at the border, surely.

'Have we lost the war?' I ask, before I can stop
myself.

'Of course not! Never!' snaps Mutti, and
although she doesn't quite bang her fist on the
table, the effect is the same. 'It's an insult to
Walther and Franz to even think it. There'll be
no talk of defeat in this house!'

I clamp my mouth shut. Even Vati looks afraid
to say anything. After a heavy silence Mutti
speaks again, more calmly. 'The Führer is too
clever to be beaten, Margot. He's devising new
weapons, new tactics, isn't he, Gerhard?'

My father looks up. 'Oh, er, yes, new tactics,'

he agrees, but the feeble tone of his voice seems a more honest answer.

★   ★   ★

Later, alone in my bedroom, I take Dieter Kleinschmidt's letter from its hiding place under my mattress.

My dearest Margot,
Love must be a kind of madness. I survive
through feeling and nothing else these
days. I refuse to let the hunger and the
never-ending tiredness take hold of me and
surround myself with you, instead. I paint
visions in my mind of your rose-leafed lips
and the dimples in your chin when you
smile just for me. I listen for the song of
your whispering voice and imagine the
curve of your hip cupped in my hand, even
if it's the memory of something that never
happened. Sometimes, they are the best
memories, as this letter shows me. Touch-
ing you across such an unbridgeable
distance keeps breath in my lungs and
makes each tomorrow bearable.
    Love shaped us both, me from the first
time I saw you, and it shaped you in the
ways you deflected me, ignored me, but
never quite enough to make me think I
should stop hoping. Hope is what I've
always needed, never more than now, in
Sachsenhausen.
    How I want to be with you, to enjoy

33

your gentle devotion. A weakness in me
says it will be soon, but I mustn't give up.
I must deny us for Mutti's sake and for
Gabbi and Silke. Do you need courage
where you are now? Are you as lonely as
me? Your silence is torment. As each week
passes it extinguishes more of the defiant
stars I search for in the evenings, wonder-
ing which is you. If the stars are eternal,
then so are you and I, as lovers in my
mind.

   With all the love I have left,
   Dieter

The letter is more painful, more heart-rending, than the first. I give way to the tears I was able to avoid while reading his first letter, yet I'm elated that love so intense actually exists. Flirting with those dangerous Frenchmen seems shallow now, lasting only as long as a dancing tune, while this letter speaks of stars in place until God ends time altogether. I know, even before I've finished the final lines, that I have to see this Dieter Kleinschmidt, have to discover for myself what kind of man is able to love a woman so completely.

I'm breaking promises. I'm being treacherous towards the Jewish girl in Poland, but I don't care. This is something I want to do just for me, to fill an emptiness inside me I wasn't even aware of until I started reading letters from that barrel. I want to be in love like he is. There, I've said it, so I'll say the rest. I want someone to love me the way he loves this other Margot.

34

The next morning I leave home before six, silently cursing every scrape and squeak as I wheel my bike through the gate. Twenty minutes later I'm at the mailroom. It's locked and the darkened space inside deserted, but I barely notice because, through the gate, I can see thousands of grey figures lined up in arrow-straight rows. Do I dare go right up to the iron bars? I wonder. I'm thinking about this so hard I don't hear the car until it pulls up behind me.

I turn to see a driver jump out of an SS limousine and open the rear door. A man my father's age answers the chauffeur's salute with a flap of his hand but his eyes are fixed firmly on me.

'What are you doing here, Fräulein?'

What reason can I give? I'm not even sure myself. 'I'm sorry, Herr . . . ' Oh God, what's his rank? The uniform is decorated with gold braid and smart enough to parade before the Führer himself. Speaking too fast I say, 'I misread the time. I work in the mailroom and I didn't want to be late.'

'Late? At this hour? What's your name, girl?'

'Margot Baumann, sir.'

'Baumann. Another Baumann works for one of my officers. A very . . . lively girl, I'm told.'

My terror subsides a little. If I can keep him thinking about my sister, then maybe I'll get away with my flimsy excuse for being so early. Just as well, too, because the grand car and the way he said 'his' officers has made me realise

35

who he is: Sturmbannführer Kaindl, the commandant of Sachsenhausen.

'Yes, sir,' I say quickly. 'That's my sister, Renate. She's secretary to Kapitän Goldapp. She talks about him all the time at the dinner table.'

The commandant chuckles to himself, and his belly wobbles beneath the uniform. 'I dare say *she* would talk about *him*, but I doubt Kapitän Goldapp mentions your sister at his own dinner table, not when he goes home to visit his wife, anyway.' And he laughs like he's told the greatest joke in the world.

By now he's looking me up and down, more bemused than suspicious. Good — he thinks I'm an idiot and he's bored with me already. He cuts the smile from his face with the deftness of a surgeon and says sharply, 'Stand away from those gates, girl. Prisoners will march through at any moment. Best you go home and come back at your regular time.' Then, without waiting for me to obey, he turns and heads for one of the wooden huts.

I wheel my bike a few metres, still in a daze. What had the commandant meant about Kapitän Goldapp? Why wouldn't he mention Renate at his dinner table? I am still puzzling over his remarks when the gates open behind me and the first squad of prisoners emerges.

I quickly pedal through the outer gate and turn towards home, but once I'm a good distance ahead, I stop by the side of the road to watch the prisoners pass. The shaven heads beneath the caps are no surprise — I'd seen as much earlier, with Lili — but I hadn't

36

remembered the guards. There are three to every squad plus another with an Alsatian straining at the leash. The snarling dog is even more menacing than the machine guns in the watchtowers.

I step forward for a closer look and a guard glances over. Just a harmless girl, he thinks, or maybe it's the uniform that makes him turn away. I'm only metres from the nearest prisoners, but it's still too far to read the numbers on their chests. Did I seriously imagine I could pick out Dieter Kleinschmidt this way?

I don't have time to call myself a fool. I'm too busy making sense of what I see. Every head is angled downwards, in defeat it seems, until I realise the truth: they're all trying desperately to keep in step, which is especially hard for the men wearing clogs instead of shoes. When a man stumbles the guards are onto him like wolves, kicking at him savagely until he scrambles to his feet and shuffles back to his place, with the dog snapping at him viciously.

Such brutality, just for losing your step! Yet I quickly forget the snarling and the shouting when the next squad passes me. Many of these men are Jews — I can tell by the yellow triangles beside their numbers. Their uniforms are filthy. And the bodies inside those rags! Wrists, hands and necks are all I can see, and maybe there's a mercy in that because they tell me clearly enough how wasted the rest of their bodies must be. 'Skeletons,' I whisper. And the faces — oh, the faces. I understand now why prisoners' letters asked for anything edible their families could spare, even potato peelings.

By the time the last of the squads have passed I've long since turned my back. There must be a good reason for treating men this way; the Führer wouldn't allow it otherwise. But when I think that one of those desolate figures might have been Dieter Kleinschmidt I can't balance things properly in my mind. I can't even do my job properly when the mailroom finally opens at eight o'clock. Every chance I get I stare out through the barred windows into the appelplatz.

'What are *they* doing?' I ask when I see a truck stop beside one of the barracks and prisoners hurry out to unload it.

Bruno comes to stand beside me, squinting through the grimy glass. 'Delivering dirty clothes,' he says. 'Prisoners wash all the SS uniforms in that building. The place is run by an old Jew who used to own a laundry.'

I wonder if this means he's better fed. I notice there are no dogs snarling at the prisoners who unload the truck. 'Jews wear a yellow triangle in front of their number, don't they?'

Bruno nods. 'Like the Star of David they wear on the streets . . . if there *are* any Jews left on the streets these days.'

Many of the wretched souls I'd seen that morning wore the yellow triangle, but I'd seen other colours, too. 'And red?' I ask.

'For communists. Green triangles are for thieves and thugs. They make good kapos to keep the rest in line inside the barracks.'

I wonder what colour Dieter's triangle is. Why is he in Sachsenhausen at all? Most of all I wonder if he's a walking skeleton being chased to work by dogs. This morning I'd turned my back when it all got too much. Now, my eyes see misery everywhere I look, and when I close them, frightened men march through my head, desperate to keep in step.

5

On Sunday I catch up with Lili beside the Lehnitzsee, which doesn't boast a single sail on its blue waters, despite the autumn sunshine. We're so bored. There are no boys, no one to do anything with. At any moment, Lili will fill the void with more talk of Jens, whom she uses as a convenient daydream, I've decided. Well, I have a daydream of my own so I get in first.

'There's a young man in the camp who writes beautiful letters,' I say as we lie on our backs on the grass.

Lili is immediately interested. 'Good-looking?'

'That's just it — I don't know.'

'What do you mean?'

'I mean I've only read his letters; I've never seen his face.'

I've got her now. She rolls onto her side, propping her head on her hand, eager for more. 'He's not an officer, is he? You wouldn't be allowed to read their mail.'

'He's a prisoner.'

'A prisoner! But Margot, there are Jews in that camp. Thousands of them. Father told me. You need to be careful . . . '

'Dieter's not a Jew, but I *have* read letters from Jews and some were just as beautiful.' And unbearably sad, some of them, I could add, but don't. Now that I've crossed the line there's no point holding back, so I tell Lili about the barrel

40

and the oil drum and the letters hidden in my raincoat.

'Margot! What if they catch you?'

'They'll throw me out of the mailroom, I suppose.'

'It could be a lot worse than that! You're helping enemies of the Reich. It's against the law.'

'Does there need to be a law against love letters?' Saying those words out loud, I hear the anger in my voice. I'm feeling oddly brave, too, for not burning everything from the barrel. I return to the subject of Dieter. 'He hasn't received any letters like the ones he writes. If I could send his letters on like the rest, his girlfriend would surely write something just as beautiful for him.'

'So these letters are to his girlfriend?' asks Lili.

'Her name is Margot. I guess that's why they mean so much to me.'

'Must be damned good letters,' Lili mutters.

Bravery makes me reckless. 'Maybe I could write him a letter. Pretend I was her. I mean, my name is Margot, after all.'

'Are you crazy? What do you know about writing love letters? It's not your business, Margot, even if your names are the same.'

'But all the love he pours into those letters is going to waste.'

'It's not sugar spilled out of a bag. This Dieter will manage perfectly well without you.'

Normally I'm the one who has to rein in Lili's mad schemes. Today it's the other way around, and she's right, of course. I'm doing what I

41

promised I wouldn't; I'm poking my nose in where I have no right to. But I'm not ready to give up just yet. 'Maybe I'd forget about writing him letters if I could just know what he looks like.'

'Much better idea,' Lili agrees.

'Really?' I sit up and turn to face her.

She's enjoying herself now, urging me on to take the edge from her own boredom. 'What do you think he looks like?'

It's strange, but I haven't pictured Dieter in my mind even once. When I take time now to think about it, Lili becomes impatient and jumps in with her own ideas. 'Definitely tall, and so handsome you'll go weak at the knees,' she teases. 'Since he's not a Jew, he's probably blond, but with soft blue eyes — not like those new posters with a soldier staring out at you like he's going to shoot. They scare me.'

I catch her playful mood. 'No, he'll have dark hair, almost black, with brooding eyes and a way of looking at you from beneath his eyebrows that shows he's just a little vulnerable.'

Before I can imagine any more, the fun falls out from under me like a trapdoor. Dieter's head will be shaved and his face as gaunt as those of the men I saw so recently. The best I can hope for is a dignity in his eyes, a light he keeps alive with dreams of Margot Lipsky. If I ever get to meet him, I'll be looking into the face of a dreamer like myself.

'What have you done so far to find out?' asks Lili.

'Embarrassed myself, mostly.' I tell her about

my early-morning visit to the camp, although I leave out the nightmare of the prisoners and concentrate instead on my encounter with Sturmbannführer Kaindl.

'Nothing like going straight to the top. The commandant could certainly arrange a meeting.'

'Lili! Be serious. I didn't exactly charm the man, anyway. He thinks I'm an idiot.'

Lili's not listening. 'The commandant,' she murmurs. 'He definitely said Kapitän Goldapp wouldn't mention Renate to his wife?'

'Something like that. I was so petrified, I didn't think about what he'd said until afterwards.'

'But he was laughing, as though there was some secret joke behind what he was saying.' Lili stretched her arms onto the grass beyond her head and begins to laugh herself. 'Oh, Margot, you don't get it, do you? I'll bet my bones your sister is having an affair with Kapitän Goldapp.'

Suddenly the sun seems only inches from my face. I fall back onto the grass beside Lili, but not to laugh. 'Poor Renate! If Mutti and Vati find out they'll kill her. The scandal! She'll have to leave Oranienburg until people forget about it — if they ever forget it.'

'Oh, Margot, listen to yourself. We're not at school anymore with those dried-up fraus worried we'll smile at some spotty boy. Don't you think it's sort of . . . exciting?'

When she puts it that way, I suppose it is, but I still worry what will happen if they're found out. Renate's not always the kindest sister, but I do care about her.

Lili and I spend the rest of the afternoon

shivering with the delicious thrill that we too might have a secret love affair one day.

I forget all about Dieter Kleinschmidt.

★   ★   ★

For days, my head is filled with thoughts of my sister's affair. All the signs are there to suggest Lili is right. Renate comes home late from Sachsenhausen almost every evening and instead of slouching into the hallway like someone who has worked extra hours, her face is flushed and happy. She has dresses in her wardrobe that never appear in the shops for ordinary women to buy. Even make-up!

Then, on Thursday, I discover that my sister and her lover aren't important at all.

Dear Mutti,
Leon is dead. His hand got caught
between two slabs of stone. Now he's
gone. He was the one who found clogs big
enough for my feet after my shoes were
stolen. He shared his bread with me when
mine was snatched out of my hand. I
couldn't have got through those first weeks
in the quarry without him showing me the
dangers. He was my only real friend. Now
I'm alone again in this terrible place where
you survive only if you have friends to
carry you when you fall, and I'm not talk-
ing about bodies and arms and legs. It's
what's inside your head that keeps you
alive in Sachsenhausen. We're all meant to

44

die here in the end and it's just a matter of how long you can bear to hold out. Men throw themselves on the electric wire when they've had enough. I've seen it with my own eyes and I cannot promise not to do the same. My body's exhausted and I'm hungry every hour I'm awake, but its loneliness that stalks me like a wolf in the night. I keep it at bay by writing letters, as many as I can afford the paper and stamps for, but you say you haven't had any from me since the first one, back in May. I don't know what's happened to the others. Maybe you won't get this one either and that thought fills me with despair, as if I'm the last person on earth, left to speak to himself alone. Your letters are the only ones I receive and I can't tell you what they mean to me. Please keep writing even if you don't hear from me.

With love,
Dieter

As I read this letter I'm wiping away tears and my hands tremble like they did when I read Dieter's first love letter to Margot Lipsky. Everything is different, though. Back then I was filled with awe and a touch of envy. Now I'm weighed down with pity for this young man I've never seen, who doesn't even know I exist, though I feel we've become friends. He needs a friend. He's lost the only one he has, the one who's kept him alive when he stumbles. I know what he means by those words, about needing

45

the strength of another human being to prop him up against the doubts, the despair, the dark voice that whispers in his ear. I read the line about the electric wire again and wince at the dread it creates in my chest.

★　★　★

As soon as I'm free of Sachsenhausen, I ride to Lili's house, shoulder Frau Martin aside when she opens the door and burst into Lili's room at the top of the stairs.

'You can't do it,' says Lili. 'Margot, are you listening to me? The risk is . . . enormous.' She draws out the last word, using her hands to double its meaning. 'Everything about it is . . . is . . . crazy, wrong, dangerous.'

'He has to get a letter. What if he gives up hope because there's no letter from Poland? I'm here, roaming around Oranienburg with nothing worthwhile to do. You're learning to be a nurse. That's helping people. I can't do much for anyone in the mailroom, except this. Dieter's struggling; he needs a reason to stay alive, and Margot Lipsky is his reason.'

'But you're not Margot Lipsky. You can't do it. He'll know straight away from the handwriting.'

'Do you know what Jens's writing looks like?'

When she hesitates, I know I've won that argument at least.

'Well maybe it won't be the handwriting, but something will give you away and then he'll think the letter's a monstrous trick. He'll hate you for it.'

'He doesn't even know me,' I mutter, trying not to sound pathetic. I've already made my mind up anyway and now I'm sorry I came here to talk about it. More than sorry, I'm angry she won't agree with me. I'm fidgety, nervous about what I'm going to do and at the same time more aware than ever of being alive. I practise the right tone in my head and say, 'I'm going to do it.'

'For Dieter or for yourself?' asks Lili.

That's it! I burst out of Lili's bedroom, take my bike from where I left it by the gate and push down on the pedals so hard my thighs are burning before I'm halfway home.

My dearest Dieter,
Love is all the things you say in your let-
ters and I am writing to tell you how much
I can't wait to be back together with you. I
kiss the paper each night before I get into
bed because your hands have touched it
and this helps me dream of holding your
hand for real again soon.

My dearest Dieter,
Love is madness and I am crazy for you. I
feel you with me, just the way you say you
feel me. I am flattered that you think of
me so much and I certainly think of you
all the time too. Don't give up, my dear-
est, they cannot keep us in prison forever.

'Awful, awful, awful.' I screw up the page and throw it at the wall. Of all the objections Lili counted off on her fingers the first she came up

47

with is the one that has me stumped. I don't know a thing about love letters. I sure as hell can't write one, anyway. I've been at it all night.

I try again to become Margot Lipsky. In my early years at school there was a Jewish girl in my class. I can't remember her name. What I do remember is her sister, who was about the age I am now. She was *so* beautiful — slim, with flawless olive skin and hair that hung down to her waist in a shimmering black rope. I never dared tell anyone — certainly not Mutti, who would have thrashed my legs with a wooden spoon — but I wanted to look like that girl.

Something happened soon after. More of the Jewish treachery, it must have been, because they weren't allowed to go to school with us anymore. Lili said she'd seen one girl in the back of a truck, being driven out of town. She exaggerated things sometimes, especially when we were younger, so I didn't know whether to believe her, but what I know for certain is that we never see any Jews on the streets of Oranienburg anymore.

That's my problem with this letter. I'm pretending to be a Jew. 'Filthy Jew,' I mutter under my breath because the words seem stuck together in my head — you can't say the second without the first. A shudder goes through my body because of what I see behind my eyes when I hear those words — rats scurrying down gutters to escape the pure German light and grimy, hook-nosed rabbis with black stubble on their chins who lean over blond-haired babies. And then the scene goes black because the films

I saw years ago never actually showed the horror that came next.

Their letters aren't like that, though. I've read dozens written by Jews, some of them every bit as loving as Dieter's, to wives, lovers, parents, to young children. The most heart-rending are the letters from men who've been selected or think they might be soon. They never actually say what they're being selected for. People I've asked only shake their heads or give official-sounding answers. 'It's a way of keeping the camp orderly and efficient,' one of the censors told me.

'The old and sick are sent somewhere else, is that what you mean?' I asked.

'Yes, Margot, that's what happens,' he answered and went back to his pile of letters.

Footsteps outside my door. Mutti's off to bed which means it's ten o'clock, and I still haven't written a single word worth keeping. At least I've faced down the Lipsky girl's Jewishness. I feel better about 'being' her now and this helps me see the mistake I've been making all night. All right, so she's a Jew, but the thing I have to lock on to is that she's in love with a young man who loves her too. I close my eyes and imagine what it would be like to receive such heartfelt letters and I want to return that affection with the same intensity.

My dearest Dieter,
Look up at the stars tonight and know that
every one of them is me and that their
twinkling is our laughter, unheard by those
close by, as ours was. Your letters tell me

49

you think of me every day, yet I knew that already for the stars shine here too and they beam your smile on me, warmer than sunshine. If it keeps you alive to have me inside your head then I am already with you and always will be. That makes you eternal, Dieter, for I won't leave this prison you've locked me in. A willing inmate seeks no escape.

You call me gentle and devoted and I cry remembering how easily those qualities came to me when you lavished ten times more on me. I have decided to store up all that we would share together now, if we were not forced apart this way. Then, when we stand face to face again, nothing will have been lost. What a thing it would be to drown in too much love and have God shaking his head as he welcomes us into his heaven. Why did I create death, he will say, when lovers like these smile at its embrace?

Life in this camp is harsh but you mustn't worry about me. It is you, Dieter, who must stay alive for the both of us. I send you my love with every word on this page and hope they end the torment you speak of. Mine only continues every day we are apart.

With all my love,
Margot

6

'Lili, let me in!'

I pound on the door with the palm of my hand and when it doesn't open quickly enough I press my forehead against the obstinate wood, hoping it might take pity on me. Above my head Herr Martin leans out through his bedroom window, but before he can complain at me making such a racket on a Sunday morning, Lili's there at the door and I sweep past her into the hall.

'What it is? Not bad news about Walther?'

'No, nothing like that,' I say over my shoulder. I'm already climbing the staircase to her room.

Once inside her bedroom I fall into her arms. 'I should have listened to you,' I confess between sobs. 'Everything you warned me about — the handwriting, even the words I used . . . He's sure to know it's a forgery. I put it in the mail for him to get on Friday and I've lain awake two nights in a row thinking of the moment he read my letter, of how hurt he must have been and how he must hate the person who sent it.'

Lili holds me, gently patting my back like a mother with a newborn baby. 'You're not a hurtful person, Margot,' she says when I leave a gap long enough for her to fill. 'You're trying to help him, even if you shouldn't have . . . ' I brace myself for the I-told-you-so, but she lets me off the hook. It's more than I deserve. 'Dieter will have torn it up and forgotten about it,' she says

51

instead. 'He'll never know it was the girl in the mailroom. He doesn't even know there *is* a girl in the mailroom.'

That's true, I suppose. I spend long enough reminding myself I don't exist as far as he's concerned and for once this is a good thing. My panic subsides and the Martins ask me to stay for breakfast.

'What put you in such a state, anyway?' asks Frau Martin.

Lili answers for me. 'Margot did something — ' she pauses, searching for the word ' — impulsive.'

'You Margot! You were always the level-headed one. Well, giving in to impulse is only to be expected when you have my daughter for your friend,' says Frau Martin, but she's only pretending to be critical. She adores Lili as much as I do.

'Is it really so bad to be impulsive?' I ask when Lili sees me to the door.

'It is for someone as innocent as you, my darling,' she says, giving me a final, comforting hug.

★　　★　　★

I cling to the hope that Lili is right and Dieter simply tore up my letter, using anger as a shield against the pain. October wipes away memories of the summer and then, ten days after I pounded on Lili's door, a postcard to Margot Lipsky falls into the barrel. Postcards aren't the same as letters — their words are starkly exposed, and I'm immediately aware of Dieter's

52

writing only centimetres from the address. I'm afraid to read it; petrified would be a better word, when I'm standing like a statue with the card in my hand, unable to move, unable to think. His words are certain to be laced with abuse for the ghoul who's used something so intimate to play a childish trick.

I stuff the card inside my jacket, where it taunts me as I move through my morning duties, until I'd rather read Dieter's abuse than go another minute imagining it. I walk out to the oil drum, planning to burn it once the searing words have delivered their message. I take a breath and force my eyes to focus.

Dear Margot,
Your letter has made me ten times stron-
ger, put some backbone into me, you
might say, and stopped the shameful tears
I shed too often in this horrible place. I
wish I could express emotion as fluently
and as clearly as you do. I carry your letter
with me to read whenever I can snatch a
moment and to protect it from thieves.
They can have whatever else they haven't
stolen already, but not your letter, because
it is the memory of you that keeps me
alive. Please write again when you can.
Dieter

I can't believe it. He doesn't suspect a thing! My letter worked, and look at the change in his mood. These aren't the words of a mind giving in to despair.

I weep with relief, laughing at myself as the tears roll down my cheeks. Relief becomes joy. 'You've done a good thing, Margot,' I say out loud. 'Maybe even saved a life.' I know damned well it's a self-satisfied joy and I must be wary of it, but under an autumn sky that has somehow become brighter and warmer, I don't care.

I wait until my tears have dried and the red around my eyes is surely gone, then return to the mailroom. Near the barrel is an abandoned desk where a censor once decided which letters would be allowed to carry their delight, relief, hope, promises, appeals, but mostly the longing of love to the eyes they were meant for. In the drawer is a stash of konzentrationslager stationery, and after a peek over my shoulder I take two . . . no, three . . . no, four sheets and hide them inside my uniform.

'How long does a letter take to reach Poland?' I ask Frau Cullmann, who's the only woman among the censors. For all the feminine friendship she offers me she might as well wear trousers.

'Five days, unless bombing has damaged the train tracks,' she replies. 'Who do you know in Poland?'

I don't answer.

'Don't tell me you have a boyfriend among the soldiers,' says Frau Cullmann.

Again I stay quiet, trying for a coy smile.

'Well, well, you'll be a match for your sister yet.' She nudges me with her elbow and goes off, chuckling to herself.

'Cow,' I mutter when she's out of earshot. Five

days to Poland, five days to return, and I should add a few more so he doesn't get suspicious. I can't send a second letter for a fortnight.

★ ★ ★

I try not to count the days. And fail. Each night I sit cross-legged on my bed scribbling phrases I like the sound of. I reread my first letter — I still have the draft copy that I poured out in a single, inspired torrent — and despair that I'll ever match it with a second. Who was I when I wrote those words? . . . *your smile on me, warmer than sunshine . . . drown in too much love . . .*

I'd been Margot Lipsky. That's the easy answer, yet I'm fooling myself and I know it. Margot Baumann wrote those words. They came out of my mind into my hand. I try again to melt the two of us together, but the gush of words doesn't come. I'll have to build this new letter more consciously. At least the other Margot's Jewishness doesn't mean a thing anymore — she'll be simply a girl in love, and the lucky object of an intense love that I'm trying to keep alive.

On a fresh page I write:

You may have been stolen from my sight, Dieter, but not even the Führer can steal you from my memory. Don't ever believe that, for I will never . . .

I stop in mid-sentence. The Führer? I want Dieter to know the most powerful force on earth can't make Margot forget him, but a censor might think there's a different meaning, that Adolf Hitler is the cruel force keeping them apart. I rub out 'Führer' and write 'devil himself', then gasp at how I've paired these two powers together. I'll come back to this later when the right words drop into my head.

How can you say you are not as fluent as me when your letters paint such a vivid picture of our love, more beautiful than the great artists have ever managed?

No, I'm getting too grand, reaching too far with my metaphors. This is a girl like me, in love, I remind myself and try again to imagine a way into the heart of Margot Lipsky.

As a girl I dreamed of meeting a man who would give me back ten times the love I was able to give him. It was a dream that lived separately from me, something I smiled at because even then I knew the difference between the magic of imagination and the numbness of being ordinary. Please live through this nightmare, Dieter, so I won't go back to the bleak and the mundane. Write to me of your misery if it helps. Something you wrote in your letters makes me think of a pact between us. Each morning when they march us to work we will be side by side.

This seems more promising, but there's a problem with what I've written that niggles at me. Much as I've tried to be another person, those words aren't just from me — they're about me. I don't know how to solve this problem so I set it aside and, combining fragments from drafts over many nights, I copy a second letter onto konzentrationslager stationery. Then, fourteen days after his postcard to me — no, his postcard to Margot Lipsky — I slip it into the pile of incoming mail.

★   ★   ★

I wait two days before I let myself check the barrel. After that I find a reason to visit it every day and feel my impatience rising each time there's nothing from Dieter. A week after my second letter he posts a card to his mother.

> *Dear Mutti,*
>
> *The socks and the biscuits were very welcome — thank you, thank you — but the cheese and the herring you listed in your letter weren't in the package. Men in my barracks say the guards and the kapos keep the best for themselves and they steal any money relatives send into the camp as well. Please do not waste the few marks you have when so little will reach me. They cannot steal your love from a sheet of paper, though, so please send a letter whenever you can.*
>
> *Your loving son,*
> *Dieter*

'There was no mention of Margot Lipsky,' I tell Lili.

We're on our way to the movie house to see *Sophienlund*, which we've seen twice before, but new films don't come to Oranienburg as often as they used to and a song from *Sophienlund* is one we dance to all the time in Lili's room.

'So you think that's proof, then?' Lili asks.

'That they hid their romance from their parents? Yes. I've thought so from the start.'

'You wanted him to write to Margot Lipsky, though, didn't you? Not his mother.'

I try for a smile of resignation and manage only a sigh.

'You were waiting for it.'

I'm starting to get irritated. 'Yes, all right, I was.'

'His letters aren't for you, Margot. You've got to be careful.'

'Of what?'

'Of falling in love with him,' she says bluntly.

'He's in love with Margot Lipsky. I know that!' I'm close to shouting.

Lili's got her patient face on, the one that says, 'I know you better than you know yourself, Margot Baumann.'

'He needs her alive in his head,' I tell Lili, wishing she would understand. 'That's why I'm writing to him. He won't give up as long as he has her to write to and me to write back.'

'Come on, we'll be late,' she says, taking my arm, while to the south a distant storm flares on the horizon and its low rumble carries to our ears on the evening breeze. Only it's not the flash of lightning we can see, nor the rumble of thunder we can hear. Bombs are falling on Berlin again tonight.

7

Dearest Margot,
The days grow cold and the nights even
colder. Your letters are my blanket and my
stove and I count the days until I hear
from you again . . .

This letter comes only a week after the postcard
to Dieter's mother. He goes on to write of the
feast the two families will enjoy when they're
released from their konzentrationslager.

I imagine myself sitting down to eat, with
you opposite me, of course, your family
and mine all around us, and no one will
know we are caressing each other's feet
beneath the table.

There are more tender words and playful
reminders of stolen kisses and the electric sweat
of near-discovery. I'm desperate to know their
secrets, partly so I can invent similar snatches of
memory to write in my replies, but mostly
because I'm so drawn into their story. It's like
reading a novel one random page at a time.

I agonise for a fortnight over Margot Lipsky's
reply.

Dear Dieter,
Like you I use the memory of us together

60

to warm my hands and feet. When it is
time for that feast you wrote about, I will
be the cook. I will do roast beef and
blintzes with strawberries. Remember this
because when you sit down to such a
meal, it will mean there is no more war
and our time apart is truly over.

I fill every line on the too small page with hope, encouragement and the love of a girl far away in Poland.

As I slip it among the incoming mail the first snow falls gently onto the appelplatz, melting the instant it comes to rest as though the konzentrationslager draws the beauty, the purpose, even the will to survive from everything within its walls.

Two days later I just make it to the mailroom before heavy rain sets in. Only my raincoat and the unteroffizier's umbrella keep me dry as I flit from hut to hut, and not even these can keep the water out of my shoes.

'My feet are blocks of ice,' I tell the entire mailroom once the final round is done.

'It'll be worse tonight,' says Bruno. 'The ache in my hip is better than any weather report on the radio. Once the sky clears there'll be frost for sure.'

All afternoon, rain hangs around outside the door like an unwanted dog. It's still there when I'm free to go home. 'Scheisse,' I mutter, unfurling my raincoat.

Then voices, laughter. I look up to see Renate run out of a door at the other end of the gatehouse with an officer beside her, holding an umbrella above her head. I can guess who he is. My sister slips elegantly into the back seat of a waiting car and, before I think to call out, Kapitän Goldapp is waving her off. Damn! I could have gone home with her. I look at the unpromising sky then trudge back into the mailroom and spend the hour it takes for the rain to ease writing a letter for Franz's birthday.

By the time I'm done the prisoners are returning to camp. I have to stand between two wooden huts near the gatehouse to let a squad pass. Is Dieter among them? Even if I knew what he looked like it's too dark to see faces. There's enough light from electric lamps to make out their bodies, though. Every man is soaked to the skin and shivering uncontrollably even as he fights to stay in step. Then they disappear through the gates. If they were the gates of hell at least there'd be some warmth to get them through the night.

★   ★   ★

'Don't they let prisoners shelter from the rain?' I demand of Vati when I'm barely through the door.

He looks surprised at how sharply I've spoken, but I don't care and let my face show it.

'The men you saw were quarry workers, most likely,' he says once I've explained. 'If they stopped production every time it rained, Margot, nothing would get done.'

Quarry workers! Dieter mentioned a quarry.

Now I'm frantic. 'But they were frozen to the bone, and bone is all that's left of them. Vati, they'll die if we treat them like that!'

'Thousands die for the Reich every day,' says my mother, who's come from the kitchen to see why I'm so steamed up. 'Soldiers fight in the rain — why shouldn't these criminals do their job in the rain, too?'

'Would you say the same if the Russians treated Walther like that? There's going to be a frost tonight. Their clothes will freeze on their bodies.'

At least Mutti winces at this, but rather than answer me she goes back into the kitchen, leaving Vati to shrug his shoulders.

I stomp upstairs to change out of my wet clothes and find Renate standing in front of the mirror in a dress I haven't seen before. It's silk, I'm sure of it. Kapitän Goldapp, I say to myself with a sniff and start towards my bed. In those few steps, though, my mind races from shivering prisoners to umbrellas in the rain and back to my sister in a dress given to her by her lover.

'Renate,' I say, before I lose my nerve, 'I need a favour.'

'Anything, darling, except my make-up.'

'Nothing like that. I was wondering if you would ask Kapitän Goldapp to arrange something for me.'

Renate turns from her reflection to face me. Her eyebrows have tightened at my mention of the captain. 'Why would he arrange something for you?'

'Because he likes you and I'm your sister.'

63

Renate glares at me. It's more clearly a warning now, so I hurry on. 'A little favour, that's all. Will you ask him?'

'That depends on what it is,' she says cautiously.

'Nothing really,' I say lightly. 'Just change the work assignment for one of the prisoners.'

'One of the prisoners? Why?'

'I don't want to say. It doesn't matter to you, does it?'

Renate continues to watch me, waiting for an explanation. When I stay silent, she loses patience and turns back to the mirror, pulling at the fabric to make the dress sit properly at her waist. She does look smart. I can't help wishing I had a dress like that.

'I'm not going to embarrass myself over some silly whim of yours, Margot. Those lazy drones in the mailroom want a prisoner to do their work for them, is that it?'

'No, it's nothing to do with the mailroom.' I wonder if I dare tell her about Dieter, but Renate is already reaching for her handbag. 'I'm meeting some officers for a drink. A car will be here any minute.' And without a backwards look, she heads for the stairs, leaving me dripping and bedraggled and dismissed as a fool.

★ ★ ★

Through dinner I can think only of the night ahead. Dieter is surely as wet as the men I saw sloshing through the gate. My head fills with even worse fears. Winter has barely begun, with

64

the bitter weeks of January and February lying in wait like the jaws of an icy monster. When my parents have gone to bed and it's time for me to pull the blankets over myself to sleep, I've never been so aware of their warmth.

★ ★ ★

Later, I wake in darkness to find Renate undressing for bed.

'What time is it?' I murmur.

'Nearly midnight. The captain asked me to go back to the konzentrationslager to finish an urgent report.'

That will be what she tells Mutti. I slip out of bed and, after closing the bedroom door, switch on the lamp.

'I don't need the light on. And open the door or the room will get stuffy.'

I ignore her and instead sit on my bed and say, 'I need to talk to you.'

'Not now, I'm tired.'

'Yes now, while Vati and Mutti are asleep.'

Renate lifts her eyes to the ceiling — or is it to God in his heaven, hoping he'll save her from this pesky little sister? 'If you want some boyfriend advice it'll have to wait until the morning.'

'It's you who needs boyfriend advice.'

Renate snaps to attention. 'What do you mean by that?'

'Kapitän Goldapp is married. What you're doing is wrong.'

'I haven't got a clue what you're talking about,

Margot. The captain's my boss, nothing more.'

'Do you really expect us to believe you're working on these nights you come home at midnight? If stupid, naïve Margot Baumann can see what's going on, how many others are talking?'

The easy confidence slips from my sister's face, but only for an instant. 'Rumours are everywhere, about everyone,' she retorts. 'No one believes half of what they hear.'

I wish I could tell her about my encounter with the commandant, but it would only lead to distracting questions, so I invent a lie. 'Even the old crocks in the mailroom are gossiping. Their old favourite, Renate, and Kapitän Goldapp — it's all they talk about, even the unteroffizier. Word will reach Mutti sooner or later.'

The trick works. Renate turns aside, unable to face me, and even though I've started our conversation for a different reason, this glimpse of her vulnerability makes me play the loving sister. 'You have to end your affair. It's wrong. I know it's hard for you to see it, but so many people will get hurt.'

Renate rounds on me. 'Oh, stop all this pure-hearted claptrap, Margot. You're right about one thing: you're naïve, a baby with your schoolgirl hair — you have no idea what love does to you once it takes hold. I'm sorry for you, really I am, for the dull vision of love you've got up here.' She taps her own forehead. 'You'll settle for what Mutti and Vati have, boring, bloodless and empty. When a love like the captain and I have comes along, marriage vows don't mean a thing; it's like a fever and nothing can stand in its way. But you'll never know anything about that, Margot; you'll never feel what I feel for him.'

Her words sting me horribly because there might be more truth to them than I want to admit. What had Lili's mother called me? Level-headed! That's how people see me, because that's how I am. The only risk I've ever taken was to write to Dieter Kleinschmidt and what kind of risk is that? I pat myself on the back and say my letters might save his life, but what use are letters against a winter working in that quarry?

Level-headed is just another word for cowardice, I tell myself. What if my cowardice extends to love? What if it makes me reach always for the safe, the contained, the half-lived? I think again about the grass fire that burned out all too soon and picture my parents' faces in the dying flames. I haven't seen them hug one another in years.

Am I in love with Dieter Kleinschmidt? I don't know. How can you love someone you haven't met? It would be wrong of me, anyway, when he belongs to another Margot. But I've experienced his letters more intensely than anything in my life until now, and knowing this makes me angry at the contempt in Renate's voice, as though I'm Margot the mouse, too afraid to grab what I want.

Something hardens inside me. I'm going to get Dieter Kleinschmidt through this winter. I don't need to answer for my motives. I don't care if they are good or reasonable or even honourable. This is something I want, in the way my sister has wanted things all her life and gone after them for no other reason.

'Renate,' I say, 'I asked you for a favour — a different work assignment for one of the prisoners. You're going to arrange it, or Mutti and Vati are going to hear about your affair.'

Renate's eyes widen, then close, slit-like, in fury. 'Blackmail. Is that what you've sunk to?'

In struggles with my sister I've always been crippled by uncertainty. Not this time. In a low, determined tone I say, 'You'll do what I'm asking, Renate.'

'No!' she cries, loud enough to be heard outside our room. 'I won't let you hold this over me. I won't do it.'

I get up off the bed and shout with equal venom, 'Yes you will!'

Before either of us can say more the bedroom door opens to reveal our parents standing sleepy and bewildered in the passageway. 'What's going on? Why this arguing in the middle of the night?'

I turn deliberately towards Renate, shaping my face into a question — *the* question.

She shakes her head defiantly.

'Well?' my father demands. 'What's this about?'

'Mutti, Vati,' I say, 'Renate is — '

My sister jumps in before I can get the words out — and they *were* ready on my tongue like the bolt on a crossbow. I was going to do it without hesitation, or doubt, or guilt.

'I'm going to do Margot a favour,' says Renate. 'I said no at first — that's what we were arguing about — but I've changed my mind.'

'What favour?' Mutti asks, intrigued.

68

Renate moves her lips and tongue but only a throaty rumble comes out, leaving me to answer in her place. 'Kapitän Goldapp has been getting her make-up from the black market,' I say. 'I want some too, so I can look nice.'

'That's what all this shouting was about?' asks Vati, unable to believe it. 'Make-up?'

Mutti draws him away with a hand on his shoulder. 'They're girls, Gerhard. Such things are important to them.'

★ ★ ★

During the days after I confronted Renate, the weather grants a little mercy while I wait for news that the switch has been made. I've told her it has to be something indoors, somewhere warm. Remembering the chimney on the far side of the konzentrationslager I suggested Dieter might help with the furnace.

'He wouldn't thank you for that,' she'd replied sourly, but didn't explain why.

I'm nervous. I look between the bars into the appelplatz when I should be delivering letters and Unteroffizier Junge will reprimand me any minute, but every prisoner I see now is Dieter. This morning they hanged a man during rollcall and prisoners were still taking down the body when I arrived for work. It's him, I thought. Oh God, what have I done? But Frau Cullmann said it was a Jew who'd tried to kill a kapo during the night.

I'm at the window again in the afternoon when Renate appears in the mailroom for the first time since I took her place. 'How are you all? I miss you terribly,' she tells the other workers. They know she's lying but smile broadly at her anyway. With a pretty face, you can get away with anything.

'Margot,' she whispers when she's close enough, 'Kapitän Goldapp wants to discuss what job would suit your prisoner friend.'

I follow her out into the cold, past the gate I've come to loathe and in through a different door of the same building. Up a flight of stairs, Kapitän Goldapp is waiting for us at the door of his office.

'Margot, please come in,' he says with a stiff smile. He's as handsome as Renate is beautiful. They'd make a good couple if he didn't already have a wife.

'Thank you,' I respond politely, squeezing past him. All the way here I've been trying to guess which jobs the captain has in mind. Out of the weather, I remind myself. Nothing less.

The door closes with the three of us inside and instantly the captain's smile vanishes. 'Sit down,' he orders coldly, pushing his own chair behind me.

But this will give him the power of height over me. 'No,' I say, 'I'd rather stand.'

'Sit down!' he roars with such force my legs give way beneath me. I'm still trying to recover from the shock when he grips the arms of the chair and leans his face close to mine. 'Now listen to me, little Margot. You think you can blackmail your sister and me, but you're mistaken. In fact, it's the other way around. Like a fool, you gave Renate the number for this prisoner you care so much about. And a number gives me a name: Dieter Kleinschmidt. That's right, isn't it?'

I strain every muscle in my face, but I can't keep the fear from my eyes. He knows he's got the right name.

'I've already sent the order — but not the one you want. Tonight, when this Dieter returns to his barracks, the kapos will be waiting for him. If he's lucky the beating will leave him able to work. If not, well . . . ' He lets go of the chair to rock back on his heels. When he looks down at me again his lips have curled into a malicious smile. 'There's a selection due at the end of the week. I wouldn't count on his chances.'

'No — you must stop them!' I'm ready to promise anything, to fall on my knees and plead in front of him. I'll beg Renate to forgive me for blackmailing her . . . anything that will stop the beating. But Kapitän Goldapp doesn't give me the chance.

'*Must?*' he cries, his eyes bulging with rage. He presses his weight onto the arms of my chair again, his face even closer this time, while I fight the shaking that wants to take over every inch of my body. '*Must* is a word you do not say to me, Margot. It's *you* who must do what *I* say. Is that clear?' He pauses briefly, and when he speaks again the rage has gone from his voice, but not the malice. 'It's not too late to countermand my order. This Dieter can sleep well tonight if you do as I say, but in the morning he will go to the quarry with the rest and you will forget your

71

infatuation with him — or you might end up in the camp alongside him, for helping an enemy of the Reich.'

A gasp from behind me. 'No, Albie.'

'Quiet, Renate,' snaps the captain.

'But you wouldn't really . . . you never said anything about . . . '

I turn around to see my sister's face has gone white with fear and something else . . . Shame.

Goldapp frowns at her irritably then seems to remember me in the chair before him. 'If you breathe one word to anyone about Renate and me, Kleinschmidt will die in the next selection.'

Although no one has said as much, for a while I've suspected that selection is a death sentence — now the captain has confirmed it. I'm utterly confused and frightened for myself now as well as for Dieter. If I could only think!

'Do you understand your position, Margot? Do you agree? Nod if your tongue won't work and this will be over. Once you accept your girlish game is finished you can go back to the mailroom.'

No one has ever pressured me this way, nor spoken to me with such venom.

'Well?' the captain demands. 'Do you agree?'

My lips want to form a simple 'yes'. I just want this intimidation to end. I look at Renate, who's doing her best to harden her face. She can't quite manage it and I see now that these two would never throw me into the konzentration-slager. That much was a bluff, at least. But it's Dieter I must think of. If I agree, then there'll be no beating and that's some relief. Things will be like they were before.

I just want to get out of this room. I clutch at words swirling inside my head. *Like they were before*, I hear again amid the storm. I can still write to Dieter, still be his Margot. But didn't I come here with different words in my head? *Out of the weather. Nothing less.* The deal they're forcing on me is no deal at all.

I stand up, making the captain step back. He thinks I'm ready to agree, yet just making him give ground like this lends me strength. I stare at my sister's lover and see death in his face. Life and death, I remind myself. I've come to appreciate the true meaning of those words like never before.

'No,' I say as coldly as anything said to me since I came through the door. 'Dieter needs a job indoors for the winter. Only when he's safe will you two be safe as well.'

Fury flares in Goldapp's face. He raises his hand as if to slap me.

'You'll do as you're told!'

There's more, but I don't take it in, because his body has betrayed his desperate need to make me submit. Renate is edgy, too. This isn't going the way she'd expected. Despite their threats, I've got the upper hand. I've had it all along and they've simply tried to cheat me out of the power I still hold over them — if I'm tough enough to use it.

Somewhere out of the rain and the snow. If I can come up with a solution, make it easy for them . . . Odd pictures flicker into my mind. Men unloading baskets from a dilapidated truck.

'Dieter can work in the laundry,' I say, trying desperately to make it sound like a demand, not a suggestion. 'As long as he's safe in the old Jew's laundry, then so is your secret.'

Goldapp still looks determined to break me, but Renate speaks first. 'The laundry. Maybe he can be moved, Albie.' Her eyes flick towards the captain, who scowls and mutters darkly, 'If you give in once to blackmail, you keep on paying.'

Renate wraps her arms around herself in a gesture I recognise. She wants all this over and done with as much as I do. 'This deal has to be the end to it, Margot. You can't go on demanding privileges for this prisoner. If you agree, then maybe Albie will . . . '

She trails off, unsure of her lover, but she's called it a deal. I'm so close to getting Dieter out of the quarry. 'Yes, the last time,' I say quickly. 'If you stick to your side of the bargain I won't come to you again. That's a promise.'

Goldapp explodes in contempt. 'A promise! The words of a schoolgirl. You say that now, but when the fellow whinges to you again what is such a promise worth?'

'Wait, Albie,' says Renate, and to my surprise my sister takes me gently by the elbow. 'Margot may be a fool, but I've never known her to go back on her word.' Without releasing her grip she shifts to stand between me and the captain. 'This is the end to it, you understand,' she tells us both firmly. 'Each side sticks to what we've decided here today. Are we agreed?'

I say yes, or maybe I simply nod. Whatever sign I give, I'm gone from the room and down the stairs before I'm fully aware of myself again, and once I do come to life, I burst through the door to the outside and throw up into the mud.

Urh! With the foulness wiped from my mouth I cry quietly to release the rest of what's dammed up inside me, and when that's gone too, I look up at the sky. A few clouds scurry across vivid blue and the cold air in my lungs feels like life itself.

I start to laugh.

8

Dear Mutti,
I've had the most wonderful stroke of luck.
My work now is in the laundry, where it is
WARM!! . . .

Dieter posts this card into my barrel late in
November. Although Renate had said the switch
was made the day after our confrontation, this is
the first evidence I trust. More news comes a
week later.

Dear Margot,
I spend my days in warmth now and for
once it isn't thoughts of you alone that
keep me from shivering. I have been
moved to the laundry where the work is
not so hard. This makes me wonder what
influence you have over the gods. Are
there more than one, Margot? For a while
I've been wondering if there are any at all.
Then a poem changed my mind. You
don't know that I wrote you poems. Just as
well I didn't show them to you because
they were awful. But this one is by a great
poet. There is a man in our barracks who
began reciting poems out loud to fight off
our living death, but some didn't like it
and cried out to him, 'Stop! Stop! What's
the point of fine words in a place like this?'

I went to him afterwards and asked him to whisper the poems to me. He's a university professor and knows much Goethe off by heart. He taught me this one.

Who has never eaten his bread with tears
Who has never, through night's sorrowful hours,
Sat on his bed and wept with fear,

He knows not you, your heavenly powers

So I still believe in some kind of heavenly power, Margot. I believe in you, that you spoke to the God who won't listen to me and had him change my work assignment to the laundry. I like this kind of God better, and wish only that He grants the same mercy to you, in place of the love I can only send from so far away.
Your loving Dieter

I write poems that I never let anyone see. Like Dieter, I cringe at how awful they are and mock myself for even trying. Each time I reread this letter I still fight tears at the way every word he writes brings him closer to me. Now I've drawn even closer, not by the hand of God but my own.

Since the laundry is visible across the appelplatz, I spend even more time staring through the mailroom window. You're going to make it through the winter, I promise Dieter, wishing my words could float across the filthy snow and through the walls until they whisper in his ear. The words should warm my own heart,

77

too, but I'm not satisfied, and I know why. I might be good at pretending when I write letters in the name of another girl, yet pretending to myself is harder. I don't just want to save Dieter's life, I want to be part of his life; I want to meet him, I want to know if he's like his letters.

I should give myself a good talking-to right now about honouring the promise I made at the beginning. But whatever hardened inside me on the night I blackmailed my own sister is building a new Margot. God, how many Margots are there going to be? And as soon as I ask the question a sly voice answers, As many as you need to make. Slough off one and emerge as another like an insect, if that's what it takes. I don't know who I'm going to end up being, but it won't be the girl I once was. The girl I used to be wouldn't dare go inside the wire.

9

I'll only get one chance at what I'm planning and it has to look like a clumsy accident.

'Excuse me, Unteroffizier, I need to replenish your ink pad,' I say casually from a spot close by his desk. I've already flitted like a bee from censor to censor doing the same with an open bottle of ink. The unteroffizier hands up his ink pad without looking at me. This is the moment. Something so simple and yet my heart is racing like a kitten's. I jerk forward with a deliberate *Oh!* as though I've stubbed my toe and . . . yes, yes, yes, the sleeve of his uniform is an oozing mess.

I gasp. 'What have I done? I'm so sorry, Unteroffizier. Oh, look at the stain. It's ruined.'

Frau Cullmann wanders over for a closer look, but no one takes charge. So *I* do.

'If we can wash out the ink before it dries . . . the thing is to act quickly.' I come around behind the unteroffizier and help him out of his jacket, all the while firing words like bullets from a machine gun. 'I'll take care of it. It's my fault, so it's the least I can do. The laundry's only a minute away through the gate.' I'm halfway across the appelplatz before he quite knows he's given the order.

And halfway is as far as I get before I'm aware of the space around me. I mean truly aware in a way I can't possibly be when gaping through the grimy glass of the mailroom. I'm standing where the prisoners line up for rollcall, which sometimes goes on for hours, where they are beaten if they speak to one another, beaten if they faint, beaten if a guard feels like beating them. I know this from the hundreds of letters I've read, but even those letters haven't prepared me for the misery that rises up from the gravel. I've had to step inside the wire myself before I can feel it, no more visible than ghosts in a graveyard, but present behind my eyes all the same. So much torment has leached into this ground I wondered if anything could ever grow here again.

Already I want to be outside the wire again. If it were only the stained jacket that had brought me this far, I'd hurry back and stammer pathetic apologies to Unteroffizier Junge. But the jacket is no more than an excuse. I set off again, ignoring the machine-gun towers with their barrels pointed at me, until I've crossed the appelplatz and pushed open a door into the half-dark of the laundry.

'Who's the chief laundryman?' I ask the first person I see.

The man whips off his striped cap before nodding towards a much older man who's huddled over a lamp while he examines a woman's blouse.

'My unteroffizier wants this seen to immediately,' I say when I reach him.

The prisoner looks up at me cautiously. I can tell by his features that he's the old Jew I've heard about, and the yellow triangle beside his number confirms it. He lays down the blouse he's been inspecting and accepts the SS jacket in its place. 'Ink. It will leave a stain.'

'My unteroffizier wants it completely gone. I'm to stay here until it's done.'

'Always the impossible,' he mutters. 'You'll be here a long time.'

I try to look annoyed at the news when in fact it's exactly what I was hoping to hear.

I shiver extravagantly and move deeper into the building as though searching for somewhere warm to wait. What I discover is a row of tubs lining one wall of a mostly open space with benches in the centre where prisoners stand sorting clothes in much the way I handle mail. Overhead, uniforms, underwear, even dresses and colourful scarves hang drying in long lines. I move among the working figures, reading numbers wherever I can. The triangles in front of each are mostly red and a few purple, which I've learned means a Jehovah's Witness. The only yellow I've seen was on the old Jew. These aren't the walking corpses I've seen near the gates, but they're underfed and sickly and I can't help wondering when was the last time any of them laughed out loud.

Damn, so many are turned away from me. I keep moving, and in a corner far from the door find an alcove partially shielded by racks of clothing. I take note and start another round of the benches. Two men have finished wringing clothes at the tubs and are now pegging them to a line lowered from the ceiling. One is in his twenties, as best as I can guess. I shift his way.

81

There's an A at the start of his number, and immediately my heartbeat rises, but when I step closer the first digit is a six.

The other figure is as tall as Walther, although the awkward way he moves his long limbs makes me think he's a teenager. No one so young could write letters like Dieter's. I start to move past the skinny boy . . . then stop in my tracks. There's an A on his chest and then a 7. The other numbers match. Blood is moving through my body the way a mob riots in the streets. His face is too pinched by hunger and weariness to be handsome, as Lili and I had joked he would be. What else had we predicted that day beside the lake when it had all been a game? The cap and the shaven head guard the secret of his hair colour and there's not enough light to learn the colour of his eyes. But what does it matter? This is Dieter Kleinschmidt.

I shift to see him more clearly and suddenly he snatches the cap from his head and stands rigidly to attention, staring at his feet. It takes a few moments to realise that I'm the cause. I shudder at the submission drilled into him. In the world of these prisoners, even the mailroom girl can evoke fear.

'You are Dieter Kleinschmidt,' I say in a voice so low none of the others can hear.

The words jolt his entire body, and despite the discipline of fear he looks up, revealing more of his face. He's so like the other boys I know — Ferdy, Jens and the rest who call themselves men while they wait eagerly for the army's call. 'How old are you?' I ask.

He's confused and deeply wary of me. Why do you wish to know? his face seems to ask.

'I must identify you properly, then I'll explain.'

'Seventeen,' he answers.

So young. Only a year older than me. 'And your mother's name?'

'Anna.'

I nod, as though with his answers he has passed some kind of test. 'Find a way to move behind those racks,' I say and walk off, taking a cigarette from the pack I've borrowed from Lili as part of a plan to make me seem older and more self-assured. I copy her grown-up elegance in the way I smoke it, all the time thinking to myself, what's taking him so long? I don't dare look around, in case it's obvious I'm waiting for him. It seems like an hour — probably ten minutes really — before he places a basket of laundry on a bench beside the racks. I make myself count out another minute then wander over.

'The kapo keeps a lookout,' Dieter whispers as he starts to fold clean underwear, 'but I'm in no trouble here as long as I'm busy.'

I can't take my eyes off him. This is really the man — the boy — who writes such loving letters to Margot. He's so different from what I imagined. I settle one question for Lili immediately. His eyes are blue, sapphire blue. So tall, too, although it's not that which made him seem awkward, I realise now. It's more that he's lost so much weight quickly and painfully. Is it any surprise there's no colour to his skin, even in the warmth of the laundry? I'm still mortified at the way he reacted so meekly when I first approached him. I don't want him to fear me; I want him to look at me.

I check for watching eyes and when the moment's right I lean forward and place a hunk of bread on the bench within Dieter's reach. His eyes go wide.

'Eat it,' I urge.

He snatches it greedily. The pleasure on his face as he swallows the bread is almost too much for me to watch. I reach forward with another piece.

'Why?' he asks.

'It comes from your mother, through a system of connections. I'm simply the last link in the chain.' This is the story I decided on. 'You told her it's no use posting anything so she's found another way.' I give him a third piece of bread and two Reichsmarks which he stuffs into his shirt.

'I'm still not sure you're real, but this bread is,' he says, and there's the hint of a smile. I could never have imagined a fleeting smile could make me so happy. 'When you said my name, it sounded strange. No — it sounded wonderful. In here we are numbers. I've seen prisoners beaten for calling another by his name.' He represses a shudder.

'I know nothing about you. Only the number I was to look for. How did you end up in Sachsenhausen?' I ask. He wears a black triangle, I've noticed. From Bruno I've learned this is the colour for enemies of the Reich.

Footsteps interrupt me. I retreat towards the

window and play the impatient messenger with another cigarette. With studied boredom, I pretend to sense the presence of the newcomer and turn to look him up and down. He wears the stripes of a prisoner but lacks the deference of the others and, if this isn't evidence enough, the truncheon wedged into his belt proves he's a kapo.

'Is the unteroffizier's jacket ready?' I ask him, mimicking Renate at her most haughty.

'The fräulein had best ask the Jew,' he answers respectfully, while at the same time letting me know such matters are beneath him.

At the bench Dieter works as though he's not there, folding items precisely and placing them in neat piles until the kapo gives a snort of contempt and saunters away.

When it's safe, I drift closer once more. 'You're so young. What did you do to end up in Sachsenhausen?'

But Dieter now stands in front of three stacks of underwear and there is nothing left to fold. He looks down at the laundry for a few seconds, glances left and right to be sure that the kapo isn't watching, then knocks over the piles. Not satisfied, he plunges his hands into the mess, creasing and crumpling before he dumps the lot back into the basket. Then he begins folding again.

I watch the whole performance wide-eyed, and when he sees my astonishment he shakes with silent laughter. I join in and, since laughter as spontaneous as this is precious, neither of us wants to stop.

'You asked why I'm here,' he says at last. 'It's because of my father. At least that's what the SS would tell you.' The way he spits out the double letters is laced with hatred. 'Vati had a boyhood friend growing up in Leipzig, a Jew name Lipsky.'

I freeze. The name has to seem new to me. How do those actresses control their faces? Dieter's not looking at me, though. He stares down at the clothing on the bench, his mind far away. 'When the laws started against Jews, the Lipskys came to Hannover with false papers so Mr Lipsky could work in my father's warehouse. For years no one knew they were actually Jews, but when the war began and it was too late to flee, he worried he'd been recognised in the street, so my father boarded up a disused corner of the warehouse. He was clever — you couldn't tell there was space behind the wall. The whole Lipsky family lived there for almost a year. It was my job to take them supplies . . . '

He pauses, eyes still focused on his busy hands while he travels deep into his memories.

'At night, you see, there were no workers. The family could come out, walk around, get away from each other for a bit . . . '

More silence. I know now how his romance with the family's daughter had begun and why his letters spoke of Margot as being a prisoner even before she was sent to Poland.

'They were careless, though. They gave you away and that's why you're here?'

Dieter lets out a painful sigh. There's a gentleness in him that I'm starting to notice in

86

the way he speaks and the way he works his hands. Not weakness, though — far from it!

'No, not careless,' he tells me. 'Unlucky. One of my father's men brought his grandson to work because the school had been bombed. He kicked a ball around the warehouse to pass the time, it came to rest in the wrong place, he heard something . . . ' Dieter raises his head to look at me, inviting me to picture the rest.

'The Gestapo came for them?'

He nods, closing his eyes in resignation. 'They dragged the Lipskys out of hiding. A truck was waiting to take them for deportation, but before they were pushed aboard they had to watch the Gestapo beat my father. 'This is what happens to Jew-lovers,' they shouted.

'Another of our workers slipped away to warn Mutti and found me home from training school. I was going to be a radio operator in the Wehrmacht.' He laughs bitterly at this. 'My father was already a mass of blood by the time I arrived and still those thugs swung their batons. I couldn't bear it, the way the rest looked on and did nothing. I snatched up a piece of wood and charged at them, smashed one on the head, but they were too strong. They made me stand close enough for my father's blood to splash onto my clothes and kept at it until he was dead. Then they took me to a cell in Hardenbergstrasse. I was sent here to Sachsenhausen the next day.'

'Your poor father,' I say and, forgetting where we are entirely, I reach across and take his hand. He reels away from my touch as though I've burned him, then relaxes and lets my hand close over his. He stares at our two hands, and I wonder if he can't quite connect what he's seeing with the warmth of my touch. He fights tears and loses the struggle.

'I'm sorry. The odd thing is . . . I didn't cry when it happened,' he tells me. 'Or in the cell while I waited for them to shoot me. Here with you, this is the first time.'

'I would cry every night if it had been my father.'

He looks down at me. 'You don't think me a coward then?'

'It takes courage just to stay alive in this camp,' I answer, surprising myself.

'That's more true than you realise. You need courage to trust people and I haven't had that kind of courage since . . . '

I almost finish for him: *since Leon died.* Thank God I stop myself.

'Trust the wrong person in this place and you pay for it. I lost my shoes that way. I let a man talk me into taking them off because it was summer back then and my feet would get hot during the night. In the morning my shoes were gone, of course, and all the bastard did was grin at me, like I'd been a fool to believe him.'

'Do you trust me?' I ask.

'Looks that way. You're the first person I've really spoken to in weeks.' His smile is like a warm chasm that's opened up just for me. Tears flood my eyes. Damn, damn. He has to think I'm just a messenger with no personal stake in his life. I remember I've brought more food for him — two inches of wurst and some dried turnip cake filched from under Mutti's nose. I fumble them out of my coat and while he scrambles to get them hidden inside his own clothing I force the treacherous sentiment out of my face.

'It's not just getting cheated, though,' he says, going deeper into himself. 'Trust becomes friendship and friends can die. In an instant they're gone and the hole it rips open in your chest never heals over. I'm too much of a coward to endure that again.'

I can't imagine being afraid to make friends. What kind of world is this camp that I've stared into for so long from behind the mailroom window?

'What can I bring you?' I ask.

'Shoes,' he says instantly. 'These clogs blister my feet and there's no warmth in them.' He removes a foot from one clog and I wince at the angry sores.

'I'll see what I can do.'

★   ★   ★

The Jew comes looking for me. 'Fräulein, it's hopeless. Tell the unteroffizier I will need to bleach the sleeve and redye it. Five days, at least.'

I make a show of disgust then flounce away without a backwards glance. Five days! Perfect. I'll need that long to get more food together to bring Dieter. And a pair of shoes — that will take time, too.

I don't see the kapo until he steps out of the shadows.

'Let me escort you to the door, Fräulein.'

89

'I know the way.'

'Yes, but you don't know about my thirst,' he says, falling into stride beside me.

'What are you talking about?'

'Schnapps,' he answers. 'If you want another visit like today, you'll need to quench my thirst.'

'I'm here on business for my unteroffizier.'

We're at the door by this time, but the kapo blocks my path. 'Did you think your little performance with the cigarette would hide what you're up to? You came to see that boy.'

'What boy? I was waiting for the jacket to — '

'Enough,' the kapo snaps irritably. 'I survive in this camp because I watch and take my chances where I see them. Don't look so scared; you can still bring titbits to your boyfriend.'

'He's not my boyfriend.'

'Cousin, acquaintance, it makes no difference to me. You care about him, that's what counts.' He grins, showing filthy teeth. Hair sprouts from beneath his cap and there's no pallid skin or hollow cheeks for him, nor the stooped shoulders of a man who lives in constant fear. His eyes have the flinty gaze of a predator and the chill of a blizzard.

'When you come to fetch your boss's jacket, what will be left of your friend? Will he even be here?' The kapo rests his hand deliberately on the protruding handle of his truncheon. 'Come back, don't come back, it's all the same to me, but that boy will die if I don't get my schnapps.'

This time I cross the appelplatz barely taking in what I see. How am I going to get a bottle of schnapps when shops haven't sold any for a year and even my father can't afford black market prices?

⋆ ⋆ ⋆

'Your sister could sort out that wretched kapo for you — or her captain could, at least,' says Lili.

The cinema is open again, for as long as the electricity lasts, anyway, and we've hurried through the snow to see what's showing. Mostly we want to be away from home and the soul-gnawing silence weekends have become now that no one will talk about the war, even though there's nothing else to talk about.

'I can't go to Renate. I promised I wouldn't bother them again.'

Lili rolls her eyes. 'What does that matter? You still have them over a barrel and they know it.'

'It's not as simple as you think,' I tell her. 'The captain's a proud man, Lili, and vicious. I think he would rather give up what he loves than lose face, especially to a girl. If I go back on my word, he'll dump Renate just to spite me, and you know who'll pay the heaviest price, don't you?'

'I hadn't thought of it like that,' Lili admits meekly.

'I have to solve this myself, with a bottle of schnapps.'

'All right, then, no help from Renate,' Lili replies. 'But that doesn't mean you're on your own. I've got an idea.'

91

10

The bierkeller is in Kanalstrasse. I've been doubtful from the beginning and I'm still not sure we should go in.

'We've come this far and your mother didn't have a clue what we're wearing under these coats. That's a good omen, isn't it?' says Lili. To her, this is a daring challenge, like we're back pinching apples from Herr Koder's tree on the way home from school.

A fog of cigarette smoke draws us in among the rowdy voices and the sweaty, beery smell of men who've escaped from Sachsenhausen for a few hours at least. Other than the bartender and the musicians, every man wears a uniform. This bierkeller is for the guards who man the machine-gun towers, who herd prisoners to the Heinkel aircraft factory and the quarry, who train the dogs and hold them, straining and snarling, on their leashes. Clusters of them sit facing one another across long wooden tables while they go about the serious business of getting drunk. I hate this place.

In the far corner a woman sings into a microphone, couples dance, and only when I see the colour and sway of skirts among the army drab am I sure we're not the only women in the place.

A soldier sidles up to us and I almost jump out of my skin. 'Come on, my pretties, let's have a look at you.'

'You can see us well enough as we are,' Lili responds sharply. She's so much better at this than me.

'Ah, but it's not your faces a man needs to see,' says the soldier, leering at us, and he makes a circle with his arms, suggesting one of us dance with him. I'd rather wrestle a bear. When Lili says no, he staggers off, laughing.

'I want to go home,' I whisper into Lili's ear.

'They're not all like that,' she says, and she squeezes my hand. It's not nearly enough to reassure me. A few smaller round tables are scattered about and that's where Lili finds what we've come for. Five soldiers are sharing a bottle of schnapps, splashing generous shots into tiny glasses and throwing the clear liquid down their throats.

'That bottle's nearly empty,' I point out.

She's already looking for others. I do the same and notice how the men push the shoulders of friends beside them, goading, shouting in each other's ears, all in good humour, but the pointing and the urging and the teasing has one aim — to force a reluctant companion towards the women sitting in twos and threes at the bar.

'We'd better get these off,' says Lili. We help each other out of our coats and drape them over a stool at the end of the bar. Immediately, hungry eyes look us over, especially Lili, who's wearing Renate's silk dress — not that Renate knows anything about it.

'It's not like this in the movies,' Lili whispers. 'These men are bigger, louder, more . . . dangerous.' It's the first hint she's as nervous as I am.

What are these men seeing when they look at me? I've slimmed down so much because of the meagre rations that I'm wearing one of Renate's dresses too, an old one, but she's always liked the way her figure attracts a man's eye and chosen her clothes to do just that. This dress shows more of my bust than I've ever dared before and I can feel the fabric tight at the waist and over my hips. I must confess to a shiver of excitement when I saw myself in the mirror.

Lili had sensed what I was feeling. 'More beautiful than you thought, aren't you, Margot? I don't know why you insist Renate got all the looks. Maybe tonight will bring you more than a bottle of schnapps.'

But she's wrong about that. I don't feel attractive in front of these men, I feel naked. When I shudder now it's not with the thrill that men might think me pretty, it's with disgust.

On the dance floor, gruff voices rise above the music, turning heads and halting conversations. Two men are arguing over a woman. One of the men is angry with her. She'd promised him the next dance, he claims loudly, and when she ignores him he grabs at her, pulling her towards him roughly, only for her new partner to snatch her back again. The woman staggers and almost falls, her lovely dress now twisted and one shoe loose under the feet of other dancers.

Peacemakers settle the dispute and the men, so eager to punch one another only moments ago, are laughing together while the poor woman bobs frantically between couples, trying to snatch back her shoe. Those watching laugh at *her*, not the men who've caused the spectacle. This is a man's world and we're fools to be here.

Lili has come to the same conclusion. 'I'm not so sure now, Margot. Maybe we should leave.' She reaches for her coat.

'No! I've got to have a bottle of schnapps or Dieter will get beaten by the horrible kapo. This was your idea, anyway, and I can't think of a better one.'

She's surprised at how sharply I've spoken. 'But these men are awful, they're drunk. They might hurt us.'

'I can't do it on my own, not the way we planned,' I remind her. 'You have to play your part.' And I grab her arm to make it clear she's staying.

'Please, Margot, I can't do it.'

'You have to. We're not leaving without a bottle of schnapps, do you understand?'

Lili has been jerking her arm, trying to free herself from my grip, but the determination in my voice seems to calm her down. 'All right, then. Let's get it done so we can go home.'

Even as we're arguing, I've spotted a chance. 'That table away from the rest. They've just opened a fresh bottle and there're only three of them.'

Better still, one goes off to try his luck with a woman sitting by herself. 'Do that trick with the cigarette,' I urge Lili. 'This is your chance to be an actress. Imagine you're in a movie like *Sophienlund*.'

Lili takes a pack from her handbag and with shaking hands slips an unlit cigarette between her fingers, flexing her wrist back and forth like we've seen blonde-haired beauties do on-screen. 'Here goes,' she whispers and sets off towards the table. I'm lucky to have a friend like her. Though she must be petrified, she swings her hips and tosses her hair playfully as though she's done this a thousand times.

The men see her coming. 'How pretty you are, come sit on my knee,' they call, and soon the pair are jostling one another for the chance to light Lili's cigarette. She shakes her head and backs away coyly when they press her to sit down. Instead, she reaches forward to grab a hand of each of the men and draws them to their feet. 'I'll dance with you both,' I hear her promise as they move past me towards the dance floor, 'but I can't choose who to try first.' Behind them, the bottle of schnapps stands abandoned on the table.

I work my way towards it, checking over my shoulder every few steps. Lili is in the arms of one of the soldiers while the other watches impatiently from the edge of the dance floor. The bottle is almost in reach. I glance left and right. No one's looking. Take it, Margot. This is the moment.

I can't move, can't bring myself to stretch out my hand and steal. I have no name for what I'm feeling. It's not simply fear or loss of nerve. It's a crippling despair that my obsession with one young man is laughable, pointless, a silly dream.

'Good evening, Fräulein,' says a voice behind me.

I spin around so quickly I nearly totter off my heels. It's the third man, the one who'd gone off to dance. Perhaps he'd been turned down. I didn't think to check once Lili began to work her wiles on his companions. Oh God, he'd been standing behind me at the very moment . . .

He's speaking to me. I hear none of it, but slowly I'm aware of the look on his face — he's flirting with me. I snatch at his words — *pretty thing, lovely hair.* He reaches out and touches where it curls back against my neck, courtesy of half an hour's determined grooming in front of the mirror. I feel myself responding in the way I often do when I'm embarrassed: I smile like an idiot.

That's all the encouragement the soldier needs, and now he's kissing me and this isn't like Ferdy, whose mouth was soft and tentative. He's a grown man, a soldier. His mouth is greedy and demanding and he stinks of beer and cigarettes. The foul taste invades my mouth. I just want him to stop, but I need that bottle of schnapps and so I do nothing. The kiss ends finally and he takes a step back. 'You don't like it, do you?' he asks.

I can't look at him.

'Silly bitch,' he sneers. 'What are you doing here if you don't like a bit of fun? Plenty of girls do, you know.' He nods towards the bar and the women waiting to dance. He reaches for the bottle, takes a swig, then sets it back on the table before lurching away to try his luck on someone more willing. As soon as he's gone, I grab the schnapps and hurry to retrieve my coat and with the bottle hidden in its folds, I slip outside into the freezing night.

97

We've done it. I've got the bottle. What now? We didn't talk about afterwards. Maybe we never quite believed we'd get this far. I think about it. Lili will look for me once she'd danced with each of the soldiers. She'll make her excuses. There's nothing I can do but wait. Three minutes, then five, and the longer I shift from foot to frozen foot the darker my fears become. I see the poor woman scrambling for her shoe and hear the cruel laughter of the men. I shudder with disgust at how the soldier gripped my arms and pushed his mouth onto mine. I've left Lili to face all that alone. After seven minutes, I go back inside.

Uproar! Men are shouting; drunken men who know only one way to settle an argument. The reek of violence hangs more pungently in the air than the grey fug of cigarettes or the stale breath of alcohol. Around the bierkeller others are turning to see what the commotion is about. Some grin, eager for the punches that are sure to fly.

'It was on the table, a whole bottle. Someone's taken it. I tell you, the bastard who took it will . . .'

I don't need to hear any more to know who's making such a fuss. I scan the crowd for Lili and to my relief I spot her hurrying towards me, her hands working nervously at the belt of her coat. 'Let's go,' she says as soon as she reaches me.

'You two — stop there!'

I turn to find the man who kissed me striding towards us, his companions close behind. 'You're together, are you? Well, now, isn't that suspicious?'

'This is my friend Margot,' says Lili.

'I don't care what her name is. You've got our schnapps.'

'What are you talking about? I was on the dance floor with your friends.'

'Not you — her!' he bellows.

'Schnapps?' I say, trying for an innocent look.

'It's hidden in your coat. Open it and let me see.'

'No,' I say, and I step back two paces only to find one of the trio has circled behind me. The musicians and their weary singer try to ignore us, but every eye in the place is watching. They want to see the soldier's hands on me, they want to see my coat forced open.

'You have no right!' cries Lili.

'I have all the right I need.' And the drunken soldier grabs at the buttons of my coat. I can only wriggle in humiliation while his rough hands roam my body.

Even the music has stopped, everyone captivated by the spectacle. Surely the bottle will turn up among my clothes, they're thinking, and then the fun will really begin. The cruelty of Sachsenhausen has taken root inside them. It accompanies them even when they leave the camp. If they had dogs with them now, and clubs to beat us with, they'd form a circle around us.

But the soldier finds nothing. Frowning, he searches one last time, groping at the pockets of my coat, feeling down the back. Finally he gives up.

'I haven't got your stupid schnapps,' I shout in his face. If I were a man I'd punch him. I don't need to, though. He's beaten and he knows it.

Lili marches me to the door. Outside the cold slaps our faces and even then Lili has to draw three deep gasps of the frigid air before she can speak. 'I thought . . . I thought you'd taken it. Oh God, what if you had and he found it on you? They'd have torn us to shreds.'

She's shaking as though she'll never stop and I feel awful for walking away from her when she needs my arm around her in comfort. 'I can't do that again,' she calls after me. 'I'm sorry, Margot, really I am, but you'll have to find another way.' By now I'm some distance from her and she has to shout to be heard. 'Where are you going?'

'You don't have to do it again, Lili,' I call to her, and I reach under a bush to retrieve the schnapps from where I'd hidden it before going back inside. 'Let's go home.'

11

There's no shoe shop in Oranienburg these days. I could ask the parents of dead soldiers if they have a pair lying idle, but that seems harder than stealing schnapps from drunken guards. The solution is closer to home, though.

Sometimes I slip into the boys' room, to get away from Mutti as much as anything else. The truth is, I'm more comfortable with my brothers smiling at me from the photos above their beds than in my own room, where Renate speaks to me only when she has to and always in a sharp tone. I guess I brought that on myself.

Walther loves hiking, that's the thing. During his last year in Hitler Youth, he tramped all over Germany in the boots our proud parents bought for him, boots that are still at the back of his cupboard. My God, they're enormous! I can hardly stuff them inside my coat like I did with the sausage and the turnip cake. I consider 'posting' them through the mailroom, but Walther took good care of his boots, making them just the kind of thing Bruno would steal. Only on the morning I'm due to collect the unteroffizier's jacket do I stumble on a way to get them into the laundry.

The kapo swoops before I'm ten paces inside. Without a care for who's watching he uncaps the schnapps, tests a little on his tongue and smiles. 'Take as long as you like. I'll even send him to you.'

Dieter joins me soon after in the same secluded corner of the laundry where we spoke before. 'What's the news from my mother?'

'I have none, only this.' I hand over morsels of black market cheese and some bread I've saved from my own ration at home. He hasn't noticed the boots and I get a childish thrill out of delaying the moment. The cheese disappears inside his shirt, but the bread he tears at immediately with his teeth, all the while looking around like a rabbit watching for the fox. To ease his fear, I explain about the kapo.

'It's dangerous to trust a man like that,' he warns, his face hardening.

'His sort shouldn't have such power,' I say. 'The Führer wouldn't stand for it. This whole place is Himmler's doing, don't you think? If the Führer knew what went on here, he'd stop it.'

Dieter laughs like I've made a joke, then sees I mean it and stares at me for so long I feel uncomfortable. At last he says, 'Maybe you're right; Himmler's in charge of these camps. But Hitler . . . Don't you think what's happened to the Jews — the round-ups, the deportations . . . ' He stops without finishing what he'd been going to say about the Führer. He's mentioned the Jews, though, and I use this to bring up the Lipskys. 'The family your father kept hidden, you must have . . . come to know them.'

Dieter's eyes narrow. I worry I've said too much, and like a fool I say even more. 'I mean, you told me last time how you took food to them at night and let them roam around the warehouse to stretch their legs. Were you able to talk?'

'In whispers, yes. We could never be sure a passer-by wouldn't hear. No light, of course, no hot food in case the aroma gave them away. But yes, we talked and I got to know them, as you say. I'd seen Mr Lipsky around the warehouse, but not his children. There was a girl, older than me.'

The tone of his voice changes and I imagine I can hear the wonder of discovering one another when he adds quickly, 'She'd lived only a few streets away for years before they went into hiding, and I'd never met her. Maybe I wouldn't have liked her if I had. Boys and girls don't think much of each other when they're twelve or thirteen.'

'That's true,' I reply with a grin. 'At that age I thought boys were worse than monkeys. I soon changed my mind though.'

He likes this and once again I fall into his smile. Oh God help me. Is this what love feels like? It's so wrong, when I've tricked him into talking about the girl he loves. 'Did she have brothers and sisters?' I ask, hoping my guilt will ease if I guide our talk away from Margot.

'Ethan and Hannah. I promised Ethan I'd teach him to sail.'

'My brothers taught me to sail during the summer holidays. Not Franz, so much — we weren't very close before he went off to war — but Walther spent hours making sure I could tack into the wind without capsizing. You must be a good sailor, then, like him.' When he shrugs, feigning modesty, I call his bluff. 'I'll bet you won races.'

He throws back his head, enjoying the way I've caught him out. 'One or two, on Rügen Island, back when the war had barely started.'

'I've sailed those waters. Vati's sister used to take her children to Binz every summer and we'd go with them. They had a dinghy with a mast. There are thousands like them. Do you know the type I mean?'

'Know it? I learned to sail in one! Then my father hired a six-metre yacht and I sailed it from Göhren to Binz with my sisters on board.'

Yes, and you camped on the shore, so close to where I slept among my cousins I've dreamed I saw you on the sand ever since I read your letter. Not that I dare say this, and besides, Dieter is fighting tears now, closing his eyes lightly to hide them. 'I'm sorry,' he whispers, knowing I've noticed. 'It's just the memory of my sisters — and Ethan, too . . . I'll never teach him to sail now. They were sent to Auschwitz. Do you know about Auschwitz?'

'It's a konzentrationslager in Poland, like this one.'

'No, not like this one. Here, they work us worse than slaves, and when we're no use anymore there's a selection.'

'I know what selection means,' I tell him. 'People don't just die in camps like this. They're taken off and killed, murdered deliberately to get rid of them. It's true, isn't it?'

'Haven't you worked that out already?' he sneers. 'Killing is what konzentrationslager are for.' For a moment I fear he must think me too stupid to bother with. 'The jobs they force on us,

104

the quarry, the factories . . . If they fed us properly they'd double production. Sometimes I think it's just a way of spinning things out, so they don't have thousands of corpses to burn all at once.' His voice is so heavy with loathing and disgust, I feel the weight of it on my own shoulders.

'Burn?' I echo tentatively.

'You've seen the smoke, you've smelled it.'

He can't mean the smokestack on the far side of the camp. That's for . . . actually, I don't know what that furnace is for. I assumed it was for burning the camp's rubbish, maybe, or a factory of some kind. Before I can question him further, I see the kapo approaching. So much for taking all the time I like.

'I have to go.'

'Thank you for the food,' he says. 'I'll make this lot last a week. Really, you can't imagine how it helps, and not just with the hunger.' He pauses, as if hoping that I'll sense his meaning, then he speaks the words anyway. 'Coming here the way you do gives me contact with the living, instead of the living dead . . . '

I'm about to walk away — I've taken the first step, in fact — when the unfamiliar bulk tugging on my feet reminds me why I came here in the first place. 'Dieter, quickly — these are for you.' I'm already bent over double to loosen the laces. 'They were my — ' I hastily correct myself. 'They're from your mother. God knows where she found them. The only way I could get them past the guard was to wear them. Look, I put on every pair of socks I own to stop my feet slipping

105

straight out of them.'

All Dieter sees are the boots. Before I've got the second one free he's pulling on the first. 'It fits. I can't believe it! These are worth a sackful of bread and cheese. Thank you, thank you.' He seems ready to hug me.

Have I ever been so happy? He looks at me as though he hasn't quite seen me until now. 'How will you get out of the camp without shoes?'

'In these,' I answer. While he's been lacing his feet into Walther's boots, I've stripped off the extra socks and freed a pair of satin slippers which I'd flattened against the small of my back.

'You're going to dance out of here like a ballerina, is that it?'

'They only have to get me through the gate. The kapo is almost here. I have to go.'

I don't want to leave. I want him to smile again like he did when his foot slipped into the first boot. I want him to ask about me . . . And then he does! He grabs at my sleeve to hold me there with him a little longer.

'Please, what's your name?'

What could be more natural than to ask for a name, yet he's caught me out and I realise suddenly how the truth will give me away.

'Renate,' I say. 'Renate Baumann.'

★   ★   ★

Once I've said goodbye to Dieter, I can't wait to get out of the laundry, across the appelplatz, out of the konzentrationslager altogether. I'm not even sure my home will be far enough away. I

106

might ride out into the countryside, mile after mile until there's no smoke in the sky and no smell.

But first I have to see the old Jew, who hands over the unteroffizier's jacket and tells me to come back in a week if the dye starts to fade. I should be over the moon — another excuse to see Dieter; a week in which to hoard my rations, to shave the end off a mettwurst or the unsweetened cake Mutti bakes to make the best use of our flour and eggs — but my mind is too full of death to think of how I'll keep Dieter alive, and I am so flustered I forget about the kapo.

'Went well, did it?' he asks from the shadows by the door. 'I could arrange a bed for you both next time,' he adds, then laughs when I blush. 'Two bottles.'

'What?!'

He steps between me and the door. 'You'll be back. Nothing surer. I'll look forward to it, in fact, because next time you'll bring two bottles.' And as though this is a part he acts out every day in a pantomime, he grips his truncheon exactly as he'd done the week before.

'But I had trouble enough getting one!'

'You managed all the same.'

I remember the soldier who had kissed me, the stink of his body, his hands all over me.

'And if I manage two, you'll only demand four,' I hiss at him.

'Ah, now you see how the world works, Fräulein. You'll get me whatever I ask for. Shouldn't be hard for a pretty thing like you.

Soldiers will hand over all the schnapps you want if you give them what *they* want.'

He enjoys my outrage, the way I want to spit at him but dare not. I've seen the look in his face before at school — the sneer of the bully who doesn't care what he can get out of his victims; it's their powerlessness he craves. I'm not a schoolgirl any longer, though. Like Renate, he's going to learn that much, at least.

'No more schnapps. I'm not selling myself on the streets so you can get drunk. You'll get nothing more from me.'

Surprise on his face. He expects me to be cowed like the prisoners who live and die at his whim. I move to push past him, but he shoves me back with a force that startles me.

'Walk away and your friend won't live to see morning.'

'One bottle, maybe I can get one more.' I'm angry with myself for giving in, making my words come out as a shout.

'Two,' he cries, even louder.

Then, without warning, the door is wrenched open and an SS corporal is standing there, backlit by the too-bright glare of the appelplatz. 'What's the shouting about?'

'Korporal Meier,' says the kapo, 'the fräulein was abusing the Jew about his work. I'm trying to explain that the man does his best, even if he's an enemy of the — '

'Shut up, Hempenstall,' snaps the corporal. 'Fräulein, what's this about?'

'Nothing, sir. A misunderstanding. We'll sort it out if you'll just leave us — '

'You're lying as well,' he says, but without the menace he turned on the kapo. 'I know this piece of scheisse. He's trying to squeeze something out of you; Reichsmarks, or is it schnapps?'

I can't keep the truth from my face.

'Thought as much,' says Meier. 'Go tickle your friends with that truncheon of yours, Hempenstall. Raise your voice like that again and I'll hang your balls on barbed wire.'

The kapo has no choice, but the glare of pure malice he turns on me drains the blood from my face.

'No, you don't understand, Korporal. We haven't finished . . . '

'You have now.' He watches the kapo slink into the gloom of the laundry while inside my head a death knell sounds. *Your friend won't live to see morning.*

'Are you ill, Fräulein?' asks the corporal. 'Come on, I'll walk you to the gate. You don't belong in the konzentrationslager, do you? Not inside the wire, anyway.'

'No, I work in there,' I say, nodding towards the gatehouse. 'Please, I don't need an escort, I — I have to speak to the Jew again . . . '

'Not today.' And taking me gently by the arm, he guides me across the appelplatz.

With every step I become more frantic, until halfway across I wrench my arm away. 'I have to go back.'

'All right, that's enough. What's going on? You're not still frightened of that scum are you?'

'Not for myself.' I shouldn't say any more, but for the first time I look at him and find that his

109

gaze is more inquisitive than suspicious.

'I'll know if you're lying,' he warns me.

I can't lie, or at least I can't think of anything that he'll believe. 'Help me, please. There's a prisoner in the laundry — not a Jew, you understand,' I say quickly, in case this makes a difference. He's SS after all. 'I read his letters, they're beautiful letters. The kapo knows I care about him and he's blackmailing me for more than I can get my hands on. You must stop him, or he'll kill Diet — he'll kill the prisoner before morning.'

'You read his letters?'

'Yes, I work in the mailroom. I'm not doing any harm. I just want to help him.'

'Because he writes beautiful letters?'

'To his girlfriend.'

'Not you, then. You're not his lover?'

I shake my head. Why do men always think of sex?

'Is he a friend of your family's?'

Another shake of my head. 'It's like I told you. His letters were too beautiful to burn with the rest.'

'And because of them you put yourself at risk like this.'

'He's the one at risk. The kapo will kill him — tonight, if I don't agree to get schnapps for him.'

Korporal Meier crosses his arms and smiles briefly at the sky. 'My dear fräulein, you don't understand how vulnerable our friend Hempenstall is within these walls. A kapo stays a kapo only as long as we have use for him. If he loses

110

the protection of the SS he will find himself back among the same prisoners he's beaten and robbed. None survive a single night and it's a grisly way to die. I've seen the bodies. So has Hempenstall. I'll have a word with him and you can stop worrying.'

I let out a huge sob of relief that folds me double. 'Sorry,' I mutter as I force long, steady breaths into my lungs. 'I'm not much good at this.'

'No, you're not, but I don't know many your age who'd try. How old are you, seventeen?'

'Sixteen.'

'Old enough for love.'

I look up at him, unsure of his meaning. He's not suggesting . . . ?

'You'll make yourself conspicuous if you come into the camp too often. Did they search you at the gate?'

'No, I told the guard I had to collect a jacket for the unteroffizier and he let me through.' I show him the jacket as proof.

'You brought things for your young man as well, though.'

I nod.

'What's your name?' he asks.

There's no need to lie now, and besides, I'm exhausted by deception. 'Margot Baumann.'

'One day they will search you, Margot, and what will you do then? The war is going . . . let's just say it isn't going as the men here hoped it would and they're nervous, vindictive. They'll beat you until you tell them who the things are for and then beat him for the hell of it.'

111

'But I've promised to bring him more to eat.'

'There are other ways. I can get things to this lucky devil. Tell me his name.'

It's the way he demands a name that puts me on guard. When I don't answer he lets out a weary sigh. 'You don't trust me?'

'I'm sorry. I trust people too easily. I told you, I'm no good in this new Germany the war has turned us into.'

'The war? Do you think it started with the war?' he asks sharply. He shakes his head and murmurs softly, as if in wonder, 'My God, to be as innocent as you.' Then the harsh tone is back just as quickly, as though he's two men in one. 'Are you going to give me a name, or is he to starve with the rest?'

'If I could just know . . . why you are helping me?'

'Because this camp withers my soul,' he replies. He looks down at me with a sadness I've previously seen only on the faces of prisoners so spent after their day's work they can barely make it through the gates. 'Then I stumble on you, a single flower in a burned-out field.'

'Kleinschmidt,' I mumble, so quietly I'm sure he can't have heard me. I clear my throat and say more loudly, 'His name is Dieter Kleinschmidt.'

12

Dearest Dieter,
I'm so pleased you have such a place to
work through the winter. I am envious, in
fact, for it is just as cold here as the win-
ters in Hannover and Leipzig. I saw Ethan
through the wire yesterday and told Mutti,
who cried at the news.

Should I mention others in the Lipsky family like
this, when they might be dead? I'm writing these
letters to give Dieter hope — so precious, so
hard to come by inside the wire. I leave the
reference to Ethan and Mutti in, then add a line
about teaching Ethan to sail. Damn. I cross it
out in frustration; how easy it is to slip up. Dieter
had only told me about the sailing lessons at our
last meeting and to mention them so soon
afterwards would surely make him suspicious.

Have I told you what strength it gives me
just to think of you? I don't have to be
with you to enjoy your presence in my life.
I remember as a little girl I wanted things
to happen, yet whenever a wish came true
I found it empty. With you, Dieter,
through all those months in the warehouse,
the opposite was true. I would wait for you
all day, and when you were finally there,
our time together burst open and grew.

Did it? Margot Lipsky would have her own answer, I suppose, but that's how it feels to me. I've written those last words by doing what I've become used to — imagining the emotions of a girl in the bloom of first love. It's not something I've had any real experience of, and that's why I have to put myself into a kind of trance. I'm beginning to wonder, though, if I'm so unfamiliar with love anymore.

★ ★ ★

Korporal Meier is as good as his word. His name is Thomas and he grew up in Berlin. I learn this about him during our meetings (after our first encounter) leading up to Christmas, when I hand over what I've saved and scrounged and stolen. What I truly want, though, is to meet with Dieter again.

'I could tell the guards on the gate I have to collect something urgently for an officer. When I come back with nothing, I can say it wasn't ready. Do you think that would work?'

'As long as you don't try to smuggle anything in,' he insists, scratching at his brow. He has a rash spreading out from beneath his hair near the temple. Years ago one of my teachers had the same thing — caused by nerves, according to Mutti. My teacher scratched constantly and the rash never went away. It's a pity for Meier because he's quite good-looking otherwise, especially when he gives one of his rare smiles. He produces one now.

'New Year's Eve would be best, late in the day.

The guards will have their minds on parties and kapos like your friend Hempenstall will get a share of their drink.'

★ ★ ★

Dieter is the first to notice when I slip in among the washing tubs and the sorting benches. The mood inside the laundry is almost jovial, simply because the striped skeletons dare look around them, even at one another. I even hear voices and not just the cautious whispers of my earlier visits. Best of all, there's no sign of Hempenstall.

I move to the secluded corner and Dieter joins me there soon after. With the kapos gone we take a risk and sit side by side on the bench where he once folded underwear for the SS.

'I'm sorry,' I say. 'I have nothing for you.'

He shrugs. 'Not to worry. Three parcels have come since I saw you last.'

'I found another way — a better way.'

'But the block leader delivered them with his own hands. Who's giving them to him?'

I shake my head. 'I can't tell you.' Meier was adamant about that. If anything should go wrong, Dieter can't give up a name he doesn't know.

'I thought I'd never see you again,' says Dieter, who looks left and right and over his shoulder in regular rotation as though he can't shrug off the habit of watching for truncheons. 'That would have been . . . a shame.' He relaxes enough to face me fully. 'In fact, I'd have traded a whole parcel for a visit from you. Well, half a parcel, maybe.'

115

He grins as he puts a price on my company and I see immediately why Margot Lipsky fell in love with him. He's so generous in giving away part of himself, even in this hellhole. There's no facade, no posturing with Dieter Kleinschmidt, unlike the boys I've grown up with. He's not a boy, that's the thing. He's had to grow up quickly to survive. When I first came to the laundry, he kept me at arm's length. All that talk of trust was life and death to him. But he knows me now and that makes him unafraid to let me see him, his needs, his vulnerability, not as an inmate but as a human being. In leaving himself unguarded, he lets another take hold.

I'm suddenly aware of how close we are — as close as I was to Ferdy when he kissed me. I see a pinkish tinge in Dieter's face and looking down find it in his hands, too. I've put it there and knowing this makes me part of his life in a way I've never been for anyone until now.

'I hope I can do something so daring and kind for you one day,' says Dieter, and for a silly moment I wonder if he's aware of all that's passed through my mind just now. But he means the parcels of sausage and cheese and cake, of course.

'You've already done your bit. You helped keep the Lipskys alive.'

'Did I?' he asks ruefully. 'Be careful, Renate. You don't want to suffer the same fate, believe me.' And he holds his arms out to show off his grubby stripes. 'An enemy of the Reich,' he jokes. 'No wonder the Nazis are so frightened of me.'

He calls me Renate. How many roles am I going to create for myself? The one person I can't be with Dieter is myself.

'They punish you because you don't hate the Jews like good Germans are supposed to.'

'Are you a good German, then, Renate? Do you think it was wrong of me to help that Jewish family?'

As if that matters to me now. There's a simple way to explain. 'I work in the mailroom. I've read a few letters — a lot, really — from Jews to their loved ones.'

'Did they change anything for you?' Dieter asks.

'They showed me there's love in all of us, that it's a human thing and pays no attention to race or religion.'

This is new to me. I've never put such thoughts into words before and at this first attempt I'm scared of what might come stampeding out of me. 'There's so much I haven't wanted to think about. There are . . . things.' What a say-nothing word. Name them, Margot, I tell myself. 'Doubts, bigger even than the Jews. I can't talk about them at home. I . . . I get so angry at what's happening to the people I love, to this town, to the Fatherland.'

I break off and look towards Dieter. Does he understand my ramblings? Does he care? 'Oranienburg used to have such good people; you'd see them on sunny days around the Lehnitzsee. They're gone now, all gone — replaced by soldiers from this camp. Some are even the same men and women, Dieter, the same names, the same faces,

117

but they've become different people. Mostly I'm angry about my brother Walther. He was taken prisoner near Stalingrad. He might be dead, but I can't say so at home, even though I see the same fear in my father's eyes. And as for my mother, she wrestles with herself until she's exhausted. Sometimes I think she'll explode with her own confusion. She wanted this war more than Vati, more than anyone I know. She couldn't wait to see my brothers in uniform. And what has she got now, for all her zeal? Instead of victories, the news is full of death. Even if Walther is alive there's no hope he'll be set free any time soon. The Wehrmacht is thousands of kilometres from Stalingrad and retreating further every day.'

If I say any more it will come out as pathetic sobs. I fall quiet to save him the embarrassment, and for a long time Dieter makes no move to fill the silence. Then, 'I know it's you, Renate.'

I don't know what he's talking about at first.

He speaks again, softly, looking directly into my eyes. 'The letters — I know you write them. I couldn't work out how you managed it, but now I see. You work in the mailroom.'

'Letters! What are you saying?' I stick a stupid smile on my face. 'I don't understand.'

'Margot is dead. She was sent to Auschwitz, where they herd Jews into bunkers straight off the trains, then gas them, thousands at a time. There are prisoners here who've seen it. No one survives.'

'But you've had letters from her . . . '

He stares at me, shaking his head. 'They haven't come from her. You wrote them, Renate.'

118

Oh no. Oh God, no. He's found me out. I open my mouth to deny it, tell him he's wrong, that I don't know anything about letters from his girlfriend. Maybe I could do it, too, if I wasn't so tired of lies, of tricks, of pretending to be who I'm not. Whatever happens, I'm going to end one deception at least. 'Renate is my sister. My real name is *Margot* Baumann.'

He turns his head away at this news and it seems he's turning away from me forever.

'Please forgive me. I should never have done it, I know, but after the first one, you wrote back about how much it meant to you.'

He does turn back to stare at me now, wordlessly, and this is worse than being shunned, worse even than being shouted at. My tongue stumbles on. 'Your letters carried so much love and . . . and when I knew they couldn't reach her . . . That's how you knew, isn't it? You didn't put a number on her letters.'

He frowns when I say this as though he doesn't understand. 'A number . . . ?' he murmurs, then it comes to him. 'Oh, yes, you mean her prisoner number. But there were other things — things you don't know about Margot and me.'

Saying the name reminds him of what I'd told him a moment earlier. 'Your name is Margot too. So when you read my letters it was like I was writing to you.'

Am I made of glass, that he sees into me so clearly?

'I'm so sorry. If there's anything I can do . . . ' My apologies sound pathetic and so far short of deserving his forgiveness. I stand up to flee only for Dieter to take hold of my skirt. 'Sit down,' he says sharply.

I obey, burying my face in my hands, hoping that what I can't see won't harm me. 'You've known from the start. Oh God.'

'Yes, from the first one. I thought some SS bastard must be mocking me and I searched every line for the cruelty, but it wasn't there. All I could see was the kindness.'

I feel a hand on my shoulder and look up.

He snatches his hand away. 'I'm sorry. I forget how badly I stink.'

He's sorry! I want to say to him, Put your hand on my shoulder again.

'Stop crying, please, there's no need. Your letters are the only good thing that's happened to me in Sachsenhausen.'

Have I heard him properly? There's no smile to reassure me — far from it. His face is solemn, his features hardened in a way I haven't seen since he warned me against the kapo.

'You have to understand, life has a different value in this camp. We're all here to die, it's just a matter of how long each of us lasts. In weeks or months, maybe a year, we're dead. So staying alive becomes pointless — do you see what I mean? That's why having something to live for becomes precious, and I was losing mine. I thought of throwing myself on the electric wire.'

I know this about you, Dieter, I say inside my head. That's why I'm here.

He's watching to see if I'm shocked, and seems disappointed that I haven't gasped in horror. 'I wouldn't have been the first. I wrote

120

the letters to Margot to stop myself, by pretend-ing, by dreaming my way back to life.'

A touch of contempt enters his voice. 'You should know the power of pretending, but my first letter to Margot showed me something just as precious — that even though she's dead, she should know that I loved her. That's it, do you see? The dead should know they are loved just like the living. Once I'm dead too, there'll be no one to remember what I felt about her. Gone, all gone into nothingness.' He throws up his hands in a burst of anger. 'I couldn't bear that. No one else knew, you see, and *that* was why I had to stay alive, my reason. Margot couldn't really be dead as long as I kept her alive in the words of my letters. I had to send them to her as though she were still alive. The hope wouldn't come unless I posted them like any other letter. It worked for a while, but the quarry . . . ' He pauses, as if recalling painful memories. 'Those SS bastards, Christ, how I hope one day I get a chance to . . . '

He forces the rage back into himself, enough to continue in a steadier voice. 'I had a friend, older than me . . . Leon, the only prisoner I've dared trust. We helped each other, urged one another to keep going, but Leon smashed his hand between two blocks of stone and they didn't even wait until the next selection, just dragged him out of the barracks still clutching his hand, and bang. I had to carry his body to the furnace, his eyes staring up at the sky. The SS wouldn't let me close them. They thought it was funny.'

He breathes in harsh, audible gasps before composure returns. 'Then the weather turned icy, and instead of one or two dead in our block each week, there'd be ten. I helped carry out the bodies then, too. They looked so peaceful, and now my letters to Margot didn't seem enough anymore. I felt myself drifting — not to the electric wire, maybe, but there's a bigger killer in this camp than hunger and sickness and beatings from the kapos.'

Dieter has spoken to his own knees through all of this. Now he breaks off and glances my way for the briefest instant before he looks away again. 'That was when the first letter came from Margot . . . from you. I read it over and over, wanting it to be from her. Oh, how much I wanted those words to be hers. But you see, Margot didn't — ' He stops abruptly to stare at me. 'I'm sorry, you are Margot too, it's all so confusing.' He laughs in a way I can't read. 'So I knew your letter was a fake and that made it easier. I should have been angry, I should have hated whoever was pretending to be my Margot, but I was sure it wasn't meant to hurt me.'

'I would never do that. Not to you, not to anyone.'

'A good soul,' Dieter says, and I'm not sure if he's being sarcastic.

'Can you forgive me?'

'Forgive you? I should thank you, Margot.'

'I just wanted to help,' I say meekly, while inside I dance and sing like a gypsy. He spoke my name without the shadow of Margot Lipsky standing between us. Even this, though, doesn't prepare me for what he says next.

'Will you keep helping me, even if it's all pretending? Will you write more letters like you've been doing? Since your name is Margot too, maybe it's not such a fraud after all.'

13

Dearest Dieter,
When there is nothing to eat I feast on memories of you, of spending time with you, even though we had to be careful no one would see anything special about us.

Dear Margot,
I am discovering the wonderful thing about love: that it is not a single emotion or something that you 'do'. The exciting thing is that someone else in the world cares for you and thinks of you all the time. This helps me here in Sachsenhausen, helps me see the other prisoners as human beings who feel the same things as me, who fear the same things, who have good in them as I think I still have some good in me. I don't keep myself apart from them as much as I used to. I am making new friends. It is because of you.

Dear Dieter,
Please, please, remember our nights in the warehouse. Use them to keep you warm in the way I used them to get me through the boredom of stillness and silence when your father's men were at work. During those long hours I played a game, guessing what your first words to me would be when

*finally you called us out into the darkness,
and how many minutes would pass before
we kissed.*

*Dear Margot,
It seems odd that the same God who cre-
ated love could let anyone live in camps
like this one. Maybe he is conducting an
experiment, to see if I can stay in love
despite all that has happened. Or maybe
there is no God, only a giant set of scales,
and now that the world is weighed down
by hatred and war, it is up to people like
us to balance things out so the whole
planet doesn't tip over into darkness.*

*Remind me of the things we did
together while you were in hiding. Even if
I don't remember those things myself they
become real when I read them in your letters. Believe me when I write these words:
Margot, your letters keep me alive.*

'How are the letters going?' asks Lili. 'You
seemed a bit . . . exhausted by it all last time I
asked.'

'I love doing it and I dread it. There are times
he is almost admitting to us both that it's a
sham. He's prompting me to make things up so
he can believe them and that puts everything out
of balance. I have to believe he writes those
letters to her, not me, and when I write back to
him I have to convince myself I'm Margot.'

'You *are* Margot,' says Lili, giving me a brief
hug as she squeezes past. We're in her bedroom

125

— not to dance, which doesn't seem right anymore, or even to talk in our usual way about boys and movies and fun.

'Honestly, what can I fit in a single suitcase?' Lili complains. 'I can easily carry two, but would they listen?' She dips her head towards her parents' room, where Frau Martin is packing her own single suitcase.

'It's a farm, this place you're going to?'

'Yes, my father's cousin's place west of Hamburg. Kilometres away from any bombs, apparently. Kilometres away from anything much to do, I'll bet.'

'You'll be up to your knees in chickens and cow manure. What am I going to do without you?' I ask pitifully.

'Write me letters since you're so good at it. You can pretend to be Heinrich, if you like.'

Heinrich has replaced Jens. A young soldier, of course. Far too young to be a soldier in my opinion — the one time I saw him he looked like a twelve-year-old playing dress-ups — but the uniform was too much for Lili.

'I do enough pretending,' I tell her, flopping onto the bed beside the suitcase, adding, 'The red one,' when Lili holds up two skirts. I continue, 'The hard part is pretending to be in love with Dieter when I am anyway.'

'That doesn't make sense,' says Lili. She stops sorting through her clothes and takes her usual place amid a nest of pillows. 'I warned you against this but you wouldn't listen.'

'Oh, Lili, is there any hope for me?'

'As a romantic, none whatsoever. As a girl with

126

her heart set on one boy, there's plenty.' Lili shifts down the bed until she is beside me, one arm around my shoulders protectively. 'Listen to me. One day, Dieter will be free of that horrible place and he'll need someone to love. He can't go on loving a dead girl forever, can he? The heart needs something more, something real and warm and kissable.'

She pauses, leaving me to fill in what hasn't been said. And, oh, how I want to believe it's that simple.

'No, it doesn't work that way with us. I've come to know him, but he doesn't know me at all, because everything I write to him is supposed to be from a different girl. Even if he does think about me, it's only as a fraud.'

'You've kept him fed and out of the winter cold.'

'Oh, Lili, I don't want gratitude — I want love. But the way things are, if he ever gets released from the konzentrationslager he'll be embarrassed by our letters and the last thing he'll want is to be reminded of the misery of Sachsenhausen every time he sees my face.'

* * *

'Hello, Walther,' I say, once I've settled on his bed. 'I haven't been in to see you for a while. Please don't give me the silent treatment just for that.'

I wait for his deep, jovial voice to answer and almost believe for a moment that the photograph above his pillow will speak to me.

'Look what I've brought.' I hold up sheets of paper. 'I've sent so many letters to Franz you must worry he's my new favourite. It's not true and to prove it I'm going to write one for you.'

The letter is Dieter's idea, or at least I've borrowed the idea *from* Dieter. Like him, I know it won't reach its destination, but writing it will satisfy a need inside me.

'I want your permission to be in love,' I tell Walther's smiling face. 'Lili thinks I'm mad. That's a bit rich, don't you think, when she falls in love at the drop of a hat?'

If I keep this up, my mother will hear and come to investigate, but I like the cheeriness in my voice. 'Life's been a bit serious lately, especially now that Lili's gone,' I admit in a whisper. 'If I took my cue from Mutti, I'd have no fun at all. You were always fun. You had me convinced there was a snake living under this bed, do you remember? And when you called out, 'It's coming, it's coming,' I climbed you like a tree.'

Once his laughter had given away the trick I'd pummelled at him with my little fists until he'd trapped my arms between us in a bear hug. How old was I then — six, seven?

I lie back on the bed with the sheets of paper on my chest and forget about writing for the moment. 'You'd like him, Walther. He's a sailor, which you would insist on if you were picking someone for me, wouldn't you?'

I think about this. Walther made decisions for me all my life — the flavour of an ice-cream, the colour of the ribbon in my hair. I wanted him to

128

choose because it showed he loved me. Letting him do it showed I loved him.

'We'll still go sailing when you come back — there'll be another person in the boat with us, that's all. I promise you won't feel abandoned.'

Here, his unresponsive face saddens me in a way I'm not prepared for, and when I speak to him again, I'm more serious. 'Even if you do come back, Walther, we won't be grown-up brother and little-girl sister anymore. That time is over.'

I feel a deep sense of loss as I say it, but not one that leaves me bereft as it might have done only a few months ago. 'You're older, you understand. Have you ever known this feeling?'

This time he does speak back to me. He tells me that he's been in love three times, I decide, and I imagine him telling me of the joy these experiences brought him.

'Yes,' I agree, 'that's what it's like: far better than a cosy fire or beautiful clothes. It takes you out of yourself and into another person who does the same to you, who's always there to touch with your thoughts. I haven't been able to tell this to anyone — even Lili would have laughed in my face. I'm happy, Walther. We're losing the war and people are dying, but there's a happiness in me I can't turn off, even if I wanted to.'

This is what I was too ashamed to confess to Lili before she left and it brings me finally to the matter I didn't know would be part of love: that it can leave me frustrated, even angry.

'There's only so much you can write about

love, Walther. I'm tired of telling Dieter how much his dead girlfriend cares for him, tired of making up their past. I want to tell him about *me*, I want to know more about *him*. Is it so mean to want that?'

No answer. I climb off the bed, touch Walther's face with the tips of my fingers, then leave the room loving my brother as much as ever. I'm not going to write the letter I promised him, though. I write to Dieter instead and, remembering what I confided to Walther, I imagine a future for Margot Lipsky that might just as easily be Margot Baumann's.

Dear Dieter,
Once we are free of the barbed wire . . .

He won't care. He won't know I'm writing for myself, from myself. There's pain in that, but the words come more easily, and since Korporal Meier can smuggle sheets of paper into the konzentrationslager as easily as bread and turnip cake, I write to Dieter whenever I have a parcel to deliver, until I lose count of how many letters I've sent into the camp.

14

'Do we know why?' asks Frau Cullmann.

The question is for Unteroffizier Junge, but my ears are just as keen for his answer.

'Stealing from the kitchen, I think,' says the unteroffizier without taking his eyes from the appelplatz. 'They were executed last night. I suppose the bodies were left as a warning to the rest at rollcall this morning.'

'Stiff as planks if they've been out there all night,' says Frau Cullmann, and the pair of them turn away, leaving me to check that my eyes are right — all three bodies strung in a neat line from the gallows are wearing dresses. I can breathe more easily. It's another matter altogether that the sight no longer shocks me.

We start work and despite the cold I put on my coat and take a sack of letters out to the oil drum. I'm choosing which to burn and which to save when the sound of hurrying footsteps makes me look up and I see Renate striding towards me, struggling into her own coat.

'There's been a call. We're needed at home.'

'Why?'

'I don't know,' she snaps. 'Forget your bike, Albie's ordered a car.'

Nothing more is said until we're on our way.

'It must be news about Walther,' I say into the silence of the back seat. 'I can't bear it.'

'We don't know that. It could be something

good; he might be waiting for us in front of the fire. Or maybe it's Franz, home on leave.'

We both know it won't be either. There's another long silence.

'Are you doing what I'm doing?' Renate asks, so softly I can barely hear over the drone of the tyres. 'Are you finding out which brother you love the most?' Her hand reaches across the seat and takes hold of mine. She begins to cry quietly while I'm strangely dry-eyed. Not yet, I tell myself. I won't let death take either of them until I hear the words spoken out loud.

A car from the Heinkel factory is parked outside our gate. Inside, Mutti and Vati are huddled on the sofa with Pastor Pforr bending over them and Frau Neiman from next door standing nearby like the single crow at a funeral. Don't let it be Walther's funeral, I beg of a God I haven't prayed to in so long. I stretch out every last second of Walther's life by stubbornly refusing to ask.

Renate isn't so patient. 'Who is it, which one?'

Vati works his way to his feet, telegram in hand. 'Franz,' he says. 'Three days ago, near Köln.'

Not Walther, then. Relief bursts through me, but only for as long as it takes Renate to fall onto the sofa, her arms around Mutti. That leaves me with Vati, who folds me into his arms as he hasn't done since I was twelve years old. Franz, the brother I've come to know so much through his letters — this link to Dieter makes his death even more terrible.

Dead, dead . . . hundreds of thousands, even

millions they say, and now a Baumann among them.

And then another thought occurs to me: Köln is on the Rhine. The Americans will surely cross soon enough, and what will happen to us then?

★   ★   ★

Black is the colour of mourning. Mutti finds enough black material among the odds and ends she's hoarded to drape our house with her sons' sacrifice, but nothing can match the blackness she carries with her into every room, every task, every word she utters.

She never actually admits that she's grieving for two, but the evidence is there in unguarded moments. 'My sons,' she says bitterly. 'The pride of Oranienburg, leaders in Hitler Youth, both of them. Walther was chosen for the big rally in Nürnberg back in thirty-seven,' she reminds Frau Neiman at the funeral, even though it's Franz's body in the coffin. 'The Führer attended personally. He passed within five metres of where Walther stood waving the swastika I sewed with my own hands.'

She brings the photographs of both my brothers from their bedroom and hangs them either side of the Führer's portrait in the hall. It's wrong and I say so.

'You hang them there like the thieves beside Jesus,' I tell her, but Mutti's jaw tightens and the picture frames stay where they are until I learn to pass through the hall with my eyes closed. I've got other pictures of my brothers, but the portrait of Walther is my favourite, taken on the day he graduated from the officers' academy. He'd been so happy, so handsome, and I've never loved him more than on that day.

Vati has his own way of coping. He works even harder at the aircraft factory and often he doesn't return until ten at night, when Mutti is already in bed. I know why.

One night I wait up for him. 'I'll heat up your supper,' I offer.

'There's no need. I ate something at the factory.'

I put the plate on the kitchen table for him anyway. 'Mutti's asleep,' I say once I've taken a seat opposite him. 'You should talk to her more. She might not be so . . . ' I was going to say 'closed off from us', but decide not to in case it sounds impertinent.

'Far away,' he says, finishing my sentence for me. 'Her mind is in Stalingrad . . . and Köln.'

'No, it's more than that. She's hiding inside herself and won't come out.'

Vati answers by closing his eyes and sweeping a tired hand over an even more tired brow.

'She's a proud woman, Margot, and stubborn with it.'

I snort more rudely than I intend to. 'Yes, stubborn,' but it's what she's stubborn about that I can't stand any longer. I've been careful so far, level-headed Margot once again. But haven't I gone past that? 'Vati, do you believe in the Führer?'

He looks up, aware of the line I've crossed, and answers with the same honesty. 'I didn't at first; too many of his people were common thugs. But Germany works best under a strong government — a king or a general — and soon we were building aircraft again and my work was important. Then came the war, which would enable us to take our proper place in Europe. I believed in him then, Margot, as much as I've believed in anything.' He's spoken these last words like a man ready to lash his own back with a whip.

'Do you believe in him now, though?' I want to know. I worshipped the man for so long myself, but these days . . . I've seen enough with my own eyes to think all his brilliant speeches were just noise meant to hide how empty he is inside. And then there's Dieter. I need to hear what others think.

Vati squeezes his eyes shut and runs his hand over his brow once more. 'Don't ask me such things, my darling. It's late, very late.' Whether he means the hour of the night or something far larger he doesn't say.

'You work too hard, Vati.'

'We're developing a new aircraft. A tank buster. Lord knows we need something to stop the T34s sweeping across Poland.'

'What are T34s?'

'Russian tanks. Thousands of them. We have so few of our own now.'

He lets that admission drift in the air between us.

'Is it true, what they're saying?' I ask. 'Will the Russians reach the border soon?'

He's finished the meagre leftovers I'd served

135

him. Arranging his knife and fork neatly in the centre of the plate he looks up at last. 'They're only a hundred kilometres from Berlin.'

★ ★ ★

With Vati staying late at work and Renate rarely home at all, Mutti and I are the only two at the dinner table most nights. We rub at each other like sandpaper.

'Oh, stop talking, Margot,' she growls one night. 'I don't want to hear your voice. I want men's voices at my table — the men I raised for the Reich.'

The odd thing is I don't feel hurt. Actually, it's a relief to hear the truth spoken aloud. I've suspected for years that when my brothers went off to join the war they took all of Mutti's love with them.

'Why don't you come out and say it?' I challenge her. 'You have no love for me and precious little for Renate. You buried some of it with Franz's coffin and the rest is freezing to death in Russia.'

'You have no idea what has died,' Mutti responds in the slow, solemn tones of someone warming to what will follow. 'My sons were the model of our race, the instruments of the Führer's grand scheme. Now look at me. I'm left with daughters who can't possibly achieve what those boys had in their grasp.'

'What use are the Führer's plans now, Mutti? The Americans are pushing their way across Germany, Berlin is bombed every night and the

Russians will destroy what's left!'

'There, see!' she cries, almost gleefully. 'Walther and Franz would be ashamed to hear you say such things. They were heroes worthy of the Führer. They would never speak like that.'

My brothers have become weapons now, but I won't fall for my mother's tricks any longer. 'The Führer's no hero,' I shout — and, oh, the release I feel through my whole body . . . 'He's a death machine. He chews up precious boys like Walther and Franz and . . . ' How long would the list extend if I recited them all? The names seem to stretch endlessly to the horizon, to the moon, to the end of what a human mind can imagine and all so pointless, so completely pointless . . .

I stand up with such force my chair topples over behind me. 'He's not worthy of my brothers. I won't let their pictures hang beside that murderer for another minute.' I march into the hall, but as my fingers close around the frame of Walther's portrait, Mutti's hands trap them in place.

'They'll stay where they are. Germany's not beaten yet, not so long as my sons stay at the Führer's side.'

I use my shoulder to push her away and reach again for the picture, but Mutti is taller, stronger, so I duck under her arm and go for Franz instead.

She moves like a leopard, pinning that frame to the wall in the same way. Instantly, I lunge for Walther again, as though we're locked in some crazy dance. I'm quicker this time and Walther's portrait comes free. Mutti tries to snatch it away, but I clutch it tightly to my chest. 'You can't have him,' I say between gritted teeth.

Mutti holds on just as grimly until one hand slips and her elbow flies back wildly.

A sharp crack. Splintered glass.

'No!' she wails, her fingers prodding at the shards as though her touch will heal the wound. On the wall, a star of tiny fractures spreads across the cheek of Adolf Hitler and, with a drop of my mother's blood running down to his chin, it seems as if the Führer himself is bleeding.

'At last,' I cry, and still holding Walther's portrait I climb the staircase to my room.

15

My mother has removed the glass from the Führer's portrait so the insult done to his face won't be seen by visitors. Not that there *are* any these days. The Neimans' house has been empty for a fortnight and others slip away every day, barely noticed, just as Lili did. Mutti doesn't demand the return of Walther's photograph and pretends not to notice that Franz is gone as well. Unless Vati arrives home in time for dinner she eats in the kitchen, leaving a plate for me on the stove. I come down to get it only after she's gone to bed.

The mailroom in Sachsenhausen is handling fewer and fewer parcels, too. First one censor is reassigned to guard the swelling number of prisoners, then another and another until only Bruno remains. I don't find him as repulsive as I once did. I almost admire him, actually. He doesn't pretend to care about anyone but himself and that makes him the most honest person in Sachsenhausen.

Towards the end of March, all prisoners' mail stops on orders from Berlin and only the wily Bruno's fast talking convinces the unteroffizier to let him continue in the mailroom instead of joining the guards inside the wire. 'Thank God, it's a nightmare in there now,' he tells me afterwards as we stare through the window at row after row of prisoners standing to attention.

Rollcall in the middle of the day!

'It's all those new prisoners from the east: the Jews from camps in Poland and Russian POWs,' says Bruno. 'At least the Ivans won't be here for long.'

'Why not?' I ask.

Bruno doesn't answer me but the unteroffizier has heard my question. 'We are merely a transit camp for the prisoners of war, Margot, until Berlin decides where to send them more permanently.'

Every day lately I've seen hundreds of the ragged souls marched in from the railway station. I never see any marched out again, though, and the chimneys on the far side of the camp billow pungent smoke around the clock.

★   ★   ★

In the first week of April, I meet with Korporal Meier to give him what little I have for Dieter — and a letter from Margot, of course.

'How is he?' I ask. 'I hear the laundry's closed down.'

Meier shrugs. 'I don't know where he works now, or if there's any work at all. He's alive, though. I saw him only two days ago.'

'Can you speak to him, ask if — '

'No, of course not,' snaps Meier before I can say any more. 'I've told you, I can't afford to go near him, especially now.'

Yes, he's told me, but I can't help hoping. 'Here,' I say, offering the meagre parcel.

But Meier won't take it from me. 'The block

140

leader won't pass on anything more, and I can't blame him either. It gets more desperate in there by the day.' He nods towards the wall and its deadly crown of thorns. 'My SS brothers are unpredictable, except in their cruelty. Yesterday a guard was shot for having sex with a woman selling herself openly for food. Dead on the spot, both of them, as a warning — but, really, they look for any excuse. It's fear of the Russians. The SS don't want anyone left alive to tell them what's happened to their comrades.'

'They're brought here to die, aren't they?' I say, aware of the smoke above my head thinning as it makes its way heavenwards.

Meier looks close to breaking down in front of me. Only more words keep his lungs working. 'The POWs are brought into a room, one at a time, to be fitted for new uniforms, or that's what they're told. When you see the rags they wear, who would object? Once inside, they stand against a wall to be measured and that's when they're shot through a hole specially drilled in the brickwork.'

'No,' I breathe. A terrible thought comes to me. 'You don't . . . '

Meier shakes his head but refuses to meet my eye. 'My job is to marshal them in their barracks, make sure they don't suspect.'

That they're about to be murdered, I say to myself. 'Can't you stop them? You could refuse duty, at least.'

He stifles a grim laugh. 'I told you of the guard caught with the woman, didn't I? He disobeyed an order and I'd be no different. Any excuse, you

141

see. It doesn't matter who dies anymore — Germans, Russians, Jews — as long as there are bodies for the furnace.'

★ ★ ★

The narrow chute the prisoners use to post their letters is boarded up, but even before the order was given there'd been only a handful each day and none of them from Dieter. Now Meier won't pass on my letters to him.

In a way, I'm relieved, because I'm fed up with being this other Margot. If we'd gone on meeting in the laundry he'd have come to know me and his other Margot would have taken her rightful place among the dead, still loved, but in the way I mourn for Franz. Lili's teasing words have never been far from my mind: *The heart needs something more, something real and warm and kissable.*

Then Unteroffizier Junge calls me to his desk. 'Margot, this mailroom is to be closed. That means you're no longer needed here at Sachsenhausen. It's a mark of your devotion to the Reich that you have remained as long as you have. I expected your father to send you away long ago.' He thanks me for my service, then he hands me his cigarette lighter. 'Could you please ensure there's nothing left in the barrel before you finish?'

My final duty for the Reich, then — burn the last of the prisoners' letters. There's so few I don't even need a sack, and once I'm outside, rather than burn them, I stuff them all into the coat I'm wearing to keep out the late-winter breeze. Once I'd imagined Adolf Hitler's eyes on me, hoping he'd forgive my sad little kindnesses. Now I wish he *was* here, so I could spit in his unforgiving eye. I slip the cigarette lighter into my coat pocket unused, making my last act in Sachsenhausen one of defiance more than kindness.

The idea makes me bold, and when the gates into the SS barracks yawn at me from beyond the outer wall, I decide the unteroffizier won't care how long I'm gone. I ask a cleaning woman for directions to Korporal Meier's quarters, and soon I'm standing at his door.

'You're lucky to find me here,' he says, once he's over the surprise. 'I have to start again in an hour.' The puffiness under his eyes tells me he's not sleeping much whatever hours he works and the angry rash has spread further onto his forehead. 'Come in,' he says when the breeze chills his shirt. There are four bunks inside, but his is the only one not neatly made.

'I've come to ask again if you'll take things into the camp for Dieter. I hear stories about whole barracks left without food for days at a time. Is it true?'

Meier sighs and looks away. It's all the answer I'll get — and all I need.

'But they're already starving.'

'No, they're dying,' he corrects me. 'As fast as squads can carry them out of the barracks.'

'All the more reason for you to help me.'

'Why just you? Why just this boy you're in love with?'

'I'm not in love with him,' I say hotly.

'You say the words, little Margot, but you don't believe them, do you?' he says, not unkindly, and suddenly, amid this macabre conversation, we're smiling at each other. I look up at him, newly aware that he's as tall as my two loves, Walther and Dieter. He's stopped grinning, but doesn't stop looking down at me through the lengthening silence. What am I seeing in his face? A longing, a need, an affection I'm yet to see in Dieter's eyes? All of these, and yet it might be none at all. I haven't known enough boys to judge, and no men of Meier's age, but something in me understands what I'm seeing all the same.

'You want to kiss me, don't you?'

'Yes,' he answers softly, but he doesn't move. I've never been the subject of a gaze so intense.

'You can if you want.' I don't need to add that this is part of a bargain. 'There's no one here, no one to see us.' I don't really know what I'm suggesting. I just want him to respond, I want to play my part, do whatever I have to do, as long as Dieter survives.

Still nothing, although his expression has changed oddly to one I have no hope of reading. I try to speak again, not even sure what words will come out. But none do because he's pressed a finger to my lips to stop me.

'Please, no more,' he whispers. 'You don't know what you are to me. If I kissed you, you would die in front of my eyes and I'd be left with nothing.' He looks down at me with such despair in his face. 'You have no idea what I'm talking

144

about, do you? When I first met you on the appelplatz I found something I thought had died in Germany, a kind of love that made your skin glow. How many like you has this war left alive? How much of what I see in you has died in Sachsenhausen alone? I won't kill that in you, Margot. It would be a crime not even God could forgive.'

He's right — I don't know what he's talking about — but the same impulse that made me speak of kisses prompts my hand to move, when I'm still uncertain what it will do. Only when my hand rests flat on his chest does it make sense to me.

Meier flinches as though I've burned him and he lets out a low groan. He leaves my hand in place, though. I follow it with my head, turning to rest my ear next to my splayed fingers. With my other hand, I reach around his waist and hold him gently.

'Oh,' he says, more a sigh this time, and I sense his arms embrace me so lightly I can barely feel his touch.

'I'll look out for this boy of yours,' he says. 'Bring me what you can and I'll get it to him.' Then he grips my shoulders, but tenderly, and eases me away from his chest.

'Your touch makes me think I'm still human,' he says. 'I can't let that delusion take hold. Not now. The weight of it would kill me.'

'You'll go back to the Russians, then? You'll get them ready for the hole in the wall?'

'Yes, I'll go back. Inside the wire, I'm already dead.'

16

According to the wireless, victory can still be ours if we hold out, but a different truth is broadcast in the faces I see on the streets. Every day there's a new rumour: that Hitler has fled Berlin; that a secret deal has been done with the Americans; that the Russians shoot every German they find. Through the second and third weeks of April I ride to Sachsenhausen whenever I have something to give to Meier, and to hear him say, 'Dieter is still alive.'

I return from one of those journeys to hear Vati's voice coming from the kitchen. When has he ever been home so early? The look on his face when I join him only deepens my frown.

'We'll have an early supper: set four places,' he tells me, and when I open my mouth to question him, he cuts me off. 'I phoned Kapitän Goldapp. Renate will be here shortly.'

She arrives, looking as worried as I am. Even Mutti doesn't seem to know what this is about. Our dinner is hardly worthy of the word, but what's worse is the way we sit disconnected from one another. What was it Frau Kleinschmidt said in her letter? That their family could never be whole without its missing menfolk. We're no different.

With his plate wiped clean, Vati addresses us as though he's called a meeting at work. 'The war is lost, we must think of ourselves.'

'No, Gerhard,' Mutti protests. 'There's still hope . . .'

'Quiet,' Vati barks at her. 'They've lied to us. The Russians are on the outskirts of Berlin and it won't be long before they're here in Oranienburg, too. We're leaving, all four of us, tomorrow morning.'

'Where will we go?' Mutti asks in a cowed voice I haven't heard before.

'To my cousin in Bavaria.'

'But the Americans are already *in* Bavaria!'

My father stares straight into Mutti's face. 'Better the Americans than the Russians.' Without another word he nods towards my sister and me.

'I'm not going,' says Renate.

'Don't be a fool,' Vati replies sharply. 'You think your captain — your *lover* — will protect you?' When Renate's eyes fly wide open, he keeps on at her. 'Don't look so shocked. I've had enough friends tell me what you're up to. Well, it's over now. You're an even greater fool than I thought if you believe Goldapp will take you with him. He'll head straight for his wife and leave you to the devil. You're coming with us tomorrow if I have to chain you to my own wrist.'

★ ★ ★

Renate cries herself to sleep and takes an age about it. I find it hard to summon any sympathy because I have a job to do before morning and I don't want a tearful sister getting in the way.

147

Once she drifts into the regular breathing of sleep, I slip out of bed, take a sack from my drawer then descend the stairs with the stealth of a spy.

In the kitchen I take Mutti's precious biscuit tin from the pantry. There's nothing inside — we haven't had biscuits for a year. Into the tin I cram the letters I haven't been able to send on: some because they've become caught in my own backlog, but most because they don't have a proper address or, more sadly, the prisoner number for someone in a konzentrationslager. I've had many of these for months, dithering over what to do about them when there's so little hope of them ever reaching their destinations.

Will there be anyone at these destinations to read them anyway, when so many are dead? I've spent hours wondering how many of the letter writers would be as devoted as Dieter. Would they pour their heart and soul into words on a page if they knew already their loved ones would never read them? And every time I doubt it, I hear Dieter's words in the laundry. *The dead should know they are loved.* He's right, and that's why I can't destroy these remaining letters. Among them are the most loving I've come across, and too much love has been burned, tossed aside, ignored and forgotten for me to treat them so cruelly. In the weeks since my last letter from Dieter, I've read them over and over to sustain me. I wonder what the prisoners who wrote them would think if they knew. Would it sustain them to know their love hadn't gone to waste?

A spade rests against the fence where I left it in readiness. I've already chosen a spot, too, in the far corner of the vegetable garden, where no one will think the freshly turned soil unusual.

'I'll be back for you once the war is over,' I promise the tin as I press it into the bottom of the hole. I tamp the earth down on top of it, then I go back to my bed.

⋆ ⋆ ⋆

I come awake to the sound of knocking at our door. No, not knocking. This is loud thumping, and it is accompanied by an urgent cry: 'Open up, we have orders from the Gauleiter.'

What time is it? I wonder, still groggy with sleep. There's barely enough light to see outside; what could bring men to our door at this hour?

Renate is out of bed already and I join her on the landing just as Vati hurries down the stairs, still stuffing shirt tails into his trousers. 'Who is it?' Renate calls after him. She gets no reply other than a shake of the head.

Mutti is with us now and, wearing nothing but our nightdresses, we go down to the hall, where my eye is drawn immediately to the four suitcases lined up along the wall. We'd packed them last night, carefully assessing how much each item would be needed. We'll have to carry those cases a long way.

Vati has opened the door and already he's arguing with the visitors. I look past him and gasp. Soldiers: two with rifles and a third with a pistol holstered on his belt. They're not SS but as grim-faced and threatening as any I've seen in the konzentrationslager.

'I'm an engineer for Heinkel — they still need me,' Vati is insisting, although it's a lie. He's leaving with us this morning and the aircraft factory can go to hell.

Renate has been into the sitting room to peer through the curtains. 'There are soldiers all along the street, going door to door,' she reports. 'What are they looking for, Mutti?'

But our mother is perplexed and can only watch the argument taking place at our door, her face as pale as the washed-out cotton of her nightdress.

At last Vati turns away from the unwelcome visitors to speak with us, but as he takes a step deeper into the hall where we're waiting, one of the soldiers strides after him, as though he's worried my father will make a run for it.

'They want me for the Volkssturm,' says Vati.

'But you don't know one end of a rifle from another, Gerhard!' Mutti responds.

'The Volkssturm? What's that?' I ask.

My parents are too busy firing words at one another, so it is left to Renate to explain. 'An army of men too old for the Wehrmacht and boys too young.'

'They want him to fight? But Mutti's right — he's never fired a gun in his life!'

'It's not so hard,' comments the soldier standing close by. 'He'll learn soon enough with the Red Army to shoot at.' He speaks of fighting like it's a game played for fun.

'You can't take him,' I say, grabbing Vati's arm. 'We need him here with us.' We need him

150

on the road west, I add silently. Three women alone; we'll be vulnerable.

My mother and sister chime in. 'Leave him with us. He's too old to fight, he'll be no use to you.'

A shout from the doorway ends our pleas. It's the soldier with the pistol. 'No exemptions, no excuses. The Führer demands that every man defend Germany to the death.' And he orders Vati out of the house.

Looking past him, I can see others lined up in the street just beyond our gate. Every German man, to the death. Aren't Franz and Walther enough for them?

'Margot, go upstairs and get your father's coat,' Mutti tells me.

By the time I return, Vati is standing in line beside the son of our neighbour from across the street. The boy can't be more than thirteen. When the first bombardment of the day begins in the distance, he bursts into tears.

'Vati, your coat,' I call, handing it to him when he turns. He ignores the frown of the soldiers eager to move on and hugs me close. He might not be weeping like the boy, but I feel him trembling from head to toe. 'My darling, the three of you must leave this morning, as soon as they march us out of sight. You must get as far west as you can, as quickly as you can. Walk day and night if you have to.' And that's all he's able to say to me in farewell before they are marched away. I stand at the gate with Mutti and Renate watching as they disappear down the street, knowing I might never see him again.

151

Once we're back in the house I repeat what Vati had said, but although Mutti nods to show she's heard, I'm not so sure she's ready to comply. We go upstairs to dress in skirts and sensible flat shoes that are the most practical for walking, but when Mutti appears from her room, she's wearing the heels she keeps for visits to Berlin and her dress is the smartest she owns.

'I'm going to see the Gauleiter,' she explains in answer to our questioning looks. 'I've known him since we were children. He can order them to release your father from the Volkssturm. Wait here. We'll leave as soon as Gerhard is free.'

★　★　★

Waiting isn't easy. The bombardment is closer today. The Red Army wants Berlin but we aren't so far away. When Mutti hasn't returned by noon, Renate and I walk to the end of Wilhelmstrasse — out of restlessness and fear more than any hope of seeing our parents heading home. When we reach the intersection where our street meets the main road I can barely believe my eyes. A human tide is passing by: a whole family piled into a horse-drawn cart; two women pulling a smaller wagon loaded with bedding and a small child perched on top, waving as though it's a carnival ride. Some women are pushing prams weighed down not with babies, but with the same things that weigh down my suitcase. The strangest sight is an elderly woman being pushed along in a wheelbarrow, her black-stockinged legs dangling over the front like a huge doll's.

152

'Everyone's leaving,' I say to Renate.

'They know what's coming,' she replies. 'The next few weeks will be chaos, with no one in charge, no one taking orders, and everyone desperate to survive until the fighting is over.'

'What's happening at the konzentrationslager?' I ask, hoping she'll know more than I do. 'Are the prisoners . . . are they . . . ' What words can I use? Are they all right? What a stupid question when they've been sent there to die.

'You're thinking of your pet prisoner?'

'Don't speak of him like that. And yes, I am thinking of him. Do you think I could go out to Sachsenhausen to — '

'No,' she answers curtly. 'We have to be ready when Mutti comes back. Your prisoner can fend for himself.'

We're heading back to the house by this time. I could defy her. An hour is all it would take, and if I can find Korporal Meier he might have news. But the matter is settled when Mutti arrives home shortly after us.

'The world has gone mad,' she declares, stepping out of her uncomfortable shoes. 'The Gauleiter is a pig, not at all like I remember him. He's terrified, too, I could see it in his eyes.'

'Will he exempt Vati from the Volkssturm?' I ask.

''No exemptions!' he shouted at me. 'Every German will fight to the last drop of blood!' That's all I could get out of him: slogans and heil Hitlers.' She sighs in defeat and although she tries to hide it, I can tell she's on the verge of tears. I feel little love for my mother and she feels even less for me, but there's no doubt she loves Vati. 'We should eat,' she says, 'then we must go.'

We're sitting at the kitchen table when a car pulls up outside. There are so few of them on the streets of Oranienburg these days, we stare at one another with no need to voice the question. Then Renate is on her feet and moving quickly into the hall, as though she knows who it is, and once she opens the door I can see why.

'Albie!' she cries, falling into the arms of Kapitän Goldapp.

'I didn't expect to find you here,' he tells her. 'Why haven't you left like all the others? The Red Army's moving quickly to surround Berlin and this town is in their path.'

The story of our dawn visitors flows out of Renate. 'Can you help him, Albie? Can you get my father out of the Volkssturm?'

Mutti and I have crowded into the doorway behind Renate, but Goldapp doesn't seem to have noticed. My sister is all he cares about.

'No,' he answers bluntly. 'I have no authority. I shouldn't even be here, but the situation is hopeless. We're getting out.' As he says this, he twists to nod at the car.

Only now do I see there are two others inside: one at the steering wheel and a woman's silhouette in the back. 'We're going to bluff our way to the west and surrender to the Americans.'

What an admission!

I'm not the only one shocked by it. Renate stands back from her lover, a hand over her open mouth. 'What if they arrest you for desertion?'

'Then I'll die quickly, which is more than I

154

can expect from the Russians once they know what happened in the konzentrationslager.'

These words weaken my knees. 'What's happened?' I demand of him. 'What more have you done to those poor people?' And it's not just Dieter I'm thinking about. I've read so many letters I feel I know the prisoners like friends, even the thousands who've never written a word.

Goldapp ignores me. 'Which of those bags is yours?' he asks Renate, gesturing to the suitcases in the hall.

She points hers out and the captain pushes past us to snatch it up. With his other hand he clutches my sister's arm. 'Come on, quickly — every minute is precious.'

Renate allows herself to be led down the short path and out through the gate, but when Goldapp opens the car door, she wrenches her arm away. 'What about Mutti and Margot?'

'There's no room. Now get in.' He leaves her for a moment to load her suitcase into the trunk.

Renate turns to stare at us, her eyes wild and her pretty face creased by indecision. Then, when the captain tries to push her into the back seat, she fights him off. 'No, I'm not going without them.'

I see the muscles go tight in Goldapp's jaw. 'Get in,' he commands.

'Please, Albie,' and she rests her hand gently on his chest, the way I've done a hundred times with Dieter in my imagination. 'There's room if one sits in another's lap. We can't leave them to the Ivans — you've heard the stories . . . '

Goldapp looks at Mutti and me for the first

time. He frowns when he recognises the black-mailing sister.

'Say yes, Albie, I beg you. If you want me to come, then you must take my mother and sister as well.'

She's put herself on the line now. Months ago, in his office, I saw the pride in this man and feared he would end his affair with my sister rather than give in to me. Dieter's life teetered in the balance that day. I can't help feeling Renate's might be at stake as I watch.

'Goldapp, we have to get going,' comes a call from inside the car.

The driver steps out into the street. 'Bring them if you must, but for God's sake, let's be on our way.'

'Fetch your bags,' Kapitän Goldapp tells us.

Mutti and I are in the hallway before I'm quite aware of what's happening. We're leaving not on foot, but in a car.

'If only he could help Vati too,' I say to Mutti. 'We could all fit if we squeezed up. I can't bear to think of him facing the Red Army. They have tanks, artillery. Listen — you can hear them now.'

But really, it's Dieter I'm thinking of. A car will have carried us a hundred kilometres away by nightfall. How will I be able to help him then?

'It's gone beyond that now, Margot,' Mutti snaps as I hover over my suitcase, reluctant to pick it up. She clamps her hands onto my upper arms and pins me to the wall. We've fought in this hallway before, but I can see in her face that she's not going to lose a second time. 'Do you want to be violated by those animals from the east?'

I go limp, made powerless by my own indecision.

'Wait here,' my mother says, letting me go. 'I've left my hairbrush upstairs, the silver one I was given as a wedding present.'

As I pick up my suitcase, Goldapp's words are loud in my ears. 'Once they know what happened in the konzentrationslager,' he'd said. What did he mean? Have all the guards run off, like him? That would mean the prisoners are locked inside the electric wire with no food, no water. They might turn on one another. Dieter is alone, vulnerable. What if he survived all this suffering, only to die just days from freedom?

I hear the door to my parents' room close above my head, and that distant sound is enough to make me act. I put down the suitcase and hurry along the hall to the kitchen and out through the back door. Then I'm running towards the fence. I've climbed over it a hundred times as a little girl and I scramble over it now as effortlessly as I had then. I land on the spring shoots of our neighbour's grass and there is their garden shed, just where it's been all my life.

From over the fence I hear them calling for me. Angry, frustrated voices. 'Margot, where are you hiding? Come out, quickly, or we'll leave you behind.'

Go, I urge them in my head. I doubt it will be long before they do. Goldapp is anxious to save his own skin.

I shiver through the afternoon in the tiny shed,

and only when the light is gone do I come out, climb the fence once more and slip back into our house through the back door. It's dark inside, and I have the place to myself for the first time I can ever recall. In the distance, the dull thunder of artillery has ceased for the night. I lock all the doors and windows then go upstairs to my own bed, wondering what I'll find in Sachsenhausen when I ride out there tomorrow morning.

17

Yesterday morning, I woke to violent hammering on our door and orders barked gruffly in the street. This morning, Wilhelmstrasse has never been so silent. It must be about the same time, since the light entering through my window is still weak. I stay in bed, aware of myself alone in the house again. I shouldn't be here. I should have gone with Renate and Mutti in the captain's car. I must be mad — but if I am, my whole country has gone mad with me. Last night I dreamed its life blood was bleeding from the swollen veins of its roads. It was the scene at the end of our street that prompted the image in my mind, I suppose. There won't be much left alive in Oranienburg, not once the last of its people flee. That's why I'm staying: so that one life, at least, won't drain away. Dieter told me once that the love he and his Margot shared would live on as long as he was alive to remember it. But I don't want to love a memory. I want someone warm and kissable and very much alive.

When the sunlight strengthens, I return to the vegetable patch and harvest tiny cabbages which have barely sprouted above ground. Digging deeper I find some wizened potatoes gone to seed. I boil them with the cabbage and make a grey green mash that tastes better than it looks. I doubt Dieter will care. The artillery has started up again. My mind is too full of other things to

159

be afraid of something so far away.

The town is eerie in its stillness as I set out for the konzentrationslager — not a car or a bike, not even a pedestrian shares the streets with me. A couple of times I see a curtain twitch aside in an upstairs room, and once I catch a face staring out at me: an old woman too frail to join the columns of refugees, or too proud to be pushed along in a wheelbarrow.

Something else is different, more than the emptiness and the graveyard quiet. I can't put my finger on it at first, but then I realise — the flags are gone, the red and black of the Nazis that adorned every house when Lili and I first walked to high school. They'd fluttered with less enthusiasm when so many of our men were lost in Russia and swastikas began to disappear from windows and front doors as the news grew worse. Today, there are no Nazis in Oranienburg. None at all.

Sachsenhausen looms ahead and already I know the guards have gone from the watchtowers. There are no soldiers at the outer gate, either. There isn't a car or a truck parked anywhere along the route where only a month ago I'd count a dozen before I reached the mailroom.

The main gate is open, but it seems wrong, somehow, to ride my bike into the appelplatz, so I leave it propped against the wooden hut as I've done for almost a year and walk through on foot.

On the way here I'd pictured thousands milling in the appelplatz — not lined up stiffly, as I've so often seen them, but relaxed and

160

chatting, as though . . . That's just it. I've imagined them all waiting for me. Fool! If the gates are open, why wouldn't they all walk free? But if they *had* walked free, I'd have seen them by now in the town and along the road to Sachsenhausen. So where are they? Where's my Dieter?

I can see some striped uniforms dotted among the barracks on the far side of the appelplatz. Two are on their feet and another three lie slumped against the wall, so still I'm not sure they are even alive. The enormity of the space shrivels me and without thinking I push my hands into the pockets of my coat, wrapping it close around me. My right hand touches something small and hard — the unteroffizier's cigarette lighter. I must have forgotten to give it back to him. I wonder where he is now.

Overhead, birds ignore me as they look for pickings then, disappointed, fly away, as so many prisoners must have dreamed of doing. The crunch of the gravel underfoot is my only companion on the lonely walk to where the gallows once stood. One of the prisoners shuffles forward to intercept me. With one arm outstretched and his hand open and grasping he begs, more in grunts and moans than words. But what little I have is for Dieter. 'Where are the other prisoners?' I ask.

He shakes his head to show he doesn't understand me and pleads again, so pathetically I take a little of the mash from the cloth I've wrapped it in and give it to him. It goes straight into his mouth. He's seen the rest and lunges at me, but I'm too quick for him, and once I'm out of reach he has no strength to come after me.

I continue walking among the barracks, where I've never ventured before, until a large number 19 painted on a wall catches my eye. Dieter's barracks! I run to the door, throw it open and immediately recoil at the stink. What *is* that smell? Not rotting flesh, I'm pretty sure of that, but the reek! I force myself inside and give thanks a second time when I see there are no corpses. It's simply that too many bodies have been pressed together into this death box for too long, fouling the floor when they couldn't reach the bucket in time and sweating into the bare boards of the three-tiered bunks. The stench remains, but the prisoners are gone.

I hurry out into the sunshine and breathe in-out, in-out, until the worst is gone from my lungs. This is when I see a woman slip into the next barracks along. She is not shuffling, nor is she using her hands to steady herself against falling. The woman wears prison stripes but she's in better shape than those I saw in the appelplatz. I wait for her to come out again, and when she sees me she stops dead in her tracks.

'Who are you? What are you doing here?' she demands in accented German. She sees me glance at the yellow triangle on her dress.

'Yes, I'm a Jew,' she tells me defiantly.

'Where are all the prisoners?'

'Gone. All those who could still walk were marched away yesterday. Any too sick to move were left behind for the SS to shoot in their beds, most likely, but the Russians are so close

162

they ran off before the job was done.'

Marched away! So I've stayed behind for nothing. 'You're not sick,' I say. 'Why didn't you go with the rest?'

'I'm a doctor. There were dozens left in the infirmary.'

'But you said they were going to shoot anyone left behind.'

She shrugs her shoulders. 'They didn't. What about you? Why haven't you fled like those cowards in the watchtowers?'

'I came back to help someone I . . . someone I care about.'

'Then we're as crazy as each other. This person was a prisoner, I suppose.'

'In the barracks just there.' I point at the number 19.

'Well, he's gone now. Do you have any matches? That's what I was searching for. My patients have no flesh on their bones to keep them warm.'

'No, not matches, but I have this.' I take the lighter from my pocket and flick it into life with my thumb. I've had enough practice, after all.

'Then you can get a fire going for us. This way.' She sets off without waiting for me to agree.

We've only gone ten steps when she stops again, turning to me. 'What's that I smell?'

I sniff for smoke and shake my head.

The doctor leans towards me, almost puts her nose inside my coat. 'Potatoes. You brought your prisoner friend something to eat.'

My first reaction is to turn away, but she's

163

right. I've missed Dieter so there's no point saving anything for him. I open my coat and show her the cloth with the mash tied up inside. Instantly, she snatches it from my hand. 'This will keep twenty alive for another day,' she says, and then she scoops a small portion into her own mouth. I must have a disapproving look on my face, because she sneers at me, 'If I collapse, they'll die.'

'I'm sorry. You're welcome to it, then.'

'Can you get more?'

I think of our garden. If I scrounge again it might give up a few more potatoes, and there are many such gardens behind the houses in Oranienburg — houses that are now mostly abandoned. 'I could try.'

'Then give me that lighter and go get what you can.'

She's ordering me about like a servant, but she's so capable, so determined, and aren't we here on the same mission after all? I hand her the cigarette lighter and she lets out a cry.

'What's wrong?' I ask.

'What in God's name are you doing with this?' she asks, holding up the lighter.

'A soldier gave it to me and I forgot to give it back.'

'But look at the damned thing, would you?'

I do as she asks and see only the lighter I've used so many times to get a fire going in the oil drum.

When I shrug, still not understanding what she means for me to see, she yells in my face. 'Don't you know what that symbol means to

Russians, to Poles, to Slavs everywhere? Do you have any idea what the SS did once the Wehrmacht had swept through country after country? Hundreds of thousands have been murdered by men wearing that symbol. Rounded up into barns and burned. Machine-gunned in pits.' She thrusts the lighter back into my hand. 'Get rid of it!'

'But it's useful. How are you going to light a fire for your patients if I throw it away?'

'They'd rather freeze to death than take comfort from the SS.'

She's being ridiculous. 'It's just a lighter,' I protest. 'Where are the prisoners you're caring for?'

The doctor glares at me, but she does want to light a fire for her patients. 'At the end of this row,' she says, pointing, but rather than moving forward we both turn back the way we've come. 'You heard it too?' she asks. 'An engine?'

'Not a car,' I say. 'Not a truck, either.'

We walk back to the edge of the appelplatz. The sound is louder now. Whatever it is, it's making its way cautiously along the road beyond the outer wall. Puffs of black smoke from its exhaust shoot upwards, marking its progress until it turns the corner and stops just short of the gatehouse.

'They're here!' says the doctor. 'The Red Army's here at last.'

The Russians! Shouldn't there be gunfire, explosions, blood? I've been living in dread of this moment for months now, but the woman beside me sounds relieved, even gleeful.

What happens now? I wonder. I've never

165

thought about it, only of Dieter. I'd imagined that we would sneak away to the west ourselves, somehow . . . Oh God, the cigarette lighter! The doctor warned me, but I was too stubborn. I pull it from my pocket and fling it away. The doctor watches it skid along the hard-packed gravel then looks at me, her face pale with horror.

'What's the matter?' I ask. 'Isn't that what you told me to do?'

But she's turned away from me now and is staring towards the gate. Following her gaze I see a lone figure walking towards us across the vast space of the appelplatz. Two more soldiers appear behind him, lean men in ragged, filthy uniforms with stubble darkening their chins, each clutching a rifle across his chest. They signal that it's safe for their companions to join them and immediately a strange truck rolls into the appelplatz. It has wheels at the front but at the back, it rides on tracks like a tank.

My eyes dart back to the first man. What had he seen?

Halfway across the appelplatz he stops, his eyes scanning the ground. I can barely breathe. Finally he stoops to pick up something, rotating it in his hand to inspect both sides. I already know what it is.

The soldier calls to his comrades, who gather round to inspect what he's found. Harsh, angry words drift across the appelplatz, which is no stranger to such voices, although these aren't speaking German and I don't understand them. The newcomers are asking questions, though, and in answer, the soldier who found the cigarette lighter points towards me.

'If you run, they'll shoot you,' warns the doctor.

I don't doubt her for a moment. I put my hands in the air like I saw cowboys do once, before American films were banned. They're still above my head when the soldiers form a circle around me — there's five of them now, all shouting angrily and pointing at the lighter in the hand of their comrade. One of them lurches forward and pulls my arms down, as though my meek surrender has only made him more furious. The roughness of his grip brings memories of the drunken guard who'd searched me for his bottle of schnapps. I'd escaped that time, but these men don't want schnapps — they want blood.

A soldier emerges from the strange truck; an officer, judging by the way the others open the circle to admit him. He listens, grim-faced. They show him the cigarette lighter and suddenly he grabs my hair. It hurts, and I cry out in pain. He growls something at me and I don't have to speak Russian to know he's told me to shut up. Meanwhile the circle of soldiers is urging him on, their hollow faces full of hatred.

Oh God, I think, as he takes a pistol out of the holster on his hip. I try to wrench myself free of his grip, but he's so strong. I'm utterly helpless and beyond the kind of fear that leaves room to think. 'I'm not SS. Please, let me go,' I whimper, but they speak no German, and I doubt they would listen to me even if they did.

The officer still has me by the hair, his pistol

so close to my temple it is almost touching.

'I'm not SS,' I cry again. 'I was the mail clerk. I looked after the letters, that's all! The letters!'

Then a loud thud explodes inside my skull.

DIETER

18

25 September 1945

Dieter Kleinschmidt walked the streets of Hannover wishing the stark evidence of defeat wasn't sketched so brutally into the jagged ruins everywhere he looked. The sun of a late-summer evening warmed his face. It was a dirty face, he knew; the day's sweat had turned the dust into a grimy paste from hairline to chin. There were nights he didn't bother to wash it off since it would get just as dirty the next day.

Now that his strength was returning, he was getting regular work shifting rubble — the occupying forces paid gangs to clear roads and footpaths and rail lines throughout the city, and the gang leaders liked the way he kept at it. If the work seemed much like the quarry at times, he reminded himself there were no dogs, no vicious guards lashing out with truncheons at the slightest stumble. There were no selections, either; those came later, in his dreams. Instead, his gang rested often and talked and laughed, shared a cigarette butt scavenged from the rubble, and there was bread in the middle of the day. Like the quarry, yes, but so unlike it his heart ached with the oddness of being alive. Oh, Leon, he said silently, then raised a powder-dusted arm to be sure the flesh on his bones wasn't a dream; that he wasn't, in fact, still slowly dying in Sachsenhausen.

The pay wasn't much, but it helped to feed his mother and sisters and buy kerosene for the lantern they used to light the basement where they lived. Their apartment building had been bombed in the terrible raids after Christmas, leaving Mutti and the girls to share little more than a hole in the ground with Frau Schatz and the Rosenstahls. To Dieter it was paradise, because he'd seen the inside of hell.

He didn't notice the English soldier walking across the road towards him until the man called out for him to halt. The large P on his armband told Dieter he was a member of the military police, but the English weren't interested in catching thieves. Mostly they watched the people of Hannover suspiciously for the crime of being German.

'Show me your papers.'

Dieter reached into his pocket for the Entlassungsschein he'd been given back in May. He'd produced it so many times the paper was fraying at the edges and the folds were so weak his precious identity pass would soon separate into pieces.

The soldier took it from him, showing a little respect for its condition at least. The gruff demand for papers was a phrase a parrot could learn but Dieter had a feeling this one spoke some German. He watched the man's eyes, trying to judge whether he was actually reading the Entlassungsschein and he was ready for the question that was sure to come if he could.

The soldier looked up in surprise. 'You were in a concentration camp?'

172

'Sachsenhausen. It says so on there.' He was about to point it out when the memory of the camp took hold of him. He told himself ten times every day he wasn't a prisoner anymore, that the SS didn't have control over every movement he made, every glance of his eyes. But part of him still wasn't convinced. At least this time he hadn't snapped to attention and stared down at his feet.

'I was still wearing the camp uniform when we reached Hamburg.'

'Are you Jewish?' The soldier had a chocolate bar halfway out of his pocket when Dieter shook his head.

'I am,' the Englishman declared proudly. The chocolate bar dropped out of sight.

'I have young sisters. They aren't Jews either, just hungry.'

The soldier relented and handed over the chocolate. 'If I see *you* eating that I'll arrest you,' he announced solemnly, but there was a gleam in his eye.

Dieter felt himself relax. This one wouldn't search him for the hell of it and slip in an 'accidental' elbow to the ribs while he was at it.

'Don't worry. I learned how to deny myself in Sachsenhausen. The SS were good teachers.'

'If you're not a Jew, then why were you there?' the soldier asked.

Dieter had been stopped a dozen times by British soldiers in their victor's uniform, most with a three-day growth on their chins like this one, but he was the first to ask that question. There was something odd about his accent, too.

'I cracked a Gestapo goon over the head with a piece of wood,' Dieter replied, leaving out the reason why — that the goon was beating his father to death.

A second chocolate bar appeared from the same pocket. 'This one's for you.'

'Danke. I'll share it with my mother. It'll be the best supper we've had since I made it back to Hannover.'

'From Hamburg,' prompted the soldier.

'Yes, Hamburg. The SS marched us out of Sachsenhausen when the Red Army closed in. They were going to drown us all in the Baltic. That was the rumour.'

'A death march. I've heard of the same thing in Poland. It was winter then. Thousands died.'

'No one counted our dead,' said Dieter. Mere numbers couldn't describe the brutality of that final march, and this foreigner wouldn't understand even if he tried to explain. Nobody did. Words simply crumbled under the weight of such meaning. 'I'm alive because of these boots,' he told the soldier instead, since that was something he *could* explain. 'Some prisoners had only wooden clogs to walk in. Their feet blistered, became slippery with blood, and once they stumbled a guard moved in with his pistol.'

A final selection, Dieter added to himself, while the anger built inside him. There were times he shook with such rage his workmates thought he'd come down with typhus. He looked into the soldier's face; he was an innocent, really, despite the gun slung over his shoulder. Best to stick to the easy parts, Dieter decided.

174

'After three days the SS ran off to save themselves. Left us to the Red Cross who took us to Hamburg. I spent a fortnight there in a tent hospital.'

The soldier handed back the Entlassungs-schein. 'Dieter Kleinschmidt. Sounds as German as beer and sauerkraut. My name is Ben, short for Benjamin. My parents chose it so I'd fit in as well. Plenty of Bens in Australia and that way I wouldn't stand out as a Jew.'

'Australia? But you're English.'

The soldier chuckled. 'Don't let the uniform fool you. I was studying in England when the war started, so I joined up there.'

'Australia,' Dieter muttered. 'Kangaroos.' He bounced on the balls of his feet for a few moments. 'And that strange creature with a duck's mouth and a beaver's tail.'

'Platypus,' said the Englishman who wasn't English at all. 'You know more about Australia than other Germans I've come across.'

That was a laugh. Dieter knew nothing about the place except for its weird animals. He was simply buttering up the soldier in case there was more in his pockets. It seemed to work, too, because they began walking in the direction Dieter had been heading when he was stopped. They were going to have a conversation, it seemed.

'How do you speak German so well?' Dieter asked.

'My grandparents were from a town near Frankfurt. Got tired of the persecution, the pogroms. It's not like Hitler invented hatred of

175

the Jews all on his own. They took their chances in New South Wales. My mother grew up speaking German at home and English everywhere else. So did I. There's a lot of that still in Sydney.'

They walked on in silence for a few moments while Ben worked himself up to the question Dieter knew he wanted to ask.

Finally, it came. 'How did you survive in the camp?'

'I had help — a friend outside the wire who could get me things,' he said, picturing a face he wondered whether he would ever see again. Margot Baumann was never far from his mind.

Ben's face creased as though a vicious pain had gripped his stomach. 'I've heard stories, terrible stories of what went on. I've seen the newsreels, too. Horrible, horrible. The men who ran those camps . . . '

'The SS were a special breed, right enough,' said Dieter. 'That's why you stopped me, isn't it? You're on the lookout for SS who don't want to answer for what they did.'

'I've got good reason, don't you think? A lot of those bastards have thrown away their uniforms and pretend now they never carried a gun. As a Jew it makes my blood boil.'

'As a German, it makes mine boil too,' Dieter responded bitterly.

In Hamburg, he'd been eaten up with the need to avenge himself and went looking for faces on the street to denounce them. Even here in Hannover, he couldn't stop checking every man he passed. There was talk those already

176

captured would be put on trial and if they were sentenced to swing, he'd give a week's rations to be there when the noose tightened around their necks.

They'd reached a corner. 'I'm heading this way,' said Ben.

'Straight on for me, to the post office.'

'The post office?' The Australian looked sceptical.

'Some mail's getting through, even from the Soviet sector.'

Ben's face darkened at this reference to the Russians. 'Good luck,' he called as he sauntered off.

Dieter felt his spirits oddly lifted by their conversation. He spent so much of each day morose and haunted by terrible memories, that he needed moments like this to stir memories of a different kind; memories of a different Dieter Kleinschmidt, one he despaired of ever being again. If he was suddenly in a lighter mood, then it seemed right that he was heading for the post office. His stride lengthened. Today might be the day.

Dieter made this walk to the post office more often than he needed to, if judged against the number of letters he brought back with him. After returning empty-handed so many times, he'd told his mother he liked to stretch his legs, but her expression told him she didn't believe a word of it. 'You should save your energy for working,' she said.

But his mother didn't know about Margot Baumann and how he'd written to her in

Oranienburg. There didn't seem any way to explain about Margot — about either of his Margots, in fact, since his mother had no idea how much in love he'd been with Margot Lipsky, and without that, how could strange, illusory Margot Baumann make any sense? He wasn't sure what to make of her himself, really; it was like grasping at a cloud. On occasions he wondered whether she was even real.

No, he scolded himself whenever he drifted into thoughts like this, he hadn't been kept alive by angels and fairies. It was food in his belly and boots on his feet that saved his life. And the letters from his Margots. When the guards had finally melted away back in April, there'd been no time to think of more than just the next day, even the next hour. The Führer was dead, they said, the war as good as over, yet the dying wasn't done with and the forced march had left him dreadfully weak.

During his weeks in the care of the Red Cross, he'd thought of finding his mother and sisters more than anything. There was only one way, and as soon as he was well enough he'd set off for Hannover, along with thousands of others who'd found themselves displaced and desperate for home. And then Calenbergerstrasse, destroyed so totally he wasn't sure where their apartment had stood until his sister Silke rose up out of the ground like a ghost from her grave and let out such a scream when she saw him that his mother and Gabriele had scrambled out of their underground home to join her — and then, finally, the relief of their arms around him.

That had been in June, and through July he'd let his mother take charge while his strength slowly returned, unable to tell her much and thankful she didn't press him. Some of the boys he'd known at school had come home by then — men they were now and, like him, forced to grow up quickly by what they'd seen and done and what had been done to them. No one was in the mood to speak of the last six years, and while many had been soldiers, Dieter sat among them as though those years had been the same for all of them. Perhaps they had.

It was with these friends that he'd found work clearing debris from the bombing, and with each brick and broken beam they lifted, the city's heart was freed a little more to become as they remembered it.

The August sun evoked memories of sailing in the Baltic — and not just for him.

'Wouldn't I love to go sailing around Rügen Island again,' said Gabbi. 'What was the place where we slept on the beach?'

'Binz,' he'd answered, and suddenly Margot Baumann was in the basement with him, as close as she'd been in the dim light of the laundry. Where had she been these past months, while he'd flickered back to some kind of life? Where was she now?

He'd written to her in the first week of September; now it was almost October. Even allowing for delays and shortages, that was plenty of time. Yes, it might be today.

Dieter took his place in the queue. Hannover's grand post office had lost its roof a year ago; now

179

it operated out of the only undamaged room to one side of the main foyer. When he eventually reached the counter the postal clerk cocked his head to one side in recognition. 'Kleinschmidt, right? You're persistent, I'll grant you that, but you know I can't make a letter turn up just because you keep asking.'

'A bribe wouldn't do any good then?' Dieter asked, enjoying his own hopeful mood.

'If there was money to be made, I'd write you a letter myself and you'd be so happy to receive it, you wouldn't care,' the clerk joked. The words were like a jab in the guts to Dieter and he must have shown as much in his face, because the clerk wiped the smile from his face in response. 'I'll go check,' he muttered.

He came back with his smile restored. 'At last there's something for you!' He handed over a slim letter with handwriting Dieter didn't recognise — which meant it wasn't Margot Baumann's. So who was it from? The envelope was addressed to him personally, not his mother or the family as a whole.

He waited until he was outside, amid the dust and the fading warmth of the cobblestones, before stopping beside what had once been a fountain to tear open the envelope. He removed a single sheet of paper, unfolded it and read:

Dear Dieter,
I hope you will forgive me for opening
your letter when it was addressed not to
me but to my daughter. What you wrote
was both a great surprise to us and at the

180

same time explained much that had
puzzled us about Margot's behaviour in
the final days of the war.

Dieter, it is my sad duty to tell you our
beloved Margot died when the Red Army
swept through Oranienburg as part of their
final push to Berlin. We are stricken with
the deepest grief, a grief I am sure you
now share. I wish there was something
from these months of suffering I could
offer you to lessen your own pain at the
news, but I have found nothing for myself
and wonder if anyone ever has.

Margot obviously cared a great deal for
you and I'm sure she would have been
pleased to hear you have been reunited
with your family in Hannover.

Yours faithfully,
Gerhard Baumann

Dieter Kleinschmidt hadn't cried when his father was beaten to death in front of him. He hadn't cried when his friend Leon was shot, still clutching the hand he'd crushed between two slabs of stone. He hadn't cried on his return to Hannover, when his mother had clung to him, whimpering, 'Dieter, my Dieter, it's really you.' But he cried that evening beside the fountain as if he would never stop.

19

After receiving the letter from Gerhard Baumann, Dieter hardly left the basement. He spoke barely a word, not even to his mother. When twelve-year-old Silke came to him for the cuddles she found so comforting, he growled at her to leave him alone.

'What's the matter? What's happened?' his mother asked, but he waved her away. 'Not feeling well,' he muttered, then rolled over on his pallet to face the wall.

In the brief, devastating letter, Herr Baumann had wished there was something from his own months of grieving he could offer Dieter, then, in the same sentence, admitted there was nothing. Dieter would have to find his own way through. He was alone, just as he'd been in Sachsenhausen after Leon died. Grief became his new konzentrationslager, one with a single prisoner, and here the dogs were just as savage, the deadly fences just as high. How would he survive this time when his saviour from the last camp could no longer help him?

'Dieter, your friends are calling for you,' his mother told him. 'Three days' work clearing the canal.'

'Not today,' he replied. 'Tell them I'll work tomorrow.' But he didn't work the next day, and the foreman of his gang was losing patience.

It was just so unfair, he railed to himself, as

though a year in Sachsenhausen hadn't taught him that 'fair' was a meaningless word. Both his Margots were dead, and the timing of Margot Baumann's death seemed especially cruel. The girl who had kept him alive must have died just as he was being released. He was free now to do something for her in return, but that wish was futile. After all, what could the living do for the dead?

'Dieter, this has gone on long enough,' his mother announced one morning.

He turned from the wall to find the basement deserted except for the two of them.

'Yes, Frau Schatz and the rest are out working, as you should be, and I've sent the girls to scavenge for firewood. You *will* speak to me this morning; you will tell me why you've fallen into this morass of self-pity.'

'Self-pity? You think I'm sorry for myself!'

'Then who?' Her tone softened. 'Tell me what's happened, Dieter. We depend on you, my darling.' She lowered herself onto the ground beside his pallet and took his hand in her own to let its warmth infuse his skin. 'You've got to lift yourself out of this mood and face whatever has caused it. Are you haunted by nightmares? Is that it? Then share them with me. My husband was beaten to death, my friends dragged away and never seen again. Do you think I can't bear to hear the worst of what happened in Sachsenhausen?'

'It's not my time in Sachsenhausen I'm thinking of, Mutti. At least, not in the way you think. There was a girl . . . ' Yes, he was going to tell her at last.

'You mean Margot,' said his mother. 'You were in love with her.'

Dieter sat up on his pallet. 'You knew her? But she was — '

'Of course I knew her, darling,' said his mother, speaking over him. 'Have you forgotten I took food to the Lipskys as often as you did? She was a lovely girl. I wasn't at all surprised when you fell head over heels.'

With a wrench of mind more than muscle, Dieter fought his way free of confusion. She didn't mean Margot Baumann. She was talking about Margot Lipsky.

'I'm right, aren't I?' asked his mother when he didn't respond. 'It was there in your face every time you spoke her name, in the way you searched out books for her as if you were a knight on a quest. It made my heart glow just to watch you. I don't know if Frau Lipsky knew the pair of you were in love, but I did. So this is why you've shut yourself away: because poor Margot died in a konzentrationslager and you didn't.'

'No, no, Mutti, you've got it all wrong,' Dieter exclaimed, pressing his forearms against the sides of his head in frustration. He let the breath drain slowly out of him until he was calm enough to go on. 'Well, you're half right,' he conceded. 'I *was* in love with Margot Lipsky. The thing is, she didn't love me. We weren't boyfriend and girlfriend like you think. All the love came from one side — mine.'

'Oh, Dieter. I never thought . . . '

He shrugged and sat up with his back against the wall, making room on the pallet for his mother to do the same.

'She knew how I felt about her. It's not the sort of thing you can hide, is it?' He laughed bitterly. 'At first she encouraged me, because she was bored after spending all day in the tiny space at the back of our warehouse. When she was let out at night she wanted someone to talk to and she seemed pleased enough to sit with me away from the others. We'd hold hands in the dark. But she was a year older, Mutti, and when I tried to kiss her she came right out and said it: I was too young for her and she didn't want me for a boyfriend. It wasn't just her, either, she said. Her parents wouldn't be happy about it. They'd let her have all the friends she liked, no matter what religion they were, but she'd always known that she could only fall in love with a Jew like herself.'

'So it's the hurt of that rejection that plagues you now, is it?' asked his mother. 'Made worse because Margot's Jewishness condemned her to Hitler's gas chambers.'

'No. I was getting over it by the time the Lipskys were discovered. That didn't mean it was any easier to listen to prisoners explain what happened to Jews in the death camps, Auschwitz especially. They all died on the day they arrived. I didn't want to believe it, but then I saw how prisoners with yellow triangles on their uniforms were beaten more savagely and picked out ahead of the rest of us at selections. It was true, I couldn't deny it. The Lipskys were dead. I grieved for Margot in my first months at Sachsenhausen, even though she hadn't been in love with me. She'd never been in love with

185

anyone, she told me. She was looking forward to it, the way you look forward to Christmas. That's the way she said it, Mutti, like she was making fun of herself — and then she was dead, without ever feeling love the way I had. That seemed unbearably sad.

'But by mid-summer I had my own problems. The starvation, the brutality, the constant exhaustion in the camp began to overwhelm me, so it became a struggle just to live through each day. My shoes had been stolen by then, which made it worse. I began to learn from other prisoners that you can comfort yourself with dreams, with fantasies. One night, three men in a bunk near me took it in turns to describe the best meal they'd ever eaten.'

The memory made Dieter grab at his mother's arm in excitement. 'It sounds crazy, Mutti, I know, but it helps, it can get you through the hunger.' Then, aware of how tightly he had gripped her arm, he let his hand drop. He hadn't said so many words to his mother in all the months he'd been home.

'I was as hungry as the rest,' he went on, 'but what I missed more than food was tenderness, affection, love. They had left behind a void I could reach into, a blackness no different from death. I didn't want to get sucked into it, as I'd seen it happen to others, so I grabbed hold of what I'd felt for Margot and during those moments when I could manage it, I escaped the misery of where I was.

'Since it all happened in my imagination, I could make anything happen, I could change the

186

past. I began pretending that Margot *had* loved me after all. The fantasy became so strong in my mind I wrote her a love letter. I even posted it to Auschwitz.'

He turned to his mother, who was weeping silently beside him. 'You must think I'm mad,' he said.

She answered him with a shake of her head.

'I knew in here,' he told her, tapping his temple with his finger. 'I knew she was dead, that she would never receive it, but it gave me a kind of joy to think of Margot reading my words. I let myself wonder what she would say in her reply, as if she truly had been my girlfriend. Then I wrote her another letter. It became part of how I survived.'

It was this second letter that Margot Baumann had found in her barrel, and he felt himself close to telling her story again.

'Oh, Dieter,' said his mother, sobbing now. 'My heart aches at what Sachsenhausen drove my poor son to do. But you shouldn't feel ashamed.'

Ashamed? No, thought Dieter. He'd never felt ashamed of his fantasies. In Sachsenhausen you did what you had to do to survive.

But now his mother was embracing him and he let everything else go. She'd hugged him a hundred times since he'd come home to her, but it had never felt like this. He'd never let himself feel the depth of her affection, that was why. He wrapped his own arms around her and squeezed her tight. 'I'm only half here, Mutti. So much of me is missing.'

'But you feel better for telling me this, don't you?' she said when they drew back.

Yes, he did, but it wasn't shame that had kept him on this pallet for almost a week. It wasn't guilt that he'd survived while Margot Lipsky had perished. It was Margot Baumann's death that had broken him in a way the konzentrationslager had never quite managed to do. He'd been going to tell his mother about her, but the moment had passed. He grieved for Margot Baumann in the way he'd grieved his other Margot during those first months inside the wire. He would think of her every day for a long time yet, he was sure of it, but the talk with his mother had allowed him to release some of his pain at least. Enough to enable him to go back to the surface, back into the light of the real world. He would survive, just as he'd learned to do in Sachsenhausen.

★ ★ ★

Late in October, winter announced itself with the first northerly winds which chilled the sweat on Dieter's brow while he picked undamaged bricks from the rubble, scraped away the mortar and stacked them ready to rebuild Hannover. All over Germany men and women were doing the same. Brick by brick they would reclaim their country, beginning each day with a curse for the Führer who'd deserted them when they had no more to give him and a shake of the head at the ruin he'd made of all they loved.

Then something wonderful came to Calenbergerstrasse, carried by Gabbi while Silke ran

188

beside her calling, 'Mutti, Mutti, there's a letter from Margot.'

Dear Frau Kleinschmidt,
I am writing to you in the hope you have heard from my father. Ethan and I are living in a displaced persons camp in Berlin, hoping he will be among the new faces that straggle in from Poland every day. We have been here since August and we have written to other DP camps hoping to find him, but so far there has been no news. We know not to look for our mother and little Hannah because they were killed when we arrived in Auschwitz.

I am also writing to ask what happened to Dieter. I hope this question does not cause you pain. Your family was very brave to shelter ours, especially when Herr Kleinschmidt paid such a price. It would break my heart to think Dieter was murdered by the Nazis as well. If he is home with you, please give him our love and tell him that Ethan still wants to learn how to sail.

If you have heard from our father, or if you know where he might be or whether he is still alive, please write back to let us know.
Yours in gratitude,
Margot Lipsky

A real letter from Margot. Was a cruel God taunting him? But she was alive! That was the

189

important thing, the wonderful thing. She'd cheated the gas chambers, and Ethan, too.

Dieter read her letter over and over, just as he'd done with the false letters in Sachsen-hausen, surprised each time at how different the handwriting was. *Break my heart . . . give him our love . . .* He choked on the words, but he knew not to read anything into them. He didn't want to, anyway. He'd told his mother the truth: he *was* over the hurt of rejection by the time the Lipskys were hauled away to Poland.

Margot was alive!

He counted four 'hopes' in the dozen lines of her letter. What chance was there that their father had survived? He found himself thinking about them almost as much as Margot Baumann, until it struck him like a kapo's truncheon that he and the Lipskys, prisoners from inside the wire, were still alive, while the girl from outside . . .

Who decided such things?

His mother answered the letter immediately and at the bottom Dieter wrote a few lines of his own. That night, he'd wept with joyful relief and at the same time with despair that there'd be no more letters like those he'd carried for months inside his filthy stripes — letters he still possessed and still read, letters that hadn't been written by this Margot he'd loved in death, but by a girl who'd now taken her place among the dead.

★   ★   ★

In December, the Lipskys wrote again.

*Dear Frau Kleinschmidt and dearest
Dieter,*
*It was wonderful to receive your letter and
to hear your news. The four of you
together must make each other strong even
as you grieve for your husband and father.
There has been no news of our father and
we must face the possibility that he died in
Auschwitz after all. Ethan and I have
decided to stay in this camp until the end
of the year, but if there is still no word of
him by then, we will leave. Since your
home remains one of the places Father
might come looking for us if he is still
alive, we will write to you when we are
settled in our new home. We aren't sure
where that will be yet. Perhaps not even
Germany. All our aunts and uncles are
gone so there is no family that ties us to
any place in this country.*

There was more, but after reading these lines
Dieter called to his mother, 'They should come
here.'

She made a face. 'Why would they come back
to Hannover when it holds such terrible
memories for them? They'd do better to start
fresh somewhere else.'

'But they'll have no family.'

'They have no family here, either.'

'They'd have us. They'll need friendly faces, a
family to be part of even if it isn't their own.

191

Margot and Ethan have lost everyone they loved, Mutti. We can help them get over it.'

His mother looked him over suspiciously. 'You're hoping something will come of having Margot back here with us, is that it?' she asked. 'You hope she'll change her mind about you?'

He shook his head. 'I don't think of her that way anymore.'

'Then why haven't you given the girls here in Hannover a single look? Don't think I haven't noticed. The war killed so many young men you could have your pick of the girls.'

'Don't talk that way, Mutti. It's my business.'

She gave him a reproachful glare but fell silent.

'It's Ethan I'm thinking of as much as Margot,' Dieter explained. 'He'd be another male here in the basement where it's all women and girls. I'm sick of it.' He risked a smile. It was true, in any case. Being the only male was another thing that made him feel isolated. 'Please write to them, Mutti; let them decide for themselves, at least.'

'No, Dieter. This basement is crowded enough already and no matter how much you say otherwise, I fear Margot will bruise your heart all over again. This time I can't agree.'

* * *

Dieter worked hard in the streets of his ruined city. That way he had less energy to think and the exhaustion helped him to sleep deeply each night. What he feared was lying awake in the

192

darkness, feeling utterly alone, even though the basement's floor was a carpet of sleeping bodies. Memories of Sachsenhausen came to him then, like ghosts, but these weren't what tormented him. Invisible amid the horror was a restlessness he couldn't name, a dark mood that stood like electrified wire between him and the moments of happiness that others seemed to find despite the hunger and the cold.

He should be happy. Margot Lipsky was alive. Yet her survival was somehow linked to his mood and knowing this filled him with shame. He could sense himself withdrawing from the world again — not as obviously as he had after the letter from Herr Baumann; he was still able to work and to play with Gabbi and Silke when they needed their brother — but his life had become a walking darkness.

The girls weren't aware that anything was wrong, but his mother was. 'Talk to me like you did before, Dieter,' she begged him. 'Sachsenhausen stole a year of your life. Don't let it take anymore.'

'I don't want it to; I don't want to be like this,' he replied, aware of the desperation in his voice.

'Then talk to me.'

But he couldn't. She didn't have the ears to hear him. Neither did his workmates or the pretty girls who sought him out, hoping for some fun. None of them had been in a camp. *You don't know what it was like!* he wanted to shout at them. *You can hold my hand, you can speak of how awful it must have been, you can listen to me describe what those bastards did to us, but you didn't know fear and hunger the way I did. You cannot ease the weight pressing in on me, unless you were inside the wire.*

On nights when even the weariness of his muscles wouldn't send him into oblivion, he fought back. He stood outside himself hoping to catch the demons as they crept into his mind. It came to him finally that there were two of them, with only one name. One was dead, one alive, but both had been essential to his survival in Sachsenhausen. He wasn't sure if his darkness came because he couldn't escape from them, or because he couldn't let them go. What he did know was that one of them, at least, might help him to find out.

'I'm going to Berlin,' he told his mother in the morning.

'No, I forbid it,' she told him bluntly. 'Berlin is in the Soviet sector.'

'Parts are controlled by the Americans and the British.'

'But to reach the city you must travel through the Soviet zone. I've heard too many stories, Dieter. The Russians hate us for what our soldiers did early in the war. They take their revenge against civilians in the street, rob them, beat them and worse.'

'I have my Entlassungsschein that says I was different.'

'Will they even read it? No, I won't lose you a second time, Dieter. You're needed here.'

'Mutti, we took in the Lipskys when they needed us. The job isn't finished.'

Dieter had an entire argument prepared in his

194

mind, invoking his father's name and insisting he'd have wanted them to go on helping the children of his old friend. He didn't use it, though, because to say another word would be dishonest. He was going to Berlin for his own sake.

'Mutti, I'm eighteen years old. I make decisions for myself now.'

His mother fought him for two more days, until he packed a bundle anyway and was ready to leave. Only then did she sigh and go to a jar hidden in the wall of the basement. 'Here, take this,' she said, handing him some money she had set aside for emergencies. 'Take the train if you can find any running again.'

Then she kissed him and said into his ear. 'Don't waste this journey, Dieter. Settle in your mind whatever is keeping you from us, and when you return this time, bring all of yourself, not the half-being who left so much in Sachsenhausen.'

20

Dieter wasn't ready for Berlin. 'A wasteland, a horror-scape,' he muttered when he reached the centre of the city. Once, on a beach — he couldn't remember where or how old he'd been — he and some holiday friends had built a city out of sand, knowing the tide would sweep it away. That was part of the fun. What he saw now was that giants had played the same game with a living city. The relentless tide of war had washed through Berlin, leaving only a wall here and there as evidence of what had once stood four storeys high. Hannover had got off lightly, he realised. In every direction, the decimation went on as far as he could see, dwarfing the beach of his memory until it seemed all of humanity would have to start again.

He slept overnight in a room shared by a dozen others, without beds or blankets. The landlord rented only enough space for a body to lie stretched out on the floor — nothing new to Dieter.

'Do you know where the displaced persons camp is?' he asked the nearest of his roommates.

'There's more than one. What type are you looking for?' came an answer out of the darkness, not from the figure beside him, but from a voice in the far corner.

'What do you mean, what type?'

'They keep the Jews in a separate camp

196

because there are SS without anywhere to go either. There've been bashings, murders.'

Dieter couldn't believe what he was hearing. 'Surely the SS aren't still after the Jews!'

Grim laughter rippled across the room until an entirely different voice explained. 'It's the Jews doing the killing now.'

★ ★ ★

A sky the colour of a gun barrel greeted Dieter in the morning, but the rain held off while he walked to the refugee camp for displaced Jews, asking directions on each street corner until he found it. In a hut beside the boom gate a woman looked him over. 'Can I help you?'

'I've come to see two friends who wrote to me from this camp. They were in Auschwitz.'

'So were half the people here,' she said, as though he was a fool even to mention the fact. 'Are you Jewish yourself?'

When he shook his head, the woman's lip curled. 'Your friendship didn't keep them out of Auschwitz, then,' she said curtly. 'You were in the Wehrmacht, I suppose?'

Dieter thought back to the men in his crowded room and the grim statement: *It's the Jews doing the killing now*. A similar fury, barely hidden, burned inside this woman, too. An entire race wanted retribution, and who could blame them? He was on the point of telling her that he'd suffered in a konzentrationslager himself, thinking to earn her cooperation, even her sympathy, but held back. Jews had been beaten more often

197

than the rest in Sachsenhausen. They were more likely to be hanged for the slightest offence, selected for the gas chamber. It wouldn't be right to claim fellowship with them now.

'Their name is Lipsky, Margot and Ethan,' he said, spelling out the surname.

The woman flicked through index cards in a box on her desk then nodded. 'They're still here. I'll write up a pass for you. Show it at the gate and they'll direct you.'

The huts inside the camp looked all too familiar to Dieter and for long seconds he hesitated. The gate attendant stared at him, but with more compassion than the clerk. He wasn't a guard, the man had explained — there were no guards in this camp, no barbed wire or Alsatians, and the only uniforms were worn by Allied servicemen who came if there was trouble. 'Do you need me to show you the way?' he asked.

'No, I'll be fine in a moment.'

'Hut seven's along that central track. Turn right at the fourth row.'

Dieter's feet seemed to understand the instruction even if his head was still muddled. He made his way along the wide muddy track that divided the women's barracks from the men's, or so he presumed, judging by the groups sitting on the steps sewing or writing letters. He was in a camp again, yet uncomfortably aware of his otherness, the only non-Jew among men and women who carried their suffering so obviously in their faces. He didn't see the anger he expected in those faces, but instead signs that their minds were far away, as his had been since

198

he'd returned to Hannover. According to his mother, only half of him had come home. Maybe only half of each person he saw here had survived Auschwitz, Theresienstadt, Treblinka and all the other camps he'd heard about. He'd deliberately stepped back from identifying with Jews like these in front of the unfriendly clerk, but here he relaxed and knew that in part at least, he *was* one of them.

Hut seven was on the men's side of the camp. 'Is Ethan Lipsky here?' he asked a man smoking a cigarette in the doorway.

The man turned to call over his shoulder, 'We got an Ethan Lipsky in here?'

The faint suggestion of movement inside turned into footsteps and then an inquisitive face peered around the figure in the doorway. 'Dieter! I don't believe it! Margot, come see who it is.'

And moments later, there she was: his Margot — or one of them at least. Brother and sister hugged him so fiercely they almost fell over. 'Oh God, you don't know what it means to see someone we know,' said Margot.

She'd barely changed in two years. Long-limbed and dark-haired, that part of her might have stepped straight out of Dieter's own memory. But she was smiling, laughing, fizzing with joy in a way he'd never seen in the warehouse. There, her face had always been hidden by shadows and darkness — but it was more than that. Here she was free to be happy in a way she couldn't be with the threat of discovery hanging over her family, and with an unwanted boyfriend to keep at arm's length. She

199

was his Margot, and yet she wasn't.

They'd come down the steps to claim Dieter and now more bodies had gathered in the doorway to see the visitor.

'Does this sort of thing happen often?' Dieter asked. 'Do people find one another?'

'Not enough,' said Margot, speaking to their companions in the doorway more than to him.

'I was sure they'd shoot you,' said Ethan. Like his sister, he wore a huge grin. 'I mean, you attacked the Gestapo like they were a gang of schoolboys. It was the bravest thing I'd ever seen.'

Brave! Dieter didn't think of it that way. 'I couldn't stand by — the anger in me was too strong.'

They'd arrived at the first death, as they were always going to do, but it wasn't one of the Lipskys they were remembering. *Your friendship didn't keep them out of Auschwitz*, the woman by the gate had sneered at him. No, it didn't, Dieter agreed, but we tried.

'Your father. Has there been any news?' he asked.

Twin shakes of the head were his answer. 'Father and I stayed together at first,' Ethan explained, 'but last winter he came down with typhus and they took him away. I couldn't find out where. They wouldn't tell you anything in those . . . ' Ethan stopped. 'But you know that, Dieter. You were in a camp yourself.'

'That's why I've come. What happened to us means we belong together. You should come back to Hannover with me, live with my family, be a brother and sister to me until we're properly

200

free of those camps.'

Before the Lipskys could respond, a man appeared around the corner of the hut and came to stand behind them. He was older, in his mid-twenties.

'This is a friend of ours, Jerzy Radzinski,' said Margot, and she shifted towards the new arrival — just a few centimetres but enough for Dieter to notice.

'You're Polish,' said Dieter.

'You'd think so, with a name like that, wouldn't you,' said Jerzy without any trace of an accent. It could have come across as aggressive, but he was grinning as he said it and Dieter found himself liking the man. 'My father was from Warsaw, but I grew up in Berlin. That made me especially popular with the SS — a Jew *and* a Pole.'

Together, they went into the warmth of the hut, where Dieter was immediately assailed by the institutional air: the men and a few women gathered in huddles, the smell of sweat and especially the rows of bunks. At least these bunks weren't crammed together, plus there were proper mattresses and the bedding was clean.

'I sleep easily here,' Ethan told him, as if he recognised the apprehension in Dieter's face. 'Sometimes there's work and we go off in a truck somewhere, but this bed is my refuge afterwards, not like Auschwitz.'

'I know what you mean. You can sleep, really sleep, because you know you're not going to die tomorrow.' It was the first time he'd been able to state the simple truth of it and he knew in that moment that he'd been right to come. To say such things to anyone who hadn't worn the striped uniform was like talking to a ghost — the words went straight through, because the listener had nothing in his experience with which to grab hold of them.

Jerzy nodded solemnly, and Dieter understood that he'd been in Auschwitz, too. 'They wanted us to know we were going to die, didn't they?' he said. 'It wasn't enough to work us worse than dogs, to starve us, to kick us when we fell. No, they had to beat at our minds, too, with the fear of death that would come for each of us.'

Ethan added, 'The worst of them enjoyed it; you could see it in their faces. Hitler was the best thing that ever happened to their kind because they could torment the defenceless all day long and get a medal for it.'

Margot had her own tales. The guards hadn't been any less brutal because they wore a skirt, apparently.

'Bastards,' Dieter muttered, as his companions related their experiences. Every description, every memory, could have been one of his own. He found himself joining the recitation, opening his entire being to the anger he'd carried home with him from Sachsenhausen, aware that his fists were clenched painfully tight as he spoke.

They shared stories until they'd emptied themselves and Dieter felt better for it. 'Hey, do you remember my promise, Ethan?' he asked, signalling a switch of mood that came to him so suddenly he felt faint. 'I was going to teach you to sail.'

'And you're going to keep that promise,' cried

Margot. 'Next summer we'll find a boat . . .'

And for five light-headed minutes they planned how they'd get hold of one and what a natural sailor Ethan would be. For those moments it was as if the war, the round-up of the Jews, Auschwitz and Sachsenhausen — none of it had happened.

Jerzy didn't join in, though, and at first Dieter guessed he mustn't be much of a sailor, yet the hardened set of his eyes suggested something more. Dieter knew that look; he'd turned his own features to stone often enough. It was the face of a survivor who'd stayed alive because he focused on what was important. By now Margot had seen it too.

'Maybe not,' she said with a shrug. 'By summer we might not be in Germany at all. Jerzy's going to Palestine. He lost his whole family, even the girl he was going to marry. We're much the same. Mutti and Hannah are dead, and if our father is gone too, we'll have no one.'

'We're done with Germany,' Jerzy announced, spitting out the word like a curse and drawing Margot and Ethan to himself with an arm around each. 'What happened these last ten years — the laws, the broken windows, the Star of David picking us out on the street — must never happen again. The only way we can live without persecution is to live among Jews alone.'

'But the Nazis are gone; it won't be like that anymore,' Dieter protested.

'Not for a few years, maybe. Then it will come again. It always has. If you were a Jew, Dieter, you'd know the stories that don't get told in homes like yours. The whole country was trying to get rid of us, every last Jew, because of what we are. That won't happen in Palestine.'

The light was fading outside and rain had begun to fall.

'Where are you staying?' asked Margot, and when Dieter shrugged, they hurried him through the misty drizzle to the hut beside the boom gate and argued with the woman behind the counter until they had permission for their visitor to sleep — 'for one night only' — in hut seven.

On their return to the hut, though, the bunks had all been pushed against the walls to make space for dancing. Women, little more than girls some of them, were arriving in twos and threes, their faces flushed and eyes shining in place of the stars, some carrying bottles to add to the number already being used to fill glasses and empty jam jars. A lively accordion provided the tunes and within an hour Dieter was drunk and completely out of breath thanks to the numerous girls he'd whirled around the dance floor. He couldn't remember the name of a single one and didn't care. Neither did they. Tonight was for forgetting and he embraced the joyful blankness of it as greedily as they all did.

One man, though, stood separate from the rest, watching Dieter with a hard look. Dieter couldn't help thinking he'd come across the fellow before, but since the spirit of this night left memory outside in the damp and the cold, he didn't bother trying to work out where and when. The next time Dieter glanced his way, the man was gone.

Then Margot Lipsky claimed him for a dance. 'I've been saving this up all night,' she said. 'We danced in the warehouse, do you remember? In the darkness, where the others couldn't see us.'

'We couldn't even see each other,' Dieter replied.

'We can now.' And Margot smiled and smiled at him, until finally he had to ask why.

'You were in love with me,' she said.

'And you weren't in love with me.'

'It seems like a century ago. We're older now — you especially, Dieter.'

'Old enough for you?'

'Maybe,' she said teasingly.

'What about Jerzy? He doesn't like that we're dancing so close.' Dieter nodded towards the other man, who stood scowling at them.

'I like him. We'll go to Palestine together, and maybe we'll get married.' Margot paused, then said softly, 'I still haven't felt a love like the one you felt for me.'

'Don't marry him unless you do,' Dieter told her immediately. 'That was the hardest thing for me to deal with when I thought you were dead. I couldn't bear thinking that you'd missed out.'

'Are you still in love with me?'

'No.'

Margot made a face. 'Not even if I kiss you?'

Dieter laughed. 'If you do, Jerzy will punch me.'

'I won't then, even though I'm tempted, just to prove something to those Gestapo thugs who thought they'd ticked us off the list of the living. But we were never meant for one another,

Dieter. It wasn't the war, it wasn't Hitler. Our hearts have someone else's name on them.'

Someone else's name. Was that really true? he wondered. 'I wrote to you,' he told her.

'From Sachsenhausen? I never received anything.'

'No, you weren't meant to. There were a lot of letters, actually. They kept me alive.'

Their banter lost its playfulness. Margot danced closer and lay her head on his chest, despite Jerzy watching from only metres away. 'I know what you mean, Dieter. It's just as well I didn't get them.' She pulled back so he could see her face. 'I don't know if I could have played that game for you. It's hard to pretend what you don't feel.'

'You did all right,' he answered wistfully. 'You pretended wonderfully well, in fact. I should kiss you for that.'

Margot drew even further back from him, observing him with a puzzled look.

Dieter laughed, knowing the story of Margot Baumann was his alone and he would never share it now. It would die with him, and knowing this with such certainty brought an odd sense of intimacy between him and his dead Margot. Could it really be true they'd met only three times?

Jerzy had had enough. He claimed Margot for the next dance and Dieter was happy to let her go. He'd let go of so much today. The walls of Sachsenhausen no longer pressed around him as relentlessly as they'd done before he arrived in Berlin. The relief was a light inside his skull.

He slumped onto one of the pushed-aside beds and let the whirlwind of laughter and music go on without him. I'm almost free, he told himself, and wondered why he'd added that treacherous word. *Almost.* But he did know why, and as the beer and the schnapps carried him into sleep, a sadness washed through him again, like the blackest ink.

21

In the morning, when Ethan led the way to the dining hall, Dieter found out where he'd seen the unfriendly face before — the man was waiting for him, flanked on either side by American soldiers with the telltale P on their armbands.

'That's him!' the man cried, not just to the MPs but to the others shuffling groggily towards the vats of oatmeal. 'He was in Sachsenhausen, the same barracks as me, after I was sent there from Birkenau.' The names of these konzentrationslager brought everyone to attention. 'Yes, the same barracks, but he had a cushy job in the laundry while everyone else worked outside in the bitter cold where they beat us for the smallest mistake.'

People were turning to look now.

'He was better fed, too,' the man continued. 'I saw the block leader give him parcels — I saw it with my own eyes.'

Dieter could have jumped in to defend himself, but everything the man had said so far was true. He thought it best to hold his tongue. But his silence only left space for his accuser to fill.

'A job out of the cold had to be paid for. You all know that. Same with extra rations. He was a spy, a collaborator. He informed on Jews!'

'No!' cried Dieter. 'It wasn't like that. The parcels came from . . . ' He faltered, not wanting to explain with Ethan at his side. At least Margot wasn't here, listening to the man's lies. She'd returned to her bunk in the women's barracks after the dance and hadn't joined them yet.

'You see?' the man crowed. 'He's ashamed to answer. He can't because it will prove I'm right.'

To Dieter's dismay, one of the MPs began to nod as if the man had proved his case.

'Whatever this boy overheard he passed on to the kapos. From them it went to the SS, and Jews like all of us here paid for it at the next selection.'

'That's not true. I never said a word to . . .'
By then, though, words could barely be heard above the swelling of hostile voices in the room.

A woman rose from the nearest table and lunged at him with a butter knife. It took both of the MPs to restrain her.

'Get out now — that door,' the older of the MPs shouted, and they hustled Dieter from the dining hall, with Ethan and Jerzy Radzinski following behind them, bellowing at the rest to back off. The accuser had slipped out with them to stand scowling and aloof a few metres away.

'It's not safe here — go that way,' the same MP shouted as he shoved Dieter towards a side door of the administration hut, where they found refuge in a back room.

'This is all a mistake,' Dieter protested. 'I never gave anyone up to the SS.'

'Your papers,' demanded the MP in broken German.

Dieter produced his precious Entlassungsschein once more, hoping it would settle matters as it

209

had done whenever he was questioned previously. 'Sachsenhausen,' said the American. 'So you *were* in Sachsenhausen. This man is right.'

Across the room, Dieter's accuser grew a foot taller. 'I told you I recognised him. He betrayed us all.'

'That's complete scheisse!' snapped Dieter. 'Yes, I *was* in Sachsenhausen, I'm not denying it, but I worked in the quarry for months, I lost friends to typhus and exhaustion, to selections. One was shot in front of me because he broke his hand.'

He could have gone on, listing starvation and beatings and the thousand daily torments, but he didn't because he'd be doing what he'd always avoided until now — he'd be claiming fellowship with those who'd suffered the most. If the look on Jerzy Radzinski's face was any measure, he had good reason to resist.

His hesitation gave Ethan a chance to speak. 'Dieter's the bravest soul in this room. His family hid mine in Hannover for nearly a year and Dieter himself used to bring meals to us after dark. He stayed for hours to keep us company and when his father was beaten by the Gestapo it was Dieter who tried to stop them. How do you think he ended up in Sachsenhausen? Have you asked him that?'

This gave even Dieter's accuser pause for thought.

'Dieter's not a collaborator, he's a hero,' Ethan declared.

Then Jerzy Radzinski spoke up. 'Whatever he did to get sent to a konzentrationslager, he could still have turned on the Jews once he was there, if it meant saving himself. He wouldn't have been the only one. I saw it myself many times, in Auschwitz.'

That was enough to tip the scales against Dieter and no matter how much Ethan argued for him to be set free at the gate, the Americans took him out through the front door of the administration hut and into a jeep that stood waiting.

★ ★ ★

Dieter was taken to a military police station. There was no barbed wire, no watchtowers, but he was a prisoner once more. They marched him along a brightly lit corridor to a cell already occupied by three others. Bunk beds lined two walls with barely enough space to stand between them. At least each bunk boasted a decent mattress and blankets. He'd sleep more comfortably here than in the bombed-out basement in Hannover — if he slept at all.

The men in the upper bunks were lying flat on their backs when he entered; one didn't even bother to glance his way, preferring the fascination of the ceiling instead. This man was older than the others, Dieter guessed — forty at least; the remaining two were in their late twenties. The man on the bottom bunk sat nervously on the edge of the mattress, elbows on his knees and with a look on his face Dieter had hoped never to see again. In Sachsenhausen, before a selection, prisoners who knew they were destined for the left-hand line sometimes sat apart, as if to avoid infecting the others with their ill fortune. The fear of death in their eyes was impossible to mistake. Impossible to forget, too.

His unwilling companions kept to themselves, meaning Dieter's first hour in the cell was passed in silence, yet he began to pick out details about them. The three had been soldiers, he decided; each had the air of hardness and discipline that military life demanded.

Finally, when Dieter rose from his bunk to stretch beside the door one of them spoke to him.

'You're a bit young to be here. How old are you?'

Dieter turned in surprise to find the man on the bunk above his own propped on an elbow and waiting for an answer. His cheek was swollen and purple just below the eye, a souvenir of his arrest most likely.

'Eighteen,' Dieter answered.

'What unit were you in?'

Before Dieter could respond, he was warned off by the wretch with death in his eyes. 'Say nothing. Trust no one.' He glanced contemptuously at the bruised face above him. 'The Americans have spies in these cells to prise information out of the unsuspecting.'

The two swore savagely at each other while Dieter tried to imagine what information a spy would want from him, but life in Sachsenhausen had taught him to heed such warnings. 'I wasn't in any unit,' he replied when the arguing died down and then said no more.

Bowls of stew were passed through the door, and shortly after the man who'd warned Dieter to stay quiet was taken away. He didn't come back and in the morning it was the turn of the oldest prisoner. When his name was called he swung down briskly from his bunk, straightened his coat and tie, and walked out of the cell with shoulders back and chin jutting forward in the manner once favoured by Hitler.

'The fool,' sneered the bruised prisoner once the door was closed. 'Too full of pride to hide what he was. They won't need witnesses against him, he'll tell them everything himself.' He shook his head at the other man's folly.

'What will happen to him?' Dieter asked.

'Don't worry.' The man laughed. 'They haven't taken him off to be shot. Nor that bastard yesterday who thought I was a spy. They've gone in front of a tribunal to decide whether they should be tried for war crimes.'

'But they can't try every soldier in the Wehrmacht!'

'Of course not. Not even everyone in the SS. But if there's a witness to a shooting or a beating, then the soldier has to answer for it.'

'Witness,' Dieter muttered bitterly. What witness he could bear to the brutality of Sachsenhausen, yet he was in this cell as one of the accused. Surely, he must have been cursed at birth.

'What happens if a trial goes against you?'

'The worst are hanged,' said his companion with unfeigned nonchalance. Whatever he'd been

213

arrested for, he didn't think he'd die at the end of a rope. 'The rest go to prison. Just pray you don't get handed over to the Russians. They don't bother with a trial, apparently, just throw you straight onto a train and ship you off to a labour camp.'

Dieter pictured the words welded into the gate at Sachsenhausen: ARBEIT MACHT FREI. Work sets you free. Labour camp was the Russian term for a konzentrationslager.

The door opened once more, mid-afternoon, to admit two new prisoners, and while the guard stood in the doorway watching them settle on the vacated bunks, Dieter tested his luck, thinking it couldn't go against him every time. 'Do you think I could have paper and an envelope? I need to let my mother know where I am. She'll be expecting me back in Hannover by now.'

'Your mother,' crowed the guard, as though it were the best joke he'd heard since the war began. He wasn't wearing an American uniform and the little Dieter had heard him say suggested he was German. For a moment he looked ready to ridicule Dieter in front of the others, until he sensed the difference between this too-young prisoner and the hardened soldiers he mostly dealt with. He said nothing more, but returned half an hour later with a pencil, some paper and two envelopes.

'I grew up in Hannover,' he said. 'Bahnhof-strasse.'

'That area's all rubble now, I'm afraid.'

The guard nodded to show this was hardly

214

news to him. 'Write to your mother and I'll see what I can do.'

As soon as the guard was gone, Dieter wrote a quick note outlining the bare facts: he was a prisoner again, due to a misunderstanding this time — and his own stupidity, of course. He should have listened to his mother's pleading and stayed in Hannover. Confused, afraid, alone, he began to wonder if he'd truly left the konzentrationslager after all.

The guard had given him two sheets of paper but he couldn't think of anything more to write. The blankness of the remaining sheet seemed wrong, somehow, and he recalled what comfort he had once derived from writing to a dead girl.

My dearest Margot,
How many letters did I write to you? It's
not an easy question to answer, although I
know exactly how many you wrote to me.
I still have them all. They are the most
precious things I have. The reason I
cannot answer my own question is because
I don't know when I stopped writing to
Margot Lipsky and began writing to you
instead. Your letters were written out of
duty, I know. They were another way of
helping me, like those wonderful boots and
the food that kept me from starving when
our rations fell to almost nothing. Your
letters were made up, pretending emotions
you didn't feel, but what you never knew
was that my early letters were pretending
too. I am ashamed to tell you this now in

215

the only truly honest letter I have written to you.

I met you face to face only three times, not enough to fall in love with someone, especially with the kapo watching us. But I did fall in love with you, through the letters you wrote to me, and even though you are dead, I go on loving you. What I learned in our three meetings is that you give all of yourself to whatever you think is important. I was important to you, so you gave everything to me, and if that meant writing love letters for another girl, you would do it. I can barely imagine what it must have cost you, to find the words when there was no heartfelt love telling you what to write.

My letters were a fantasy, too, but not in the way I let you believe. Somewhere in all our pretending, I stopped loving Margot Lipsky and fell in love with the girl who wrote such beautiful, loving letters. If you were still alive to read these words, you would probably be angry or feel tricked and betrayed. You didn't agree to be loved, only to pretend love in return. You might have had a boyfriend through all those months when you wrote to me, and to hear that I loved you as much as I ever loved Margot Lipsky would have been unwelcome, so I never dared tell you the truth. I didn't want your letters to stop and that made me a coward all over again. Please forgive me, but I am only realising

216

*now that you had become the Margot I
lived for in Sachsenhausen. Only when I
admit this to myself does it make sense
how much your death has affected me. All
pretending is ended at last, even to myself.
I want you to know this, even though it is
too late, and you are gone. But as I told
you once about another Margot, the dead
should know they are loved.*
    Dieter

He folded the page and slipped it into the
remaining envelope, for no other reason than to
keep it safe. He wouldn't be posting it, so he
didn't bother to write anything on the outside.
No, wait, he thought before he'd dropped the
pencil into his pocket. And, fighting tears, he
copied the last words of his letter onto the
envelope where an address would normally be
written. Yes, they seemed right somehow.

22

The bruised soldier was called out of the cell before noon and didn't return. After another bowl of stew the key rattled in the door again and the three remaining inmates sat up as one, united at last, if only in apprehension.

'Dieter Kleinschmidt,' called the guard, the same man who'd given him the pencil and paper. As he walked Dieter to the end of the corridor he asked, 'Did you write to your mother?'

Dieter took the two envelopes from inside his jacket, checked which was addressed to the post office in Hannover and handed it to the guard. 'Sorry, I have nothing to give you for the stamp.'

'I'll manage. What about the other one?'

'Oh, er . . . no, I have nowhere to send this one,' he said, tucking it back into his jacket where it rested against his chest.

'They say the evidence against you is from Sachsenhausen,' said the guard. 'That's in the Soviet sector. You'd better come up with a good story.'

They were approaching three more men who'd been brought from their cells to wait outside a door. Their fate lay on the other side, presumably.

'Good luck,' the guard whispered then fell silent.

God help me — the Soviet sector . . . Dieter could only stare at the floor at first, afraid that if he saw his own desperation reflected in the eyes of the others he'd embarrass himself. Finally, he did look up, only to find one of the three staring at him in utter dismay. And no wonder, for Dieter recognised him: he'd been a guard in Sachsenhausen.

There were other reasons for Dieter to remember him, too, but before he could step closer, or even say a word, the door opened, drawing the prisoners into a space that might have been a schoolroom or the meeting hall beneath a church. At one end stood a large table, with three empty chairs waiting for the men who conferred solemnly nearby, although they paused their discussion to examine the new arrivals with unsmiling faces. Two wore American uniforms with the braid and epaulettes of officers, the third seemed lost inside a dark suit many sizes too big for him and a thin tie held in place by a silver pin. He might have been a doctor or an accountant, but considering where they were, Dieter decided he must be a lawyer of some kind. Today, these three were his judges.

'Dieter! Dieter!'

He turned to find Margot and Ethan calling and waving from among a row of chairs set aside for onlookers. They would have rushed to hug him if the guard hadn't called to them sternly, 'Verboten!'

To the right of the judges' table stood another, this one strewn with papers fussed over by busy figures bent at the waist, one a woman in khaki with the US flag sewn onto the sleeve of her jacket. More lawyers, presumably. The rest of the

219

room was filled with chairs arranged in rows facing the judges, two occupied by the Lipskys and many others filled by men and women who'd come to . . . to what? Dieter asked himself. To give evidence or to glare at the monsters who'd carried out the Führer's orders all too willingly, he supposed.

On the left, a single row of chairs waited for the prisoners. Dieter was told to sit in one just as the three judges took their places and the room fell silent.

'This is not a trial, but a preliminary hearing to determine if any of you have a case to answer,' said the man in the middle in passable but heavily accented German. 'Who is to be dealt with first?'

Order had somehow been restored at the lawyers' table, and a lieutenant answered, 'The man calling himself Abel Heisner, sir.'

'Which of you is Heisner?'

The prisoners glanced left and right until the guard from Sachsenhausen rose reluctantly to his feet. His name wasn't Heisner — Dieter was certain of it. He'd seen the man often enough, watching Dieter from a distance at first, which had played cruel tricks on his mind when guards held the power of life and death in their unpredictable hands. Now the tables appeared to have turned: the guard stole another glance at Dieter, and once again seemed terrified of his former prisoner.

Across the room, the lieutenant accepted a typed sheet of paper handed to him by the woman in khaki, now sitting calmly with more documents laid out in front of her the way a nurse keeps instruments ready for the doctor.

'Members of the tribunal, this man calls himself Abel Heisner, but in fact he is Thomas Meier. He was a guard in the konzentration-slager at Sachsenhausen.'

'No, that's wrong,' said the prisoner. 'I was never in Sachsenhausen, never a guard in any konzentrationslager. My name is Heisner.'

'But your papers are false. The stamp is one this tribunal has seen on many documents, made by a careless forger who used the wrong lettering in his forgeries.'

The lieutenant walked to the judges' table and laid the identity papers before the nearest, who nodded then slid them across to the next while the lieutenant returned to his place.

'Yes, I bought forged identity papers. I had to. The real ones disintegrated because bridges were destroyed and we had to swim so many rivers on the way back to Berlin. That was in the early days of the occupation. The Russians were shooting any men they found without papers. This is a matter of mistaken identity. I was a corporal in the Wehrmacht, part of General von Zangen's division in Holland and, later, on home soil when the Americans forced their way eastwards. There's a soldier from my unit here who can vouch for me.'

'A witness? We'd best hear what he has to say, then,' said the president.

Only three seats from Ethan Lipsky, a man rose to his feet. 'What Abel says is true, sir,' he declared without flinching. His name was Betz,

221

he told the judges. He gave the number of his unit and confirmed where it had served.

'Do you have any photographs of yourself with Korporal Heisner from that time?'

'Not with me today, sir. I . . . I didn't think to bring them.'

The judges looked sceptical. 'Any documents to show there was an Abel Heisner in your unit?'

The witness shook his head.

The lieutenant at the lawyers' table had been biding his time, as though he had expected the witness's testimony to prove worthless. He held up a second sheet of paper handed to him by his assistant. 'Sir, I have a statement made by Frau Else Baumgartner, a Jehovah's Witness who was imprisoned in Sachsenhausen in 1940. She was assigned to clean the SS barracks for much of her time in the camp. She says here, 'I was released in 1944 and went to live with my sister whose husband had died in Sachsenhausen two years earlier. Six months after the surrender, I saw a man in the street who looked like one of the guards I had cleaned for, Korporal Meier, although he was no longer wearing his uniform. My sister said we should follow him and that was how we found out he had changed his name to Heisner. My sister wanted to know if he was the one who had killed her husband and so we called in the military police and had him arrested.''

The third member of the tribunal spoke now for the first time. 'Whether this man is Heisner or whether he is indeed Korporal Meier, Frau Baumgartner's statement offers no evidence that this Korporal Meier had anything to do with the death of her brother-in-law.'

The scales had tipped a little in Meier's favour, or it seemed so until the energetic lieutenant took yet another document from his assistant's hand, this one many pages thick. 'Members of the tribunal, I have in my hand a report compiled by the War Crimes Investigation Team assigned to the Brandenburg region. On page seven it reads, 'More than thirty former inmates of Sachsenhausen have corroborated evidence that, in the final months before surrender, Russian prisoners of war were systematically murdered in the konzentrationslager.''

The lieutenant broke from quoting directly and, holding up the report, he went on, 'Details are given of how it was carried out and who did the shooting. There is no Korporal Meier named among them, that is true. However — ' he paused and advanced once more to the judges' table ' — with the help of witnesses, a list has been compiled of guards who took the POWs to the killing chamber. This time the name Meier does appear.' He set the report on the table and pointed with his finger for the first of the judges to see.

'I am *not* Meier,' the accused man insisted. 'I had nothing to do with these deaths. Those women want to settle scores, like so many these days, and if they can't find the real culprit they'll point the finger at anyone who looks the least bit like him. They don't care that innocent people will suffer so long as they can feel avenged.'

The man spoke well. Dieter was almost convinced, even though he knew damned well the prisoner *was* Meier.

'Is Frau Baumgartner in court to support her statement?' asked the man in the dark suit.

'No, sir,' the lieutenant replied without the confidence he'd shown till now. 'When we went to find her, she was no longer living at the same address.'

'That's as convenient as the lack of documentation from Herr Betz,' the tribunal member muttered. Speaking to the lieutenant, he said, 'So there's no one here who can identify this man as Korporal Meier?'

A long pause, then a sigh from the lieutenant. 'No, sir.'

But there was, of course, and Meier knew it. Despite his best efforts, his eyes were drawn to Dieter Kleinschmidt, who sat so close to him their outstretched hands could have touched.

The power of life and death, Dieter realised. This is what it feels like. There's no gun in my hand, no selection line, but I can decide this bastard's fate with a handful of words. *I was there. I saw him. He was one of the guards.*

Yet he didn't and not out of squeamishness. The Americans could hang as many SS monsters as they could find and he didn't care much if it was fair or legal. Dieter said nothing because in the terrible weeks of April, when he'd helped carry two, three, sometimes four emaciated bodies out of his barracks every morning, precious parcels had continued to come. The block leader hadn't given them to him. They'd just appeared in the filthy bedclothes of his bunk, or on the ground beside where he was sitting. He'd never actually seen Meier deliver a single one, but he'd been close by too many times for it to be anyone else. He'd been Margot's messenger.

The members of the tribunal conferred, examined the papers in front of them, glanced at Meier and conferred again until heads were nodding and all three straightened in their chairs. 'Abel Heisner,' said the president, 'if you are, in fact, Thomas Meier, then you have a serious case to answer. However, the issue of your identity has not yet been resolved. We rule that you are to be freed until and unless an eyewitness can attend this tribunal to identify you as an SS guard in Sachsenhausen.'

Meier fell back into his chair and rested his head between his hands until Betz, the friend who'd lied for him, came forward and helped him to his feet. They were heading towards the door when the young woman in khaki slipped a new folder in front of the lieutenant, who flicked it open with a flourish and called, 'Dieter Kleinschmidt.'

Dieter stood instantly, as though commanded by a kapo with his truncheon raised, and just as quickly regretted it as he swayed, light-headed and afraid his legs would give way beneath him. He used skills honed during endless rollcalls on the appelplatz to stay upright while the lieutenant tried to pick up something from the file. It fell apart in his hand. Dieter's Entlassungsschein had finally separated into four pieces, forcing the lieutenant to reassemble it on the table like a jigsaw puzzle.

'It says on your identity paper that you were

an inmate at KZ Sachsenhausen?' he said, the inflection in his voice turning the words into a question. 'Do you recall this man?' He nodded at Meier, who hadn't yet reached the door.

'Lieutenant, we've already dealt with that case. Please proceed with the new one,' the tribunal president instructed him.

So Dieter was saved from answering. He'd already made his decision anyway and he didn't bother to watch Meier disappear through the door. He had his own fate to worry about now.

'You don't deny being in Sachsenhausen, though,' said the lieutenant.

'I have no reason to deny it,' Dieter shot back at him, and the moment of defiance felt good — he'd get through this on his feet, no matter what they did to him.

The lieutenant reached for the only other item Dieter could see in his file — a single, closely typed sheet of paper. 'This is the statement of Hiram Bessermann, made before an officer of the investigation team yesterday. It says that through the last winter of the war, you received preferential treatment in the konzentrationslager, that you were assigned to indoor work that didn't require arduous labour. Is that correct?'

'I worked in the laundry.'

'There are many statements from inmates, not just at Sachsenhausen, which claim such work went to those who performed favours for the SS and the kapos who ran the camp for them. What favours did you do to earn such an easy work assignment?'

'No favours. I did nothing to earn it. It was

just luck.' But even he could hear in his voice that he was hiding the truth.

'The deposition from Herr Bessermann also says you received food parcels even after the mail system in the camp had broken down.'

'How could he know if the system had broken down? No one told us anything. The whole camp ran on rumours, and with so much of Germany invaded, fewer people were left to send us things. I was one of the lucky ones.'

Luck again! Was that the best he could come up with? He could tell the three judges were thinking the same thing. So could the lieutenant.

'Do you honestly expect this tribunal to believe all this good fortune was mere chance? You were spying on other inmates, weren't you? As more and more guards were sent off to the fighting and the kapos struggled to maintain order, they turned to willing accomplices like you to tell them who was stirring up trouble among the prisoners, isn't that right? And in return, they kept you alive.'

'No! Dieter would never do that!' Margot Lipsky was on her feet and Ethan, too, beside her. 'He was the one who kept *my* family alive. If the Kleinschmidts hadn't hidden us as long as they did, Ethan and I wouldn't be here right now.'

'Do you have any direct evidence to contribute to this case?' the tribunal president asked patiently.

Margot did her best, but she'd been in Auschwitz, not Sachsenhausen. The judges told her to sit down, leaving only Dieter to speak for himself.

'It's not true. I didn't make any deals,' he repeated. Yet without a better explanation, he knew few in the room would believe him.

There *was* an explanation, of course. A mail-room worker had come across his letters to a girlfriend, even though the girl he wrote to wasn't actually his girlfriend. She'd done it because her name was Margot, the same as the young woman who wasn't really his girlfriend. She'd risked her own life because of the coincidence of their names. It sounded preposterous, even to him. How could he make the judges believe such a story. 'Do you have nothing more to say to the tribunal?' the lieutenant goaded him.

Already the three heads were leaning in to confer. Dieter's heart sank. They would surely hand him over to the Russians for trial.

Then there was movement in the doorway. It seemed Thomas Meier hadn't slipped out with his friend after all. He came forward quickly, calling to the judges, 'I wish to speak.'

'Your case has already been heard,' said the president.

'Not about my own case, about this boy,' Meier cried, raising his hand to point at Dieter. 'I *was* in Sachsenhausen.'

'No — stay quiet!' his friend shouted, but it was too late. They'd all heard Meier condemn himself.

'I know I denied it just now,' he said, 'but I can't let . . . it would be too much.' He shook his head as if to clear it. 'I knew this boy in the konzentrationslager, although he didn't know me. That was the deal I made with the girl. *I* can tell you how he survived.'

The lieutenant signalled to a military police-man at the back of the room to escort Meier to the cells, but the president waved him away. 'Speak up then. What is Kleinschmidt hiding and who is this girl you mentioned?'

'A mail clerk, hardly more than a schoolgirl. She got him the job in the laundry. Her sister was having an affair with a captain in the commandant's office. She blackmailed them to get Kleinschmidt out of the quarry where so many died. The food parcels came from the girl, too. I know because she asked me to deliver them to the block leader in the boy's barracks.'

'In return for what favours?' demanded the lieutenant. 'Did you demand sex from this girl?'

'Must you always think the worst of a man?' Meier asked in a voice heavy with disgust. 'I'll answer for what I *did*, but to exploit that girl . . . It was payment enough to find one small flame of devotion still alive amid the depravity.'

'Devotion?' queried the tribunal president.

'Devotion, empathy, call it what you like.' He looked on the verge of collapse, as if it was an effort just to stay upright. 'No, she deserves better than that. Someone should say it no matter how out of place it sounds in this room. The girl was in love with him,' he said fiercely, nodding at Dieter in case there was any doubt. 'Deeply in love,' he added, as though these additional words were for himself alone.

23

A winter breeze scurried through Berlin, whipping up dust from the damaged buildings and peppering it in the faces of the men and women on the street. No one lingered in the chill longer than they had to, which was why the solitary figure outside the railway station stood out. He seemed to peer through slitted eyes at the building's broken facade, as if afraid that what was left of it might fall on him if he ventured inside. In his hand, a letter fluttered like an indecisive heart. Yet Dieter Kleinschmidt was not afraid to go into the station — he'd faced down too much fear for such a matter to concern him — he just didn't know if he was ready to go home.

In his pocket, he carried a new Entlassungsschein signed by the president of the tribunal which had found he had no case to answer. Beside it lay enough of the occupation currency issued by the Americans to buy a ticket to Hannover — a gift from the same man. Just as well, too, because he had to get home quickly. His mother would be worried out of her wits if his letter from the prison arrived before he did.

But thinking of his mother just now had stirred up her words of farewell. She'd called him a half-being and told him not to return until he was whole. She was right; he couldn't go on living with part of himself still imprisoned in

Sachsenhausen. He needed to end that part of his life. Wasn't that the real reason he'd come to Berlin?

He'd said goodbye to the Lipskys outside the tribunal.

'Oh, Dieter, will the war ever be over?' Margot asked as she clung to him.

'When you reach Palestine it will be, for you two at least. Write to me once you're there. I like your letters.' Again he was playing games with her when he shouldn't. Margot knew very well that she hadn't written him a single one, but when she opened her mouth to demand an explanation he said quickly, 'Send a photo of Ethan sailing in the Mediterranean.' Then he hugged the boy and the moment passed.

'What about you?' Margot asked. 'Will you stay in Hannover?'

'Maybe I'll go to Australia,' he said, surprising himself. He knew where the answer had come from, though. He often thought of Ben, and his tale of a family transplanted to the other side of the world where they still spoke German at home and where Jews had no fear of pogroms or the konzentrationslager. He wasn't a Jew, but maybe the war wouldn't be over for him until he too left Germany.

'Goodbye, Dieter.' The farewell came with a tender kiss on the cheek.

'Goodbye, Margot.' They would never see each other again, he knew.

The parting had stayed in his mind all the way to the station. He'd said goodbye to one Margot, only to find the other walking beside him. He took out the letter he'd written for her and read it over and over, the way he'd read those she'd sent him inside Sachsenhausen. He couldn't take this letter home to Hannover and at the same time he couldn't simply open his fingers and let the breeze turn it end over end until it was trampled underfoot. The words of Korporal Meier echoed like a constant drum inside his head: *She deserves better than that. The girl was in love with him.*

Dieter searched out the same word in his own handwriting. He'd been in love with Margot Baumann and there, outside the station, he felt the loss of her more keenly than ever before. No, he couldn't go home to Hannover until he'd conquered the raw hurt of her death. His eye fell on his own words again until it came to him — what he must do to face down that pain. *The dead should know they are loved.* He would lay this letter on her grave. Only then could he be a whole human being once more.

★ ★ ★

Dieter arrived in Oranienburg in the afternoon of the following day, driven in a horse-drawn cart by the farmer who'd found a bone-chilled stranger sheltering in his barn and taken him into his house for the night. 'Can't say I know where the cemetery is,' the farmer told him once the pair had unloaded his cart. 'It's a fair bet they've had to open a new one, anyway, to make room.'

He'd have to ask the grieving parents where to

find Margot's grave, Dieter realised. He began to stop passers-by to ask where they lived. The first few shook their heads and one man even spat at the name and hurried off, cursing. Perplexed, Dieter grew wary of whom to ask until he spotted a kindly looking face among the women on their way home from the market. 'Excuse me, I'm looking for the Baumann family.'

'Which one?' she responded. 'There are two that I know of in Oranienburg.'

'Oh, er, this family has two daughters.'

'I know them,' she answered with a sad nod, 'but you'll only find one daughter there now, and she's more trouble to them these days than she's worth. Poor Gerhard, he has barely any family left.'

'Yes, I heard the news,' he muttered.

'Wilhelmstrasse,' said the woman, pointing the way. 'I'm not sure of the number but the front door is forest green.'

Dieter was soon in Wilhelmstrasse, scanning each house he passed until he spotted a green-painted door. His steps slowed in anticipation as he approached; he was about to see the house Margot had come home to each evening while he fought for sleep in the barracks. He'd never thought to imagine it before, but nothing he might have imagined in Sachsenhausen prepared him for what he found. The house itself was no different from those to the left and right. Twin windows looked down at him from a second storey, there was a fence, a latched gate and a metre or two of garden, now overgrown and the weeds burned by frost. It was the crude markings daubed onto the fence and the walls of the house that shocked him. Swastikas — four, five of them, he counted, with foul graffiti scrawled across them. Someone had tried to scrub away two giant letters painted on the door, but they were still visible. SS.

None of the other houses had suffered such abuse. Did he have the right one? But he'd walked the length of Wilhelmstrasse and this was the only green door he'd found.

Then he sensed movement through one of the upstairs windows. Had it been Margot's room? Had her mother come to dust her daughter's things, seeking comfort amid the pain of memory? There was both comfort and pain in remembering the dead; no one knew this better than Dieter.

He walked the final few paces from the gate and knocked — three sharp raps.

'There's someone at the door,' a man called from deep inside the house. Surely Margot's father. It wasn't an appeal for his wife or daughter to answer the knock, however. Dieter heard fear in those few words.

Now there were footsteps descending stairs, the mother or the sister hurrying down from the bedroom, most likely. Urgent whispers in the hall. Yes, the Baumanns were afraid, and Dieter was willing to guess they'd been visited by more than night-time prowlers with pots of paint. He stepped back a pace or two in case his tall frame intimidated them, and when a curtain twitched in the sitting room window, he turned to let the spy get a good look at him.

A face stared out through the gap — an eye, a cheek, part of the brow above and the jaw below. It was enough, though, for Dieter to know it instantly. The face was Margot Baumann's.

THE
DEAD
SHOULD
KNOW
THEY
ARE
LOVED

24

22 April 1945

I feel pain, sharp and shocking. The officer must have slammed the pistol into the side of my head to stop me struggling. The gun is still trained on me. A twitch of his finger and I'm dead. I listen for the blast, afraid of its deafening roar as much as the bullet. His grip on my hair is so strong I can't break away, can't wrench my head back from the barrel. I can't even turn to plead with my eyes because my tongue has stopped working, and what use would it be anyway when they can't understand me? I'm crying with my mouth open, but the only sound is an animal moan from deep in my throat. With a turn of his wrist, he forces me to stare down at the gravel. The circle of braying soldiers has fallen back in case the bullet goes astray. This is the end. I'm going to die here on the appelplatz.

There *are* words, though. *Someone* is speaking. The voice is higher-pitched than those of the soldiers, shouting over the top of them. From the corner of my eye I see feet beneath the hem of a striped dress. The Jewish doctor! She's broken through the ring of men around me to argue with the officer. He's yelling at her to get out of the way, but the doctor won't budge. Instead she hammers him with words I can't understand. But *he* can. The officer speaks to her — another command to back away. The pistol is still hard against my temple. I tense myself for the burst of pain.

More shouting. The doctor sounds angry, but I don't hear desperation — more the cutting blade of contempt. She's not begging for my life; she's challenging the officer to explain himself. He growls at her, but this time it's not the snap of command. He's arguing back.

The doctor cuts him off with another volley of words, harsh and dismissive. I can see her well enough now to watch as she counts off things on her fingers in some kind of list. She points at the barracks where the both of us were heading before the sound of an engine drew us back to the appelplatz. More talking and now, oh blessed God, the officer lowers the pistol. He lets go of my hair and I collapse onto the gravel, shaking and crying.

I'm not going to die after all. The most wonderful relief seeps slowly through my body, though I am aware of an ache where the gun slammed into the hard bone between my ear and my cheek. I touch it tentatively and feel a swelling and the dampness of blood, but what do I care as long as I'm alive?

My sense of the world grows wider. Solid male bodies still form a ring around me, towering above me, each one topped by a surly, hate-filled face. The officer might have spared me, but these men aren't satisfied. I had an SS cigarette lighter; I have to be punished.

First one calls to the captain, then a second and a third until it's all of them and the loudest is the soldier who found the lighter. He holds it up for the captain to see. 'SS,' he sneers, pronouncing the letters in German.

I climb unsteadily to my feet and start towards the Jewish doctor. Two soldiers block my path, cursing me savagely. The circle shifts and tightens, sealing me off from my protector. She says something, but this time it's the soldiers who reply. *Shut up* doesn't need translation.

Trucks have begun to enter the konzentration-slager. The men around me wave one closer. When it stops, the soldier who found the cigarette lighter climbs into the back. Soon he returns with something in his hand; a camp burner, it looks like — the type we used to heat soup in the Bund Deutscher Mädel.

The Jewish doctor intercepts him as he rejoins the circle. It's not hard to guess at her words. What's he up to? she wants to know. Why does he need a camp burner? He brushes her aside. When the officer asks the same question, though, he receives an answer from half a dozen mouths at once. Their tone is heavy with malice.

'What are they doing?' I ask the doctor.

She won't answer me, and dread takes hold. I try to escape between two soldiers who are watching their comrade set up the burner, but they're too quick for me and now they take hold of my arms. One of the soldiers has wedged something into a pair of pliers which he holds over the burner's flame.

They wrench me around so I can't see what's happening. It's only when the officer orders my sleeve to be pulled back, exposing my arm, that I guess. Now the man with the pliers is standing in

241

front of me and I see at last what has been heated over the flame — the unteroffizier's cigarette lighter. Even from a distance I can feel the heat radiating from the metal.

I spy the doctor standing outside the circle of soldiers and cry out to her. 'Stop them. Please, don't let them hurt me.'

'It will hurt, but they won't kill you,' she calls back.

They have hold of me, so many of them I can't move. The pliers move closer. The red-hot lighter hovers over the white flesh of my forearm. I watch in horror.

But the man hesitates, and I wonder if he can't bring himself to do such a cruel thing. Yet his face is still alight with malice. He says something to his comrades. The officer frowns, but other voices rumble in agreement until finally the officer shrugs as though it's nothing to do with him.

The doctor speaks now, her voice higher and more frantic.

'What is it?' I cry again. 'What are they saying?'

She's too busy shouting at the soldiers to answer me. She beats at their backs with her fists, but she might as well be hammering at a brick wall.

Hands grab my hair. My head is wrenched back and other hands lock around my skull so tightly I can't move. Only my eyes are free. They see the pliers and the cigarette lighter coming closer, closer. The vicious face behind it is smiling, the lips speaking words I don't understand. I struggle with all the energy left in my body, to no avail. I scream and scream and scream until the lighter presses into the skin of my cheek, delivering pain like I have never known. Then darkness.

⋆　⋆　⋆

I'm moving. Someone has an arm around me and is half carrying, half dragging me along the path between barracks. The only sound is the rasp of my breathing and the crunch of gravel under our shoes. We turn in at a low building no different from so many of the barracks and as soon as I stumble inside the stench of bodies is in my nostrils again. The sudden change from bright sunshine to the unlit barracks leaves me blind but it doesn't matter; I don't care where I am, I don't care who else is here. My face — dear God, my face hurts so much.

'Don't touch it,' warns a voice when I raise my hand. It's the Jewish doctor. She's helped me this far but now she dumps me in a corner, not even on a bed, and walks away. I don't care about this either. I have no energy left. I lie down on the hard floorboards, yet this just doubles the agony and I can feel myself about to faint again. Maybe I do. For a while I drift in and out, though whether you would call it sleep I don't know. I should be grateful that when I'm unconscious, I don't feel anything.

⋆　⋆　⋆

I don't know how much time has passed. Outside, the light has changed, clouds have moved over the konzentrationslager. It's raining, I think. My energy has returned and with it an interest in where I am. My eyes roam the room. There are no bunks here, only single beds, each with a figure lying still. It's the stillness that catches my attention first of all — that and the near silence. So many people all in one place would usually create a murmur, but here no one speaks. And there's that smell again. It's more pungent than in Dieter's abandoned barracks, where the staleness of the absent bodies lingered. This place smells of illness, of living bodies in the slow process of decay.

The only person I can see standing is the doctor as she moves from bed to bed. I sit up, instantly regretting it when the pain sharpens beneath my left eye. I touch it and quickly regret that too. The gasp of pain brings the doctor to my corner.

'Can I have a drink of water?' I ask.

'Get it yourself,' comes the blunt reply, and when she sees the shock and the hurt in my expression she adds, 'None of this lot can get their own water. That's why you're here. To help them.'

'But my face!'

'It will heal,' she snaps at me without sympathy.

I try to explore the burn again with my fingers. How big is it, how bad?

'I've told you, don't touch it. The scar will be

244

worse if it gets infected.'

Scar! I've only thought about the pain until now. 'You mean it will leave a mark forever?' And when she won't answer me, won't even look me in the eye, there's a new pain, not from my cheek but from deep in my mind. Disfigured. I'll be ugly for the rest of my life.

'Why didn't you stop them?' I demand.

The doctor looks down at me for a moment, as if considering how to respond. Then she rolls back her sleeve to expose her forearm in the way the soldiers had done to me. 'Do you see that?' she asks casually, nodding down at her arm. Following her gaze I see numbers in the stark white of her flesh. 'Jews were tattooed like this when they arrived in a camp — those who didn't go straight to the gas chambers, anyway. My countrymen were going to brand you the same way. It didn't seem so bad, but when that bastard started on about your face instead . . . ' She shrugs. 'I did what I could, but they wouldn't listen.'

The matter-of-fact way she's spoken about it overwhelms me and I lie down again, crying as bitterly as I've ever wept in my life. Disfigured, ugly. What man would ever look at me?

'No, you've rested long enough,' says the doctor.

Long enough? Is she mad? I'm going to stay like this forever.

'Get up,' she orders, and when I still won't move she pokes at my legs with the toe of her shoe. 'You've got work to do.'

'Work? But I'm a patient!'

The doctor squats down beside me. 'What's your name?'

When I tell her she takes a firm grip on my shirt, pulling me closer while she speaks straight into my face. 'Margot, do you understand why those men were going to shoot you?'

'The cigarette lighter,' I answer, since it's obvious. 'You told me to get rid of it but I wouldn't listen.'

'Yes, and if those soldiers had been Russian you'd be dead.'

'But they *were* Russians. It was the Red Army, you said so yourself.'

'They're part of the Red Army, but they're Polish, like me. That's why I was able to talk to them. Now listen to me, Margot: those soldiers didn't spare you because you're a lovesick fool looking for your boyfriend. What's one more dead German to them? And that lighter would get anyone else shot five times over. No, they spared you because they don't want to wipe the arses of the sick and the dying.' She waves her free hand in an arc taking in the entire infirmary. 'That's how I convinced them to let you live. Who's going to wash the bandages? I asked them. Who's going to empty the stinking buckets of shit? Were they going to do it? You can guess their answer to that. You're alive because I need you to do those things and a hundred other jobs that are too much for me alone. It could be days before the Red Cross get here. I'm going to keep as many of these poor souls alive as I can and you're going to help me. If you're not happy with the bargain I made, I'll give you back to those

246

soldiers, because one more dead German doesn't matter to me, either. Now get up. The officer gave me matches. We need a fire to boil water. That's your first job.'

25

Her name is Ania. She's from Warsaw, she tells me. 'Do you know about the ghetto in Warsaw? Do you know what your countrymen did to my people?'

I shake my head. 'I'm one of the lucky ones, one of the few,' she says and doesn't explain any further.

These are the only words she says to me other than, 'Help that man to the latrine, put more wood on the fire, wash this.' She works without stopping, hour after hour, and I haven't seen her eat anything since the scoop of potato and cabbage she took from me before the soldiers arrived. I don't know how she keeps going. I'm so hungry my stomach feels like it will collapse in on itself. And because she never stops, I'm not allowed to rest either.

My cheek is agony. I knock it three times in the first hour, once so badly I become light-headed and have to sit on the floor until my head clears. Getting back to my feet seems like the hardest thing I've ever done. I'm careful now when I bend over patients in their beds, very, very careful.

When the boiled water has cooled enough to drink I distribute it to the patients. Most of them need me to help them sit upright before they can sip from the cup and that means putting my arm around them and lifting. It's not that they're heavy — they're as light as children — or that they stink, which they do; it's the feel of their bodies, so frail, mere skin and bone. I'm afraid I'll crush them. I've seen prisoners close up in the laundry, all of them underfed, their faces gaunt and the veins on the backs of their hands standing out through translucent skin. They were healthy compared to these poor souls. I'd stood watching as squads of men were marched out to their long day's work in the quarry. Skeletons, I'd called them. But the figures in these beds are like corpses dug up from a graveyard. And so cold. I hold their hands between mine so they can feel warmth for a few moments at least. Some notice and thank me with a blink of their eyes, others are too far gone. They are ghosts who somehow draw breath.

I cry for them. I can't help it, can't stop. I go from prisoner to prisoner and my tears spill onto their filthy uniforms. Many are going to die, no matter what Ania does for them. She sees me red-eyed and looks ready to open me up with her sharp tongue, but instead she explains, 'The SS stopped feeding the sick a week ago. They reasoned that they were going to die anyway so why waste food on them?'

'But these are human beings! How could they treat them like this?'

'It's easier than you think. Once you no longer see a man as human, you can do what you like with him. That's one war the Nazis did win: the battle to change how Germans saw their fellow man.'

She thinks I was defeated in that war, too, and

with the deepest shame I admit she's right. For a long time I despised the Jews. For so long they weren't human the way Germans like me were human. If I hadn't read their words and pretended to be a Jewish girl in my letters to Dieter, I might still think of them that way.

Ania continues on her rounds, leaving me to cry all the more as I move from bed to bed, tipping water into desperate mouths, stoking the fire too, even though my cheek burns when I stand close to the flames.

In the evening the soldiers arrive with a vat of soup. I slurp down a bowlful and wonder if there's ever been a pleasure like I feel in my stomach right now. Ania does the same then refills the bowl and thrusts it into my hands. 'Only a spoonful for each of them to begin with,' she warns me. 'Their digestion needs to start up again. Too much at once and they'll die in more pain than if they were left to starve.'

She's worried about dysentery, too. 'Once they're eating again, they'll start shitting. We have to keep this place spotless or disease will spread and kill them all.'

Another job for me. Some patients vomit up their single spoonful of soup and every speck, every drop of saliva is mine to wipe up. They wet their beds, too. I have to slip soiled bedding out from under them and wash it in a tub. Will this day never end? It must be after midnight and I simply can't stand up anymore. I retreat to my corner and fall asleep on the hard boards before Ania can protest.

In the morning she wakes me with the same prodding at my legs and before I can heave myself up to a sitting position she tosses something onto the floor beside me. I think it's more bedding to be washed until I see the stripes.

'Put it on,' says Ania.

But the prison dress is so rank I can smell it from two metres away and it's sure to be infested with lice. 'No. What's wrong with my own clothes?'

'We need more wood for the fire. You'll have to scrounge whatever you can from the empty barracks.'

'Why do I need that filthy dress to gather firewood?'

Losing patience she drags me to my feet. 'Girls like you are the spoils of war. If you want those soldiers out there to leave you alone, then pretend you're a Jew and hope they don't notice how well fed you are.' She hands me a pair of scissors. 'Here, you'll need these too.'

I stare at her blankly.

'For your hair. No prisoner had hair like yours.'

I can't believe what she's saying. I snatch the dress from the floor. 'I'll wear this, but I'm not cutting off my hair.'

'Suit yourself,' she says, 'but get moving. The fire is almost out.'

I shudder at the way the dress clings to me and picture lice crawling out of every seam. I

251

take a cap from where it hangs above a patient's bed and shove my hair under it as best I can.

I'm barely ten paces from the infirmary when I see the first of the Red Army soldiers, this one wearing baggy brown pants and a jacket with the Russian hammer and sickle sewn onto the sleeve. I avoid eye contact and practise walking with a stoop. Pretending again. Pretending to be a Jew. Once I'd done it to help Dieter. This time becomes more personal when a truck turns in between two barracks up ahead and I hear crying, even a stifled scream. Sticking close to the wooden wall, I move towards the corner until I can poke my head around. Two girls no older than me are huddled in the back of the truck. A crowd of soldiers — Polish, Russian, I can't tell — bellow at them to get down. When they refuse, one man jumps into the truck and grabs the nearest girl with enough force to wrench her arm out of its socket. He dumps her over the side like a sack of potatoes and only then does the second one move to avoid the same treatment. Their clothes are torn and the second girl is struggling to cover herself with what's left. They've been beaten, too, I see. I pull my head back so the soldiers won't see me, but not before I glimpse the men's faces: rapacious, eager for their turn.

I go straight back to the infirmary and hack at my hair with the scissors until not a strand is more than a centimetre long.

★ ★ ★

I sleep when I can and not always at night, which means I lose track of time. Have I spent three days in the infirmary, or four, perhaps even five? On one of those days, the Red Cross arrives. Their doctor agrees with Ania that our patients are too weak to be moved, but they bring better food and more hands to share the load.

'The nurses can do your work now,' says Ania.

'Are you saying I have to leave?'

'No, I'm saying you don't have to stay.'

I turn away towards the window. There are no Red Army uniforms in sight, but Ania knows why I'm staring. 'You'd be safer in the camp, that's true, as long as you wear that dress,' she says. Then she laughs. 'Crazy, isn't it? For years those stripes marked me out for the gas chamber. Now they keep you safe.'

'Should I take off the yellow triangle?'

'Why? Does it offend you to pretend you're a Jew?'

'No. I've done it before. It's just — I don't want you to feel . . . insulted.'

She thinks about what I've said and looks me over curiously. She has one of those intense gazes that can make you wither like a cut flower, but I've done everything she's asked of me through these long, weary days and I'm too exhausted to feel any more shame.

'Many Jews pretended they were gentiles to stay alive,' she answers finally. 'I can't object to the opposite now, can I?'

I unpick the yellow triangle anyway because it doesn't feel right, any more than pretending to be Margot Lipsky in my letters to Dieter did.

With the Red Cross nurses to help, I can take short breaks in the sunshine now. The second time I slip away, Ania follows me into the light and I think she's going to tell me off. Instead, she offers me a cigarette from the packet a Polish soldier gave her yesterday. She enjoyed speaking her own language with him, I think. Maybe he's from Warsaw too and they talked of places they both remember. I'm a poor companion in that regard, but I take a cigarette and light it from the match she uses for her own.

'How did you end up with a cigarette lighter from the SS?' she asks.

'It was Unteroffizier Junge's. I borrowed it sometimes to do my job.'

'Your job?'

'I worked here in the camp.'

Ania's eyes go wide and her face darkens.

'Not in this part,' I explain quickly, nodding at the rows of barracks. 'I worked in the mailroom.'

'The mailroom,' she repeats, then she leans in close. 'Margot, don't tell anyone that you worked in a konzentrationslager. Don't tell the soldiers here in this camp or new friends you make after the war. If you have children one day, tell them you were a nurse, or a typist in an office.'

'But all I did was deliver the mail.'

Ania shakes her head. 'I'd advise anyone to do the same, but for you it will be especially important.'

Why? I wonder, but before I can ask she comes forward to take my head between her hands. 'Here, let me see your face. Mmm, it hasn't festered.'

254

'Does that mean there won't be a scar?'

'I'm afraid not. The dead skin will harden and peel away as new skin grows underneath. You'll only know how bad it is after that.'

I can't help it, I'm crying again, but this time she seems to understand. 'With make-up you'll be able to hide the worst of it.'

'Make-up! Where am I going to get make-up in a country that can't even feed itself?'

She has no answer for this and her mind is on other things, anyway. 'What did you mean about pretending to be a Jew? You said you'd done it before.'

'I wrote letters to a prisoner, pretending to be his girlfriend. She was Jewish.'

'Ah, the mailroom. You could read what the prisoners wrote. Doesn't sound like something you should have been — '

'It's not like you think,' I interrupt. 'He knew I was doing it. It was a way to raise his spirits, to keep him alive. He liked to believe they really were from his girlfriend.'

Ania leans back against the wall of the infirmary. 'It's not the strangest story I've heard from a konzentrationslager. This is the boy you came back to find, I suppose.'

'Yes.'

'You're in love with him.'

'Everyone seems to think so.' I look at my hands, at the ground, anywhere but at Ania, then answer properly. 'Yes.'

'What does he think about that?'

'He doesn't know. We've only met three times.'

'Three times! You barely know him, then. How

255

can you be in love with him?'

'Because of his letters. He's so honest and playful and — '

Now it's Ania who cuts *me* off. 'No man could win my heart with words on a page.'

I've never imagined us talking like this. She's grown a hard shell around herself to survive, as Dieter did, but now there's the merest crack and, whether intentionally or not, she's letting me see the woman inside.

'You've been in love, though,' I say, hoping to keep the conversation going.

'Three times,' she answers quickly. 'I married the second one.'

This is a teasing thing to say, to suggest that she'd been unsatisfied, perhaps even betrayed her husband, but I know what this war has done to people's lives and, despite the way she's driven me without sympathy, I know Ania, too. 'Your husband was killed, wasn't he?'

'In Warsaw. He was caught with a map of the ghetto. It didn't matter that he'd drawn it up to help the housing committee fit so many families into so few streets. To your soldiers, he was planning a revolt.'

'I'm sorry,' I say automatically, but I don't like the way she's said *your soldiers*. The only soldiers I think of as my own are Walther and Franz. 'One of my brothers died near Köln,' I tell her, 'and the other's probably dead. We just haven't had the news yet.' I want her to know that death has cut away the ones I love, too.

She knows what I'm doing. 'Your brothers were soldiers in the Wehrmacht?'

When I nod, she grunts dismissively, as though they got what they deserved. I could get angry. Maybe I should. Franz and Walther believed they were fighting for their country. But I've had no one to talk to for so long — and no one to speak with about love for even longer.

'So you met your third love after your husband was killed?'

'In Auschwitz. They sent me there after the ghetto was destroyed.'

'But how can you still be alive? All the Jews in Auschwitz were gassed.'

'I'm not a ghost, Margot,' she says, and despite the horror we're speaking of, she finds enough joy in being alive to hold out her arms and turn in a circle in front of me to demonstrate. 'Who told you we all died?'

'Dieter.'

'Your young man, again. He's half right, at least. The old, the sick, the very young, yes: they died straight off the trains. But there was a factory near Auschwitz making rubber tyres. It needed workers.'

'How young? I mean how old? Would someone my age be chosen to work in that factory?' I'm thinking of Margot Lipsky.

'Not chosen,' Ania corrects me. 'In Auschwitz you were selected.'

'Yes, I know what the word means. Selected to live or die.' My words are solemn, but inside I'm rejoicing. Oh, Dieter, your Margot might not be dead after all. This is wonderful news.

Yes, wonderful news for Dieter, but even as I wish he was beside me to hear Ania tell the story,

257

I ache with what it means for me. I want Dieter for myself. For months I've hoped that when the war is over and we can meet freely, he might find in me all the things I wrote to him about in another girl's name. There's not much chance of that if she's alive to claim his love for herself.

★ ★ ★

There's a patient I check every morning before anyone else, a man who could be fifty years old or as young as twenty. Illness and starvation mask a person's age, I've found, or perhaps the truth is that anyone reduced to skin and bone and too weak to sit up in bed seems much older than they really are. I have a special reason for visiting him. His eyes are soft and needful, like Dieter's, and his hands are long-fingered, also like Dieter's. Simply from how much of the bed he takes up, I know he must be tall. The real Dieter might be dead, of course — I have no way of knowing — so in my mind, this man takes his place. I won't lose hope as long as he opens his eyes each morning to look at me. It's superstition, I know; it's like making a bargain with God the way our pastor warned against when I was still young enough to listen. I don't care. Dieter spoke of hope and how important it was for prisoners in this camp. Well I'm a prisoner of Sachsenhausen now and I must survive the best way I can.

When I'd first seen the resemblance to Dieter, the man couldn't even turn his head and I'd had to walk around the bed just to get a single spoonful of soup between his lips. Most of it spilled out again onto the bedding. He'd been one of those I cried over, a corpse counting out his last breaths. He's stronger now. Ania's told me to give him three spoonfuls and most of it goes down his throat, making his Adam's apple work in a way I used to think grotesque. Now, I see any sign of life as beautiful, especially when I have a special reason for this man to stay alive.

Lately he's more aware of the sounds and movement around him. Another sign of life. The first time I lift his head and shoulders enough to get an extra pillow beneath them, he rewards me with a weak smile. The next day it's a whispered thanks — in Polish, according to Ania, who's noticed my interest in him. She speaks to him and he responds with a question that leaves him breathless.

'He wants to know if his nurse is pretty,' she translates for me.

'Can't he see the scar on my face?' To my surprise, this is the first time I've thought of it all day.

'Starvation can damage the eyes. He can see you, but not clearly. His vision will improve once he's better nourished.'

'So he's going to be all right?'

She shrugs and speaks to her countryman in their language.

'What did you say to him?'

'That if he's alive in the morning, you'll give him a kiss.'

★ ★ ★

259

He is alive in the morning and starvation hasn't damaged his memory. 'Daj buziaka,' he says and I don't need Ania to tell me that he's asking for the promised kiss. I peck him on the forehead.

This becomes a game we play each morning. He can raise his arms now and I'm careful in case he gets any ideas, but our ritual must mean a lot to him because only his eyes move as I lower my face to kiss him.

★   ★   ★

Adolf Hitler is dead. The Führer, we called him, at home and in the classroom, as though his name were too sacred to use in ordinary speech. How I once loved him; he was one of my three great loves. Now, it makes me sick to think that I believed in him so completely. His death is like a weight lifted from my soul and I wonder how many other Germans feel the same. I'm in no position to ask them right now. I'm surrounded by Swedish nurses and Poles and Russians, all cheering as the news spreads throughout the camp. Every horn of every truck is blaring and soldiers fire their rifles into the air. The war will soon be over, they say. Only the will of a single man has kept it going for so long.

There's been too much noise, too much excitement to visit my Polish patient and already it's mid-morning. But I'm not worried. He'll be alive, just as somewhere in Germany Dieter is safe as well. I don't need to make a bargain with God to believe it.

When I finally arrive at the Pole's bed, his

sight has recovered enough for him to recognise me. He says something I can't understand — probably a complaint about the time — then points to his forehead while his lips curve into a bashful smile. His age is clearer now. He's still in his twenties, I'd guess, maybe only a few years older than Walther. He's become like an extra brother for me, along with his secret role in keeping Dieter Kleinschmidt alive. I lean over him to administer the sisterly kiss, but suddenly he pushes me away and begins shouting in angry, animal screeches that bring one of the nurses running. She doesn't speak Polish either, so his fierce protests make no more sense to her than they do to me.

I approach him again, arms outstretched and speaking in a soothing tone. He resumes his screeching. 'Get away! Don't come near me!' His meaning is plain in any language.

Ania has arrived and she rushes over to stand between us. The distraught patient speaks to her in quick, agitated Polish.

'What is it? What's he saying?' I ask Ania, taking a step closer to the bedside.

'No, you'd better stay back,' she says. 'He doesn't want you near him.'

'Why? What have I done?'

'It's your face. He can see you clearly now.'

'Oh God, am I so ugly?' I slap a hand over my cheek, even though it hurts to touch it still.

'No, Margot. That's not it. It's . . . ' She hesitates. 'You'd best see it for yourself,' she says, turning away.

I look again at my Polish patient, but he turns

away as well. The nurse who'd stood by all this time stares at me in pity. She knows what Ania is talking about but won't tell me either. I back away. I'm running between the beds. There are no mirrors in the infirmary, so I run outside into the sunshine. I hurry to one of the windows and stand before my reflection.

My hair is a shock and I'm weary around the mouth, and older, by years, it seems to me. But it's the scar that draws my eyes and I see immediately why my Polish patient pushed me away. Only now do I understand what those soldiers did to me. They hadn't simply burned my face for the pain it would cause. They had a harsher punishment in mind. They'd wanted to brand me, as the Jews were branded — not with a tattoo but with the twin lightning bolts of the SS. Staring back at me from the windowpane is a face scarred with the most hated symbol in Europe.

26

17 December 1945

It's him. Dieter is here. Did he see my face? I wonder. Maybe be doesn't know it was me.

But I'm fooling myself. He's pounding at the door now. 'Margot! Margot Baumann. I saw you in the window. You're alive!'

No I'm not, says a voice that speaks to me all too often.

What's he doing here? No, no, no, this wasn't supposed to happen.

There's movement in the hallway. I rush from the sitting room and find my parents huddled there, halfway between the kitchen and the front door. Mutti sneers at me, 'Another drunken Russian come to gawk at your face.'

'No, this one is German,' says Vati. 'And listen, he's calling Margot by name.' He looks at me, his expression questioning rather than a glare of blame.

'It's the boy who wrote to me back in September. Don't you remember? I made you reply.'

Vati had done what I begged of him. He'd even come up with moving words to make it seem he was grieving for me. It can't have been too hard when he grieves for Franz and for Walther, too, and even Renate, whom he won't see again, most likely. Yet he hadn't asked how I knew Dieter or what he meant to me. Nor had

263

Mutti, who'd returned from Hamburg by then. Once the letter was posted, they'd forgotten all about him.

'What's he doing here if we told him you're dead?' Mutti asks now.

'Margot!' The shouts come from the side of the house now. Dieter is looking for a way in. He'll be peering through windows. Oh God, he mustn't see my face. Vati runs into the kitchen to lock the back door, leaving me alone with my mother.

'This is a fine disturbance, when all we want is to be left alone.'

'The letter was supposed to keep him away, Mutti. I don't want him here, I don't want him here, *I don't want him here!*' Am I lying or telling the truth. I'm torn in two.

Vati rejoins us in the hall. 'Everything's locked. He can't get in.'

Dieter must have come to the same conclusion, because he's gone back to the front door, calling my name more frantically now. 'Open up! Tell me what's going on!'

Vati moves closer. 'Go away! We don't know what you're talking about.'

'But I saw Margot in the window. Why did you lie to me, Herr Baumann?' He raises his voice. 'Margot, can you hear me? It's Dieter Kleinschmidt. Tell your father to open the door.'

Vati glances over his shoulder. Shrugs.

'No, no,' I hiss at him. 'He mustn't see me.'

'Who is this boy?' Mutti wants to know. 'Why is he going on this way?'

What answer can I give? That I loved him

more than I thought it was possible to love anyone. That, despite what I say, I still do. 'He's someone I knew at the konzentrationslager,' I answer meekly.

Mutti stiffens at the word and goes into the sitting room. I follow in time to see her part the curtains an inch or two. 'Now look. He's brought half the street out to watch the spectacle.' She sweeps back into the hall, snapping at me as she passes, 'As if we're not under enough suspicion already, thanks to you.' To Vati she calls, 'All this attention is dangerous, Gerhard. The Ivans will come to investigate.'

'I was thinking the same thing. We have to let him in.'

'No — please!'

But he's already reaching for the latch. At the last moment he glances back at me with a nod towards the staircase. I move without thinking, and by the time Dieter finally sets foot in our hall I'm on the landing outside my bedroom.

'He shouldn't be here.' I say it over and over, as though this alone will make him go away. Didn't he get Vati's letter? He must have, because he'd accused my father of lying to him. But if he thought I was dead, why has he come?

Dieter's voice fills the hall below. He's here, in the house I haven't dared leave for months, the only place left to me. Has he changed? The glimpse through the curtain showed more flesh on his face and he no longer had the rounded shoulders of a prisoner cowering in front of the guards. I didn't have time to take in anything else. Now I long to see more. Instead of going

265

into my room I linger at the top of the stairs.

'Yes, Margot is alive,' Vati is saying.

Damn, damn! He should pretend it was Renate at the window. Now they're talking about the letter. 'It was Margot's idea. She didn't want you to come looking for her.'

That's the truth, at least. Oh, Dieter, why couldn't you let me stay dead?

'What you're saying doesn't make sense. We were friends,' he says, his voice calm, as though he simply wants them to understand. '*Good* friends,' he says again.

No, Dieter, not friends, I want to shout down the staircase. *No one loves a boy the way I loved you and still calls him a friend.* I take one step, then another, down the stairs, but all I can see in the hall below is legs. This is a mistake. I'm horribly exposed like this and if he hears a creak on the stairs, he'll bound up two at a time until he's standing close enough to touch, close enough to stare, close enough for me to see his eyes grow wide in disgust.

I back away into the bedroom, lock the door and cross quickly to my bed, avoiding the mirror I once shared with Renate. She could have it all to herself now, if she were here. Only God knows where my sister is these days. With Kapitän Goldapp, I suppose. The pair abandoned Mutti once they'd reached an area controlled by the Americans. She found shelter in Hamburg and ate at Red Cross kitchens until August, when she'd come back to Oranienburg with a cartload of others who preferred to take their chances in the Soviet zone rather than face the winter without any place to live. Not that it was much better here once the swastikas started to appear on the walls of our house.

I should be grateful we are together, really, when millions are still separated from their loved ones. I should be grateful we are alive at all. For months I feared Vati must be among the dead, but he'd survived his days in the Volkssturm and been put to work clearing rubble in Berlin until the Russians sent him home.

I crawl across the bed, pressing myself into the corner, knees to my chest and arms wrapped tightly around them, my scarred face pressed into the cave of my body where no one can see it.

Downstairs, my parents have taken Dieter into the sitting room, where their voices are too faint for me to make out. I'll stay here, then, until they talk him into leaving. Minutes pass, then I hear the telltale creak of floorboards outside my door.

Dieter! I can't help it: a lightness takes hold of me at the thought of him so close.

I spring off the bed and cross the room. I won't let him see my face, I tell myself. I'll talk to him through the door. I listen eagerly as his footsteps come closer.

'Margot, open this door!' It's Mutti's voice.

Reluctantly I turn the key in the lock and Mutti invades my sanctuary.

'He's demanding to see you. We've explained the letter was your idea, but that only made him more agitated.'

'What have you told him about . . . ' I touch a hand to my face.

'Nothing about the way those animals marked you. Only that there's a scar and you're sensitive about it, that it's the reason you won't see him. But he won't listen. It makes no difference to him, he says.'

Oh, how I wish that could be true. 'No, Mutti, please make him understand,' I beg. I clutch at my mother, wanting her comfort, wanting the warmth of her. How strange it feels. We haven't touched like this for months. She lets me rest against her, even slips an arm around my shoulders, yet she remains stiff and I immediately feel awkward in her embrace.

'We've tried, Margot, but we're wasting our time. He won't leave until you speak to him.'

I step away from her. 'I'm not coming down.'

'Why not? He won't stay a minute once he's seen your face.'

The cruelty of what she's said makes me more determined. You'd think she would know this about me by now. But Mutti knows so little about me. This is the dead Führer's personal legacy to my mother: that the only child left to her is the one she knows least about.

'How can I come down?' I ask her, hoping still that she will understand. 'Look what's happened since I returned here from Sachsenhausen. Neighbours spit on me in the street. Friends I've known since kindergarten shout 'Nazi' in my face. Strangers come in the night to paint the SS logo on our door. All because of this.' I point to my face. 'I'd rather Dieter thinks I don't care for him than have him see the mark on my cheek.'

Annoyed, my mother departs, leaving the door

ajar. I move to close it, only to halt when I come level with the mirror. I know what I'll see if I turn and do it anyway, stepping closer, then leaning forward until my face fills the glass. Of all the things they could have done to me . . .

My mother is right. One look and Dieter will leave this house and never think of me again.

I'm still in front of the mirror when Vati appears at the top of the stairs. 'May I come in?' he asks from the doorway, and after I nod my consent he settles on the end of Renate's bed. 'I must say, this Dieter is an impressive young fellow, even if he's making a nuisance of himself.'

I break away from my reflection to sit on my own bed opposite him. There have been times lately I've wanted to curl up in my father's lap like I'd done as a little girl. Without him, there'd be no love for me in this house at all. But, for now, I know all too well he is here for the same reason as my mother. He wants to solve the problem, he wants Dieter to leave for his own sake, not mine.

'He seems to care for you a great deal,' Vati goes on, trying to strike the right tone. 'I'm not surprised he's upset at how we've lied to him. In his position, I'd want an explanation, too.'

I meet his gaze and shake my head.

Frowning he falls silent. Clearly he is searching for the right words to convince me.

'You met him at the konzentrationslager, is that right?' Without waiting for me to confirm it, he continues, 'He must be careful about drawing attention to himself. The Russians show little mercy towards men who worked in the camps.'

He lets me contemplate this before coming to the point. 'If he's risked so much just to visit your grave . . . '

'My grave?'

'That's what he told us. He said he's come to leave something on your grave.'

Instantly I want to know what it is, to claim it as my own; I want to hold it against my chest, even if the memento is no more than a withered flower.

'Consider the position he's placed himself in, Margot. At least speak to him, so he can leave again quickly and quietly, before . . . ' He leaves the dire possibilities to my imagination.

'Vati,' I say coldly, 'Dieter wasn't a guard, he was a prisoner.'

I could have prepared the ground, I could have spoken more gently, but his manipulations have made me angry. I've set out to shock him and I can't deny the satisfaction I feel when his eyes fly wide open.

'A prisoner! Margot, what were you doing in that camp?'

'I was helping him. Just one, Vati, just one of those poor souls.' And now I'm weeping as a voice shouts inside my head, *You did so little, Margot, even when you knew what was going on inside that camp.*

Vati shifts from Renate's bed to my own and slips an arm around me, just as my mother did, but when he speaks, his words surprise me. 'A prisoner. The guards were SS. No wonder you don't want him to see your face.'

'Oh, Vati, I don't care how ugly this scar has made me, it's what I'll see in his face that I can't bear. Whenever he spoke of the SS, his hands would tighten into fists. The rage in him frightened me. How can I let him see what they did to me?'

'But, Margot, he doesn't have to see your face,' he tells me. 'Cover your cheek like you did in those first weeks after you came home, before anyone knew what you were hiding.' He rises from the bed and strides purposefully to the dressing table. 'Where's your sister's scarf?'

He finds it in the top drawer and brings it over to me. It was a gift from Kapitän Goldapp, but not so precious that Renate bothered to take it with her. 'Dieter knows only that a scar has disfigured your face. It's natural that you want to keep it hidden. Once you've spoken to him, he can go home, happy to have found you alive. Then you can write to each other, keep your friendship going that way.'

Vati has no idea what he's just said. I want to scream at him. How many times did I write to Dieter, and always in the name of another girl? How would he know who was writing to him when the name at the bottom would be the same? I'll never hide who I am in that way again. Never!

'No letters, Vati,' I say, to calm myself. An odd urge to laugh takes hold of me. How absurd the world is. What I'd wanted more than anything when I wrote those letters was to see Dieter face to face. Now he's here and eager to see me, and it's the last thing I want.

Or is it? My father's idea entices as much as it frightens me. I take the scarf from his hand. 'I'll be down in a minute.'

27

Leaving my room isn't so hard, nor is navigating the stairs that take me down to the hall. It's when I reach the doorway into the sitting room that I hesitate. A framed photograph of the Führer once hung on the wall where I'm standing. The Führer, our great leader. He's been dead for almost a year and I've known he was a callous monster for longer than that, but I still give him the grand title. Ania was right: the Nazis *did* win the war inside our heads.

If the photograph were still on the wall, I'd look for my reflection in the glass, as I used to do unconsciously all those years I hurried past on my way out the door — a final check to be sure I looked my best. Today, I want to know if the scarf still covers my face like the harem girls Lili and I saw in desert romances at the cinema.

I wish Lili were here to calm me down, to come with me into the sitting room, to be someone else for Dieter to look at so it's not just me. I've had two precious letters from her, but she's not coming back to Oranienburg, not while the Ivans snatch girls off the street and no one dares to stop them. I'm alone in the hallway. I listen for voices, but the sitting room is mostly silent and the few words that do reach me seem forced. They're waiting for me. I put one foot in front of the other until at last I'm in the doorway. Three faces turn and immediately Dieter is on

273

his feet, towering over me, so solidly present in the room I flinch and back away. It's too much. If he comes any closer I'll flee to my room, but he sees how nervous I am and stays still, his eyes locked onto the silk concealing much of my face and his own face full of questions.

Hold off for a while, Dieter, I beg silently. Let me look at you and fill my head with memories for when you're gone. There's more flesh on your bones, although you are still painfully thin. There are no fat Germans these days. Wiry, muscular, that's what you are, and there's healthy colour in your skin. Your hair has grown, too — it's dark, almost black, just as I'd imagined it. At last I am seeing you as you really are. Lili was sure you'd be handsome enough to make women go weak at the knees, but your mouth is narrow and your lips too thin to be a movie star, and around your eyes there's the same weariness I discovered in the pane of glass when I learned the truth about my scar.

I sit beside Mutti on the sofa and Dieter returns to his chair. 'Your parents have told me what happened in the last days of the war,' he begins. 'That you were separated from your mother and sister in the confusion, and you couldn't get away in time.'

I shrug, not committing myself.

'It's not true, though, is it?' says Dieter, looking only at me. 'You stayed deliberately.'

'No, you have it wrong,' Mutti breaks in, eager to correct him. 'Margot became stupid with fear. She was afraid to come with us, so she hid herself, thinking the Russians wouldn't find her.

274

She couldn't hear us calling and then it was too late, we had to leave . . . '

But I *had* heard her calling me to Kapitän Goldapp's car. I'd simply ignored her, as Dieter does now. 'The Russians didn't find you hiding, did they, Margot? They didn't take you out to Sachsenhausen, either. You were already there, looking for me.'

When I nod, my parents lean forward in surprise.

'No, that can't be true!' my mother exclaims.

'Are you saying you hid yourself away on purpose?' my father demands.

But it's like they aren't even in the room.

'When you reached the camp, though, I was gone. I'd been marched away to the north with the other prisoners.'

'A prisoner!' cries Mutti. She's more shocked than my father was.

Dieter turns to her. 'Yes, Frau Baumann, I was a prisoner in Sachsenhausen and I might have died there if not for your daughter. Margot found me work out of the cold, she brought me food and . . . and other things as well.' He glances down at his feet and, following his gaze, I see Walther's boots, worn and filthy but undoubtedly the same pair.

His eyes search me out again. 'More than those things, you kept me alive in ways only the two of us know about,' he says softly.

There is a long silence, then Dieter says finally, 'The wound on your face . . . Was there a bombardment when the Red Army took the town?'

I shake my head. 'The Wehrmacht had fallen back to defend Berlin. It happened later, at the camp. Everyone was gone from there, too, or that was the way it seemed. I met a doctor who'd stayed behind to help the sick . . . '

I tell him about Ania and how she stopped the Polish officer from shooting me. This is news to my parents. I'd told them how my face was branded but not of the gun held to my head.

'You were saved by a Jew?' Mutti asks, as if this cannot be.

I'm disgusted that Hitler's voice still speaks inside my mother's head. 'Yes, a Polish Jew,' I snap at her, because she's had plenty to say about the Poles, as well.

What's happening to me? Rage and fear and love take hold at once, then let me go just as quickly. My sails are flapping in a gale; I'm a boat so far from safe harbour, so far.

'Ania needed help to care for the starving. That was why she saved me. Oh, Dieter, did you see them, the Jews? They were left to waste away. I stayed in the camp, working with the Red Cross. It wasn't safe anywhere else, even after the surrender — and with the scar on my cheek . . . I didn't dare show my face.'

He frowns when I say this and I am sure he is about to ask why — why should I be bothered about a scar when so many others bear wounds from the fighting? But I rush ahead with my story before he can voice the question.

'I worked with Ania until the end of June, but by then the Soviets were turning Sachsenhausen back into a prison for the men they'd rounded

276

up. The Red Cross were told to leave. I could have gone with them. Actually, I was riding in one of their trucks on our way out of Oranienburg when I asked the driver to stop here for a few minutes.'

I'd come back for the tin of letters in the garden, letters that are still there as I've had so much else to cope with since then, but I leave these other letters out of my story and tell Dieter what my parents already know. 'I didn't expect anyone to be here. Mutti and Renate were safe in the American zone, I hoped, and I was sure Vati must have been killed fighting with the Volkssturm. It was like staring at a ghost when I saw him through the window.'

'I know how that feels,' says Dieter and he offers me a teasing smile that I can't help but return from beneath my veil.

'I'm sorry for the way we lied to you, Dieter, really I am, but when your letter arrived things were very bad for us. Men and women came every day to cause trouble — not just soldiers, but townspeople, even neighbours who've known us for years.'

'I saw the graffiti,' Dieter says. 'But why? Why has your family been singled out?'

'We've become scapegoats,' my father replies. 'There's barely a family in Oranienburg that hasn't lost a son or a husband.'

'But you've lost your sons,' says Dieter, and I stifle a gasp. Mutti refuses to acknowledge that Walther is surely dead as well. Sometimes I think she only returned to Oranienburg in order to be here when he knocks on the door.

But Dieter notices none of this. 'Why do they single you out, Herr Baumann?' he repeats.

'It's her face,' says Mutti, clearly anxious to get this whole encounter over with. All she wants is for Dieter to leave. I hate her.

Dieter turns to look at me again, his expression bewildered, and I feel his eyes wanting to pull away the silk scarf.

'The scar was no accident,' my father explains. 'Some Red Army soldiers burned it into Margot's cheek on purpose, to mark her out, to punish her. They branded her with a symbol of Germany's power over her enemies. But now we all hate it, now it *is* the enemy, an ugly part of the madness that destroyed our country. Even those who haven't seen it on Margot's face know it's there. She worked in the konzentrationslager. That's what they say about her and she can't deny it. No one asks what job she did, no one cares. The symbol on her face makes us all the target of their rage.'

'What symbol? What are you talking about? Why would they pick you out, Margot?'

'Because I was stubborn and stupid,' I answer through welling tears. 'The unteroffizier gave me his cigarette lighter whenever I had to burn some letters. I ended up with it in my pocket. That's what they used.'

'They burned you with a cigarette lighter?'

'Not the way you think, not with the flame. The unteroffizier was SS, Dieter. His lighter had the . . . ' I can't bring myself to say it. 'On the side. Do you know what I'm talking about?'

There's no going back now, no hiding from

278

what I have become in the eyes of the world. I reach for the pins holding the scarf in place.

I could close my eyes to avoid the revulsion on his face when he sees the symbol of his torment seared into my skin. Instead I find a perverse strength inside me, like the condemned prisoner who refuses the blindfold.

His eyes have gone wide as I knew they would and I prepare myself to fall into them, to disappear, to die, for I will be dead to him forever after this moment.

'The SS,' he breathes. 'No, Margot, no.'

And suddenly he's on his knees in front of me, his hand moving towards my face. I *do* close my eyes now, as his fingers trace the mark on my cheek. There's such tenderness in his touch when so many times I've wanted to gouge at the skin with my fingernails. I open my eyes and find him weeping.

'You, Margot, of all people. You don't deserve this.'

'But I do, Dieter,' I answer him. 'I burned those letters, thousands and thousands of them, all full of love and desperation. I was naïve, I was blind; I thought the Führer was Germany's saviour. I let him steal away my brothers and any hope of happiness. He robbed me of everything and I'm not even one of his victims — not like you, Dieter, or the Jews left behind in Sachsenhausen. This is my punishment.'

'No, you shouldn't think that way.'

'But I do. There are days I wish I *was* dead, like Vati's letter said I was.'

'Don't wish yourself into a grave, Margot.

That's what I came here expecting to find, but here you are — alive.'

His face is full of so much else he wants to say and oh, how I want to hear it, but Mutti breaks in, and I can tell she is embarrassed to see us so close, so intimate. 'It seems a strange thing to travel so far just to visit a grave,' she says. She's trying to guide him towards his reason for coming, for once he has delivered whatever he was going to leave on my gravestone he'll have no reason to stay.

Dieter returns to his chair, saying, 'Actually, Frau Baumann, I wasn't planning to come here at all. My journey was to Berlin, to visit a friend who survived when I thought she must surely be dead.'

I'm immediately alert. A friend. She!

He sees me staring. 'Yes, Margot is alive,' he says, and there's no hiding how delighted he is to tell me.

'Of course she's alive — she's sitting in front of you,' says my mother, frowning.

'He means someone else, not me,' I snap at her, and only manage to confuse myself. Who am I, which Margot, when I was both? It was hard enough when the other was dead, but she's come back from the grave, just as I have. But how can I talk of these things to Dieter while my parents listen to every word, and how can I tell him what I feel when Margot Lipsky is alive to speak for herself, meaning any words of love I speak will be so nakedly my own?

Emotions swirl around me and I hardly know which one to grasp. I should be happy that

280

Margot Lipsky is alive, not only for her sake but for Dieter's. But I'm *not* happy. I want to shout to him, to my parents, to the whole world, 'I wish she'd stayed dead!' And for this I feel such shame.

Why does God tease me like this? Dieter, my Dieter, has seen the mark on my face and instead of fleeing in disgust as I'd imagined he would, he touched my cheek with . . . with . . . For those moments it seemed like love. Yet now I must give way to the girl I kept alive in his heart by offering love from my own.

But I'm too much of a coward to make a scene. Instead, I listen quietly as Dieter describes the fate of Frau Lipsky and Margot's little sister in Auschwitz and the uncertainty about her father, probably dead of typhus. Only Margot and her brother, Ethan, survived. Two remaining from a family of five. What rapacious killers have been leading my country. I'm almost relieved when anger takes hold of me.

Across the room, my mother shoots an exasperated blast from her nostrils. 'I've heard those stories,' she remarks. 'Personally, I think they're exaggerated, all this propaganda about what was done to the Jews. How could so many have died? The numbers they're claiming, it's ridiculous. And life in the konzentrationslager wasn't so cruel. Look at Margot's job in the mailroom. Prisoners could send mail, receive parcels from home. I've heard there were orchestras, concerts.'

'Yes, there was an orchestra in Sachsenhausen,' Dieter says calmly, although there's an edge to his voice that will cut my mother to pieces if she's not careful.

She doesn't take the hint. 'There, you prove my point.'

It is several seconds before Dieter responds, and the pause makes his next words even more devastating. 'The orchestra played every time they hanged a prisoner on the appelplatz,' he tells her, making no attempt to hide his contempt. 'I was in one of those camps, Frau Baumann. I know what they were like. You have no right to speak.'

'Listen to him, Mutti,' I implore her. 'You know nothing of what went on in Sachsenhausen. The stories are true.'

'I won't stay silent when people are using these lies, these exaggerations, to punish the Fatherland.'

The Fatherland! My mother is still fighting the Nazis' war. 'Please, Mutti, don't say any more.'

'You're an ignorant woman,' says Dieter, and I can't blame him, but the insult draws my father into the argument.

'You will not speak to my wife that way. You are a guest in my house and if you hope to remain any longer, you'll keep a civil tongue.'

Dieter glares at my father, yet seems to understand he has spoken only as any husband would. There's no apology, though. Why should there be? 'The Lipskys aren't waiting around for Germans like you to change,' he tells my parents. 'Margot and her brother are leaving, to make a new life in Palestine.'

Palestine! I presume that he'll go with them and I say so.

'No, that journey is for Jews alone. I'm going back to Hannover to take care of my mother and sisters. I'd hoped Margot would come with me.'

'Margot Lipsky,' I prompt him, for there was an instant when our names became confused yet again.

'Yes,' he says, looking across at me. 'She would have been someone to . . . ' His voice trails off, leaving me to finish silently for him. Someone to love. But then Dieter ends the sentence with his own words, surprising me. 'Someone to talk to.'

Talk to! About what? I wonder. About love? Is that the same as being in love? To me, it sounds dangerously close to writing letters about love.

'Margot, you should come back to Hannover with me instead.'

It takes a few moments for me to understand what he means. He fills the silence himself with more words. 'No one knows you there. You can make a fresh start.'

Leave Oranienburg! The idea terrifies me. It would mean leaving the only sanctuary I have in which to hide from a world that hates my face, but even as I cringe in terror at the thought, its colours change. Black becomes a field of green. No one knows me in Hannover and the scar on my cheek can stay hidden until Dieter's friends get to know me. New stories can be told, ones that don't dress me in an SS uniform. All of this is only the side play to what Dieter is asking, though. He wants me to go with him, to *be* with him.

My father leaps to his feet. 'What nonsense are you talking now? Margot is all we have left. Do you think for a moment we'd let her go?'

Dieter is on his feet, too. We all are. 'I'm not asking you, Herr Baumann. It's for Margot to decide. What kind of a life does she have here, anyway? She'd be better off with me.'

They're shouting now, three voices that I don't hear. Mine wouldn't be heard, even if I spoke the thoughts in my head. Instead I say them silently to Dieter. Why do you want me with you? Is it because you've lost your other Margot once more? Am I to be her substitute? Because I can't do that anymore, and before I realise what's happening, I've uttered the words out loud. 'I can't do it, Dieter, I can't.'

His face falls in disappointment, and I want to snatch back my words, because they don't mean what he thinks they do. Damn, damn. The sitting room is so crowded. My parents want Dieter to leave, but I wish that they would disappear, so I can tell him that I love him, that I've loved him since before I saw his face. I want him to know that the letters I wrote weren't pretend at all; they came from my heart.

He is speaking to me again, appealing to me directly. 'You saved my life, Margot. It wasn't just the quarry and the winter cold. You saved me on the march out of Sachsenhausen, too. Men in clogs couldn't keep up, and when they fell the SS shot them where they lay. I survived because of the boots you found for me.' He pulls up the legs of his tattered pants to show me. 'Now it's my turn. This town is your quarry. I can get you out. You can come to Hannover and live with my family.'

He wants me as a sister, is that what he's saying?

But before I can speak, my mother cries, 'Walther!' as though she's seen his ghost. Perhaps she has, because she's pointing at the boots, now worn away to almost nothing on Dieter's feet. 'Those are Walther's hiking boots. It wasn't Renate after all — it was you, Margot. You stole them!'

I've seen disdain in her eyes when she looks at me, but never hatred, not until now. I don't care. 'Yes, they're Walther's boots,' I shout at her. 'I took them to Dieter in the camp, smuggled them in on my own feet.'

'How dare you! He'll need them when he comes home.'

'Walther's not coming home,' I tell her, aware of the dangerous ground I'm treading on. Again, I don't care. 'Those boots were part of the shrine upstairs, a shrine to a dead man, Mutti. Walther died in a camp no different from Sachsenhausen, the kind you won't believe exists.' And I'm crying as I say it because it's the first time I've acknowledged the terrible truth out loud. I will never see my beloved brother again. The things I loved are gone, all gone.

Mutti turns to Dieter. 'Take them off!' she screeches. All the guilt and shame she carries inside her is focused on Walther's boots. And just look at the state of them! How pointless to want them back now. Suddenly I am overwhelmed by the futility of everything we've been through.

The scene is interrupted by a banging at our door. Voices, Russian voices, one of them with enough German to demand that we let them in.

My parents and I exchange looks, drawn together once more by our shared apprehension.

'I have to let them in,' says my father, already moving into the hall. Mutti follows, then Dieter and finally me, but not before I've wrapped the scarf around my face.

The door is opened to reveal a commissar in the baggy brown pants of the Red Army. Behind him I can see soldiers with rifles. The moment is so like the morning the Volkssturm came for my father, I imagine time has somehow doubled back on itself.

'I have reports of a stranger visiting this house,' says the commissar. He's the same man who's been here before to harass us, especially after the huge double S was painted on our front door.

Mutti looks immediately towards Dieter. She wants to give him up — she would in an instant, if she wasn't afraid of what it would mean for the rest of us if we were found to be harbouring a 'spy'.

Dieter steps forward. 'I'm the visitor. I've come to see this girl because — '

The commissar cuts him off. 'Identity papers,' he snaps, thrusting out his hand.

Dieter passes him a folded piece of paper that looks brand-new. My own papers and Mutti's and Vati's are yellowed and worn from being examined so many times.

'This is issued by the Americans,' says the commissar.

'Yes, only yesterday, in Berlin. Before that I

had an Entlassungsschein to show that I — '

Again the commissar isn't interested in his explanation. 'Outside,' he orders, and when Dieter doesn't immediately comply, he grabs his arm and thrusts him towards the uniformed men waiting in the cold.

'No, you can't take him like this,' I protest, and I push past my parents until I'm standing toe to toe with the commissar. He is surprised at first by the sight of me with my face swathed in Renate's scarf, but then he snatches it from my face, as so many delighted in doing in the days when I still dared venture into the streets.

'Ah, the SS girl,' he sneers. He takes his time inspecting my branded face all over again, wallowing in the self-righteous contempt I'm so familiar with.

'Dieter hasn't done anything wrong. You have no right to take him.'

The commissar laughs at this and, at his nod, his men march Dieter away from our door towards a truck waiting in the street.

'Where are you taking him?' I demand.

There's no answer except the cough of the engine starting up. I hurry along our path and through the gate, but that's as far as I get. Already I can see faces at windows. If I run after the truck, they'll be in the street, shouting at their favourite 'Nazi' before I've turned the first corner. What could I do for Dieter anyway? With my scar exposed for all to see, the Soviets would only go all the harder on him.

I retreat to the hall, and Vati closes the door behind me. Dieter's gone, just as they wanted.

'You have to go after him,' I tell Vati. 'He needs someone to speak up for him.'

My father raises his hands palms upwards as though to say, *What can I do?*

'Vati,' I say, 'for years you watched the SS bring workers to your factory. You knew they were starved and beaten, but as long as they built your aircraft you said nothing, you did nothing. Well, there's no factory now, there's no Luftwaffe to fly them, there's barely any Germany, but it's not too late to do something for one of those prisoners. Find out where Dieter's being held, tell the commissar why he came to Oranienburg. Vati, bring him back here to me.'

'No,' Mutti argues. 'It's too dangerous. They'll arrest you, too, Gerhard. Stay here.'

She grabs his arm and tugs him towards the sitting room, but he tells her to stop. She doesn't, and a ridiculous tug of war begins between them until, with a violence that shocks all three of us, Vati thrusts his open hand into my mother's chest, slamming her against the wall.

Not another word is spoken while my father takes his coat from the hook by the front door and walks off into the cold afternoon.

28

The silence continues through the hours I wait for Vati to return. What is there for my mother and me to talk about? I imagine this silence going on for the rest of our lives.

I retreat to my room. I'm shivering, not just because our house is unheated, but because I'm afraid of the news my father will bring back with him. Something else makes me shiver, too. If Vati does bring Dieter back to this house, I'm going to say things I've never said out loud before. I don't care if my parents are watching; I'm going to take his hand and then lift my face to his, close enough to kiss. I'll know in an instant from the way he responds. Words, the touch of his skin, maybe as little as the rhythm of his breathing. Only then can I think of Hannover.

The light is fading and still there are no footsteps on the path to our front door. Cooking smells rise from the kitchen. Once Mutti has gone to her room, I sneak downstairs to find a plate waiting for me under a cover. I feel warmer after eating and snuggled inside the dressing-gown Walther gave me one long-ago Christmas. It's too cold to stay up, but I won't sleep, not until there's news. I lie in bed and wait in the dark, too anxious to read, aware of every sound . . .

★   ★   ★

I wake to the winter sun flooding my room with light.

Vati! Has he come back? Does he have news of Dieter? I hurry out to the landing and see my father waiting for me at the bottom of the stairs.

'Did you bring Dieter back with you?' He shakes his head while I descend the stairs. 'What happened? Where is he? Have the Soviets hurt him?'

When he says nothing I drop onto the bottom step, my head in my hands. 'He shouldn't have come.'

Vati sits on the step beside me and drapes his arm over my shoulder. I lean into him, the only comfort I have left in the world.

'They'd taken him to the commissar's office for questioning,' my father begins.

I sit up stiffly. Questioning! People have been beaten, even killed while being 'questioned'. There are new stories every week.

Vati can see from my face what I'm thinking. 'Dieter's all right. They roughed him up a little for the hell of it, that's all.'

'You've seen him?'

'Yes, I waited well into the night, and finally the commissar agreed to see me. They knew by then your Dieter was no spy. They'd found a letter in his pocket, something he'd written in Berlin when he still thought you were dead. That was why he'd come to Oranienburg, he told them, to leave that letter on your grave. The commissar made jokes about it.'

'Where is he now then? Why didn't you bring him back here?'

Vati sighed through a half-smile. 'The Ivans suspect everyone, even if there is no evidence. It seems to be in their nature. Dieter was put on a truck. By now he'll be in Berlin. From there, he's to go home to Hannover, and if he's discovered in the Soviet zone again he'll be arrested.'

So Dieter is alive, he's safe. Once that was the only news I needed to hear. Not any longer, though. He has been here, in this house, and now . . . Now there is so much more to say. But I've missed my chance. We never had a moment alone in which I could say out loud that I love him, that the letters from Margot weren't made up, that they flowed from my heart.

Despair has rendered me silent and beside me my father shifts uncomfortably. 'There's no need to be afraid for him, Margot. I saw him onto the truck myself.'

'Did he say anything? Did he have any message for me?'

'There wasn't time, but he did give me the letter.'

Letter? I stare at him.

'The one that convinced the commissar he was no spy. The one he was going to leave on your grave. He wrote it to tell you things he couldn't say while he was still a prisoner in Sachsenhausen.'

I want that letter. I want it more than my life. 'Where is it?' I'm ready to rifle through my father's pockets if he delays another second.

'I left it for you on the mantelpiece.'

I'm on my feet in an instant and through the door into the sitting room. 'Where is it?' I call in

291

frustration. 'There's no letter here.'

Vati enters the room. 'I left it here,' he says. Face creased in confusion, he checks to the left of the fireplace, while I check to the right. 'There was no name on the envelope. Just some words he'd written.'

I thought I was finished with letters, yet this one has me frantic. 'Where is it, Vati? Did you put it inside your coat instead?'

He shakes his head firmly. 'No, the mantel-piece.'

'Then who's taken it?' I shout into his face. There can be only one answer.

'Mutti!' I rush back to the bottom of the stairs and shout, 'Mutti, that letter is mine. Give it to me!'

There's no reply and I sense she's not in any of the bedrooms upstairs. I barge into the kitchen, bellowing even before I emerge through the doorway, 'Mutti, Dieter wrote that letter for me, not you.'

I feel ready to kill her, I'm so enraged — but the kitchen is empty. Then I glimpse movement through the window by the sink. Mutti is outside in the frost-dusted garden. Her back is towards me until I tap on the glass. Only when she turns do I see the flame.

'No!' I burst through the back door, desperate to stop her, but by the time I reach her Dieter's letter has been turned to ash.

'How could you do this?' I scream. 'How?' I scoop some ashes from the ground and fling them at her. 'That letter was for me!'

I begin to swear at her, calling her names no

girl should ever use towards her mother. And then Vati is outside, too. He grabs me by the shoulders. 'Control yourself, girl,' he implores me.

My mother doesn't say anything. She doesn't need to. She's lost her boys in the flames of war and with another flame she has evened the score. A final victory for the Führer.

I struggle free of my father's grip and turn to face him.

'What did it say?' I demand. 'What was so important he wanted my dead spirit to read it?'

My father shakes his head. 'I didn't read it, my darling. It was for you.'

I turn my eyes to my mother. 'What about you, Mutti?'

She shrugs, but I can tell by the look on her face that she *did* read it — and that she will never tell me what it said.

'Liar,' I snap at her. 'That's why you burned it, so I'll never know.' And these last words shatter me with the terrible truth: I will never know what was in Dieter's letter. The flames have done their work, just as they did each time I took a sack of letters out to the oil drum.

I make it to my room before the tears come. There's some satisfaction in that, at least; Mutti didn't see me cry. But that doesn't change what she's done to me, what she's stolen. The letter she destroyed might have expressed the love I longed for, the love I would demand from Dieter if I were to go with him. Yet they might just as easily have been words of farewell and a final thank you for the letters that helped to keep

293

Margot alive in his mind, the Margot he never knew was me.

I'll never know. I'll never know!

Where is he now? How far away? All I can be certain of is that the distance grows larger with every minute I lie here on my bed. How far away is Hannover? Whatever the distance, it is too far for a girl with SS branded into her cheek to travel. The end of the street is too far for that girl.

But distance isn't the reason I can't go after him and neither is the scar on my face. It's because I don't know if he loves me.

I fight misery for an hour, wondering how I will ever win a long war against it. Then there's a knock at my door. 'Margot, I have something for you,' comes Vati's muffled voice.

I don't want it, whatever it is. I'm on the point of telling him so, when the door opens anyway and my father's face appears. 'I found the envelope,' he says.

I sit up as he crosses the room to join me, a white rectangle in his hand. 'Your mother tossed it aside when she opened Dieter's letter. I thought you might want it.'

I take it from his hand, not eagerly but tentatively, almost afraid to touch it. I know there's no letter inside, so what use is it to me?

'It doesn't have your name on the front,' my father reminds me, 'but he did write something.'

I glance down at the envelope in my hands and see the familiar handwriting. It's a few moments before I take in what it says.

'When he wrote those words, Dieter thought

you were dead. He insisted I tell you that as he climbed into the truck.'

I read the words again. I know them, I remember the first time he spoke them to me, in the warmth of the laundry in Sachsenhausen. The words had been for a different Margot — but these are for me alone.

THE
LAST
LETTERS

18 Beal St
Brookvale NSW 2100
AUSTRALIA

4 April 2016

The Director
Jewish Museum
Lindenstrasse 9–14
D-10969 Berlin
GERMANY

Dear Sir,
I am writing to you about some correspon-
dence from the Second World War which
may be of interest to you. Unfortunately
the letters are not in my possession and I
cannot guarantee that they even exist, as I
will explain below. If they do, however,
your organisation is in a better position to
retrieve them than we are, in Australia.
  My mother grew up in Germany during
the Nazi years before migrating to Sydney,
where my brother, Walther, and I were
born. She was always secretive about that
part of her life. Mother is now in her nine-
ties and suffering from dementia, which has
seen her relapse into her native German, a
language I no longer speak well.

Lately she has become agitated and keeps repeating a particular story about some letters. She claims there are dozens of them buried behind a house at Wilhelmstrasse 21, Oranienburg, in the Brandenburg region north of Berlin. My mother says she dug the hole in a corner of the garden and no one else was ever aware of what she'd done.

I think this information may be of interest to you because when I asked her who wrote these letters she answered, 'The prisoners, even Jews.' I have researched Oranienburg on the internet and it seems there was a concentration camp on the outskirts of the town. Hence my letter to your museum.

Of course, her story might be nothing but the product of a failing mind. I apologise if this turns out to be the case, but please let me know if anything is discovered.

Yours sincerely
Lilianna Musgrave

Jewish Museum
Lindenstrasse 9–14
D-10969 Berlin
GERMANY

8 June 2016

Dear Ms Musgrave,
Thank you for your letter of 4 April. I am
pleased to tell you that, acting on your
information and with the cooperation of
the current residents of Wilhelmstrasse 21
in Oranienburg, a team from the museum
has unearthed a biscuit tin filled with let-
ters dating from 1944 and 1945. All the
letters are written on the stationery that
concentration camp prisoners were
required to use at the time and, as you
suggest, all seem to have originated from
the Sachsenhausen camp only a short drive
from the house. A moving memorial com-
memorating the dead now stands on the
site.
    Records show that the house was occu-
pied by the Baumann family during the
war. The same records indicate there were
two daughters in the household — Renate
and Margot, both of whom would be in
their nineties now. Is either of these

301

women your mother? I note you did not reveal her name, so let me reassure you she would not be in any trouble.

The museum is in the process of identifying, as best we can from camp records, the people who wrote these letters and also the people to whom they were sent. We have not yet uncovered the reason why these letters were retained by your mother or how they came into her possession. If she still has lucid moments, we urge you to ask what she remembers.

About half of the letters were written by and addressed to Jews. We have already matched some of the letters to men and women who are known to have died in the camp during this period and hope to trace the relatives of all eventually.

In view of the special help you have afforded this museum, we would be happy to assist if you want to conduct further research into this period of your mother's life.

Faithfully,
Dr Chaim Zimmermann

18 Beal St
Brookvale NSW 2100
AUSTRALIA

27 June 2016

Dear Dr Zimmermann,
We are pleased that the buried letters have
been recovered and we wish you every suc-
cess in tracing the loved ones of the
writers. My brother, Walther, and I would
like to know how our mother got hold of
those lost letters as much as you do, espe-
cially now that I have come across some
similar letters while going through her pos-
sessions. All are written on the stationery
you describe and all were written by our
father to our mother, who was born
Margot Baumann, as you guessed. This
has come as an enormous shock to us for
we had no idea our father was a concentra-
tion camp survivor. Our parents rarely
spoke of that time in their lives and we
respected their silence, especially since my
mother's face was scarred during a bomb-
ing raid. Surgery here in Australia
managed to disguise the worst of it, but
traces remained on her cheek to remind of
a time that must distress Germans of their

303

age. What we are now discovering calls into question the story they did tell us of how they met in Berlin during the final year of the war and later married after Margot learned our father was in Hannover and managed to join him there, walking much of the distance, then asking for him at every street corner until she found him.

The letters are currently being translated in full and once this is done I will send you copies in case the contents are of interest to your researchers. I hope you understand that the originals are too precious to us to let you have them. Among them we found a plain envelope with no letter inside which has been carefully preserved in a small picture frame. No address is written on this envelope, but instead some German words which Walther and I recognised immediately. They are the words our mother had inscribed on our father's gravestone when he died in 2001: *The dead should know they are loved*. It seems certain now that the inscription meant more to them both than the obvious sentiment and, for this reason, we wish we could read the letter that this empty envelope contained. But, alas, it seems lost to us.

Your offer of help with research is much appreciated as we are keen to find out more about our parents. Sadly, my mother cannot reveal anything further. She passed away earlier this month and now lies at peace with her beloved Dieter beneath the same headstone.

With gratitude,
Lilianna Musgrave

Acknowledgements

In addition to Lisa Berryman and the wonderful team at HarperCollins, the following people helped me in the writing of this novel, either by offering comment on early drafts or providing historical detail: Kate Moloney, Julia, Bede and Siobhan Moloney, Pav Zielinksi, Leonie Tyle, Anne Hegerfeldt of Hamburg in Germany and Bethan Griffiths who was my guide on the day I visited the former concentration camp in Sachsenhausen.

We do hope that you have enjoyed reading this large print book.

Did you know that all of our titles are available for purchase?

We publish a wide range of high quality large print books including:
Romances, Mysteries, Classics
General Fiction
Non Fiction and Westerns

Special interest titles available in large print are:
The Little Oxford Dictionary
Music Book
Song Book
Hymn Book
Service Book

Also available from us courtesy of Oxford University Press:
Young Readers' Dictionary
(large print edition)
Young Readers' Thesaurus
(large print edition)

For further information or a free brochure, please contact us at:
Ulverscroft Large Print Books Ltd.,
The Green, Bradgate Road, Anstey,
Leicester, LE7 7FU, England.
Tel: (00 44) 0116 236 4325
Fax: (00 44) 0116 234 0205

SUMMER AT MOUNT HOPE

Rosalie Ham

Rural Australia, 1894: Phoeba Crupp lives with her squabbling parents and younger sister Lilith on a small farm. Her father is an eccentric ex-accountant who moved his family from the city in order to establish a vineyard, a decision her mother bitterly resents. But Phoeba has loved it there since the day they arrived and she met Hadley and Henrietta Pearson, a brother and sister from a neighbouring farm who instantly became her closest friends. At their mother's urging, Lilith throws herself into trying to find a husband, but Phoeba resists until circumstances push her towards the world of men and money. As Phoeba awakens to the realities surrounding her, she comes to realise that the friendship of those near to her may count for more than she could ever have imagined.

AMBER

Deborah Challinor

When Kitty Farrell is offered a trinket by a street urchin, her impulsive response will change both of their lives forever, and place an unexpected strain on Kitty's marriage. For the past four years, she has sailed the high seas on the trading vessel *Katipo* with Rian, her wild Irish husband; but when they return to the Bay of Islands in 1845, they find themselves in the midst of a bloody affray. Their loyalties and their love are sorely tested, and Kitty's past comes back to haunt her when she encounters the bewitching child she names Amber. As the action swirls around them, Kitty and Rian must battle to be reunited as they fight for their lives and watch friends and enemies alike succumb to the madness of war and the fatal seduction of hatred.

THE OCEANS BETWEEN US

Gill Thompson

London, 1941: A woman is found wandering and injured after an air raid. She remembers nothing of who she is; only that she has lost something precious. As the little boy waits in the orphanage, he hopes his mother will return. But then he finds himself on board a ship bound for Australia, the promise of a golden life ahead, and wonders: how will she find him in a land across the oceans? In Perth, a lonely wife takes in the supposedly orphaned child. But then she discovers the secret of his past. Should she keep quiet, or tell the truth and risk losing the boy who has become her life? Set in London and Australia, this novel is inspired by real events, and is a story of human spirit and enduring love.